In Spite of All Terror

V. M. Knox

For Sarah and Elizabeth

Also by V. M. Knox

The Clement Wisdom Series:
If Necessary Alone
Where Death and Danger Go

"Victory at all costs,
Victory in spite of all terror,
Victory however long and hard the road may be,
for without victory, there is no survival."

Winston S. Churchill
Speech to The House of Commons
13th May, 1940

England 1940

1

Tuesday 3rd September

'lement!'

He heard her calling but he did not lift his head.

'Clement! There's a telephone call for you!'

He took a deep breath and looked up. Of course he would go. That was his job. He laid the shovel down and, reaching for his handkerchief, mopped his brow before walking down the path towards the back door. Perhaps it was the warmer than usual September weather, but he felt every one of his forty-nine years.

His wife had already left the doorway as Clement entered the house. She was standing beside the kitchen table stringing some runner beans. He glanced at her hands. It always amazed him how her fingers prepared the vegetable; the swift, deft action of the sharp kitchen knife cutting and slicing with the precision of years. He walked along the corridor to the small table by the stairs and lifted the receiver.

'Reverend Wisdom speaking.'

'Clement, this is John Winthorpe.'

He thought for a second.

'Johnny Winthorpe. Say you remember seminary school, Clement?'

'Of course, forgive me. It must be more than twenty years, Johnny.' He paused. All the fun and fellowship of his younger days at Oakhill Theological College flooded back and he found himself smiling at the memories. Johnny Winthorpe, voted the man most likely to advance. Intelligent and good-looking, he could always attract the attention of people, his charm equally effective on men as it was on women. But Johnny was ten years Clement's junior and, unlike himself, had been too young to fight in the Great War. That distinction alone made Clement feel as if he inhabited a different generation.

'Is everything all right?' he asked.

'Absolutely! Archdeacon Winthorpe, actually.'

'Congratulations,' Clement replied, but he couldn't resist a smile; nothing, he mused, had changed in twenty years. 'What can I do for you, Johnny?'

'I've put your name forward for inclusion in a new initiative. Can't say much about it at this stage. Would you come up to London on Thursday? We could meet, have some lunch and I can fill you in. It would be good to see you again, Clement.'

'Thursday?'

'Yes. It may be best if you stay overnight, what with the blackouts. You can stay with the rector of Christ Church, in Mayfair. He's a friend of mine. Can you be at Victoria Station around eleven on Thursday? I'll have a driver pick you up. Just stand at the cab rank. He'll find you.'

'I suppose so.'

The Archdeacon hung up.

Clement replaced the telephone receiver. An "initiative" Johnny had said. He must mean a council, Clement thought, one that wanted him! He had finally admitted to himself that *All Saints* Anglican Church, Fearnley Maughton, East Sussex and tending the garden was his present and his future. But the war was changing everything, and the unexpected call from Johnny Winthorpe had made his heart race. He felt the smile fall from his face. Perhaps it had more to do with shortage of manpower than any special ability he may possess.

'Clement?' Mary called. 'Are you going out?'

'That was Johnny Winthorpe,' he said walking into the kitchen. 'Do you remember him? We were at theological college together. He's an Archdeacon now.'

She stopped stringing the beans, the knife held in suspended readiness. 'What did he want?'

Clement stared at the prepared beans floating in a bowl of water on the table in front of her. Whilst admitting, even if only to himself, that he felt excited at the prospect of being involved in something bigger than the Church Wardens' Committee, he remained perplexed at receiving such a call at all. 'He's put my name forward for some committee. I have to go to London on Thursday.'

'What sort of committee?'

'He didn't say.'

He saw her lips tighten at the corners. It was the smallest of reactions, but he knew from experience what it meant. Thursday was their day together.

'Well, I better get the rest of these potatoes dug.'

'Lunch will be ready in half an hour,' Mary said.

He nodded. Placing his hand on the doorknob he paused, 'Perhaps we could go to Lewes on Saturday?'

'You have a wedding and a baptism on Saturday, Clement,' she said, her hand reaching for the next bean.

Leaving the house, he walked back along the path. He would make it up to her and her disappointment would not last - that was one of the things he loved about Mary. A vicar's life was never routine and she knew that. Especially so in wartime. He picked up the hoe, pondering the new initiative. He could not imagine why Johnny would ever think of him. Swinging the implement, he chipped out a cluster of potatoes and brushed the soil from their skins. He had been the vicar of *All Saints* for twenty years and he had long given up on career advancement. He raised his head and looked over the roof tops of the houses and shops of the village. Not that he was unhappy. Quite the reverse, in fact. He had found contentment here with Mary. Fearnley Maughton was a pretty village and every season brought its own special delight; in winter the snow made the village like a Christmas card scene while in spring and summer the potted flowers and long hours of daylight brightened the most tedious day.

He breathed deeply and stretched his back. But spring was past and the autumnal leaves were already changing colour in nearby Maughton Forest. Up to his left, the church and surrounding graveyard stood on top of a low hill. It was only a short stroll from the lychgate to the front door of the vicarage. Down Church Lane was the High Street and turning left, past the police station, was the common. For him, Fearnley Maughton was more than just bricks and mortar. The village was his family. During his twenty years at *All Saints*, he had shared their sorrows and joys, held their hands and their confidences, baptised, married and laid to rest more than he cared to remember from almost every family in the district. But lately, there were too many memorial services for mere boys who would never have a funeral. He shook his head at the sadness and waste of young life. Returning to his work, he chipped again at the soil and reaching forward, tossed a fistful of potatoes into the nearby wheelbarrow.

'Insanity!' he muttered, his mind recalling his time in the trenches. But the current madness worried him. There was something sinister about this war, that despite all the carnage of the Great War, he hadn't felt then. Perhaps it was his age giving him a more mature perspective, but he didn't think so.

His mind turned to the villagers whose lives had already been tragically impacted. Clive Wade, the village baker, had lost two sons already. Just boys. One had been a soldier, lost in Norway; the other, a merchant seaman whose ship had been blown to pieces in the Channel. As children those boys had both been choristers at *All Saints*. Clement visualised their eager young faces, as innocent as fresh snow in their white choir robes. He let out a long sigh.

What had their deaths accomplished? There was no answer. Not in this life. Sometimes, especially when he was alone, walking on the Downs, he silently wrangled with God about the premature passing of innocent life. Yet despite the unanswerable questions, Clement truly believed that God had a plan for His world and it would - in God's time, not theirs - be achieved. He smiled remembering his own conversion and the man who had changed his life.

Chaplain Edwin Ross had been the army priest at the hospital in Paris where he'd been sent after being wounded in '15. Clement recalled the man's words as though he had heard them only yesterday. "Generals", Edwin Ross had said, "do not concern themselves with the fate of the individual soldier or they will lose sight of the battle. But God works in reverse. God uses the individual to reach the many." Those words were etched on Clement's mind like the sound of his own name. Initially, they had spurred him on, believing that the Almighty's purpose for him was as a chaplain in the trenches. But by the time he had finished his theological training, the war was over. 'The time for adventure is gone, Clement Wisdom,' he muttered to himself chipping at the ground.

He bent down again, his hand reaching for three more potatoes. He stopped, mesmerised by the way his boots had sunk into the earth. In his mind he could see the trenches; death and dysentery; the endless mud; and the sad hollowness which always accompanied those memories leapt from his subconscious. Straightening, he tossed the potatoes into the barrow, then turned his gaze to the wide blue sky above his head and forced himself to think on the happy memories of that time. That was when he had met Mary. While walking through St James's Park one day, he saw her feeding the ducks. In that moment, he knew there would never be anyone else.

The sound of several aeroplanes overhead broke in on his thoughts. He squinted, his eye searching for enemy fighters. The noise grew louder. Clement waited, his eyes fixed on the sky. But the planes were *Hurricanes*. He breathed a sigh of relief. Until recently, the war had been confined to Europe but with the withdrawal of troops from Dunkirk, and the increasing number of terrifying air battles he had seen over southern England, he knew this war would be different.

Clement checked his watch and stared back at the sky. The *Hurricane*s were no more than specks now. It was the third squadron he'd seen this day and it was not yet one o'clock.

He looked at the mound of potatoes in the wheel-barrow. It was enough for several day's meals. Collecting his tools, he pushed the barrow towards the house, put the potatoes into a bin beside the door then wheeled the barrow back towards the garden shed. Beside it was the Anderson Shelter. He glanced at it. He had been required to erect the half-submerged structure, although, in his opinion, erect was not quite the correct verb. Should they ever have to use it, he wondered whether, in fact, the thing could prevent death or if it was more likely to contribute towards it.

Clement scrubbed the soil from his hands in the washhouse sink and went into the kitchen. Sitting down, Mary placed the plate on the table in front of him.

He stared at the sausages. It was the third time this week. He had hoped that they would have some real meat. Remembering the newspaper pictures of Europe's destitute children, he chastised himself for thinking such thoughts.

'I'm sorry, dear,' Mary said. 'But young Stanley says that we are lucky to have sausages.'

Clement didn't know how she did it. The woman had a sixth sense that the British Army could only hope to emulate.

'No doubt his father has better fare for his dinner,' he said.

The kitchen was silent.

'I'm sorry, Mary. That was uncharitable of me.'

'Well, I wouldn't want to say anything about that,' Mary added, removing her apron and sitting down.

'For what we are about to receive may the Lord make us truly thankful,' Clement prayed and picked up his knife and fork.

'I'm not happy about you going up to London, Clement. And it has nothing to do with Thursdays being our day out. You know the Germans are targeting the airfields - especially those in the south - and the train line is so close to Kenley Airfield. If only one Nazi bomber was even slightly off course, the railway line would be destroyed.'

'I think it would be good for me to see what others are suffering while we live in our quiet and safe corner of England eating home grown vegetables. Even Stanley Russell's sausages would probably be considered a treat in London.'

'I would hardly call East Sussex a quiet and safe corner of England.'

'What our boys are doing in the skies is nothing short of extraordinary. Mr Churchill said we owe them much. But it seems to me that the raids are decreasing every day. Who knows, it may all be over by Christmas.'

'Just don't volunteer for anything that is dangerous. You did your bit for King and country last time,' Mary said.

He reached across and patted her hand. 'They must be hard up for clergymen if they have called on me.'

2

Thursday 5ᵗʰ September

Clement's friend, Peter Kempton had offered him a lift into Lewes. Crossing the Ouse River, they motored through the narrow streets and down the hill towards the railway station. The place was congested with people and luggage. From his timetable, Clement knew a train from London had recently arrived, but the numbers of people astounded him. For a moment the noise of the excited crowd sounded like the squawking seagulls he remembered from his childhood home in Rye. 'Poor souls,' he said, remembering that people were being encouraged to leave the major cities. It was just a precaution, so the authorities were saying. He made a mental note to raise the issue of billeting evacuees at the next church warden's meeting.

Peter slowed the car as Clement stared at the disenchanted faces, his heart sinking. Anxiety had orchestrated a degree of chaos. It was palpable. The newspaper photographs of European refugees with defeated eyes flooded his mind. It was unthinkable that the Germans should invade, yet here before him was the portent of things to come. He shuddered, visualizing the people of Fearnley Maughton being subjugated under the Nazi boot. He had never really believed the Germans would reach England, but now he began to feel that it may be unavoidable.

The car pulled up at the only space available, a little distance from the station entrance.

'I'm sorry, Clement, this is the closest I can safely park,' Peter said.

'So good of you to drop me off.' Clement opened the car door.

'My pleasure. I had to come through Lewes anyway. I'm in court in Brighton for the next three days.' Peter closed the boot, his thick wide fingers grasping the handle of Clement's worn leather suitcase. 'Don't forget your gas mask,' Peter said reaching for the small box. The two men shook hands.

Clement watched his friend drive away.

Clement liked Peter Kempton. For the country vicar, friendships are easily formed in a close-knit community, but only real friendships survived the bane of village life: gossip. And Peter Kempton - the village solicitor and Clement's regular chess opponent - had become a good friend. They had always been on good terms, but it had been the tragic death of Peter's wife in a car accident in Switzerland two years previously that had truly forged their friendship. Clement had sat with the grieving many times, but in the privacy of his study he had witnessed the crushing effects of grief in this stern-faced, unrelenting solicitor of the court room. He suspected it was a side of Peter Kempton few ever saw.

Turning, Clement saw the billowing smoke of the approaching train. He hurried for the crowded platform.

For the first hour of the journey he read *The Evening Argus*. Censorship kept local papers uninteresting, particularly those around the coastal towns. He put the paper onto the seat beside him and stared through the window at the passing countryside, wondering what lay ahead in London. If the Germans invaded he considered the council would be short lived. He did not believe Hitler to be a religious man. In fact, he had heard that Herr Hitler was removing the Crosses from churches and replacing them with swastikas. Clement pursed his lips at such heresy. Leaning his head back, he closed his eyes, the rhythmic sway of the train lulling him into a half-sleep.

A sudden jolting of the train woke him. He checked his watch. Two hours had passed. The train inched forward, as the tall metal roofs of London Victoria came into view. Alighting, he joined the flow of people heading for the ticket collector.

Outside a queue was forming for the cabs. Clement scanned the surrounding crowd. He had not expected to see so many people in military attire. Even women wore uniforms he did not recognise. His gaze passed from one to another. Glancing at the buildings on the opposite side of the street, he saw that all the windows were taped and walls of sandbags surrounded doorways. People hurried along as though there was nothing unusual about any of it. He thought London an alien world.

A face he recognised appeared in the crowd; the energetic gait, the broad smile, the extended hand even at several paces distance; Johnny had not changed. But the Naval Officer's uniform surprised Clement.

'Clement! How good to see you! You haven't changed a bit!'

'Johnny!' Clement said shaking the man's hand. 'Or should I say Archdeacon?'

John Winthorpe laughed. 'Clement, I would consider it an insult if you didn't call me Johnny.'

'I wasn't expecting to see you here. Its good of you to come personally.'

Johnny waved his arm in the air and a car parked at the top of the street outside a public house swung into the traffic. Turning, it pulled up beside them and Johnny opened the door.

'How is Mrs Wisdom?' Johnny asked.

'She is well, thank you. Although, not too happy about me coming up to London.'

'And you have family?'

'No. We were not blessed that way.' Clement turned to stare out the window, the subject of children one he did not wish to continue. In the early years of his marriage it had been the source of much sorrow, especially for Mary. But as the years had passed anguished tears had been replaced with stoic acceptance until finally age denied parenthood.

'She worked at The Admiralty, didn't she, before you took her away?'

Clement nodded. 'A secretary. So what is this council about, Johnny?'

There was a slight pause.

'I don't recall saying it was a council. Be that as it may, we are on our way now to meet a man who has an idea which we all believe is feasible.'

Clement's gaze followed the line of sandbags surrounding the great Abbey and the Houses of Parliament.

The threat of forthcoming invasion had transformed London. If the crowds at Lewes station had not convinced him that the war was on England's doorstep, London's streets left him in little doubt. Johnny's prevaricating words resounded in his ears as the car crossed the street and entered Whitehall.

'I wasn't aware that to be an archdeacon one also had to be a politician.'

Johnny laughed. 'I have arranged for you to stay overnight with James Moore, the rector of Christ Church in Mayfair. You shouldn't experience any problems there for your wife to worry about.'

'Thank you,' Clement said, but he didn't believe encountering street villains was what Mary had had in mind. 'The meeting is being held in Whitehall?' Clement asked as the car sped along the street.

'Nearly there.'

Just short of Trafalgar Square the car pulled up and Johnny jumped out. Clutching his small overnight suitcase, Clement followed Johnny across the street and through an elaborate doorway in an elegant, beige-stone building of some considerable size. Beyond the double doorway was a narrow entry foyer and a flight of uncarpeted stairs. Clement sensed that whoever occupied them, the offices above were neither ecumenical nor frequented by the general public.

Johnny strode ahead up the stairs to the third floor. Leaving the stairwell, he pushed open a door. Beyond was a wide, plush corridor of timber panelling and thick carpets. Johnny, it seemed to Clement, was not only familiar with the place, but perfectly at home. Striding along it, and without knocking, Johnny thrust open another door.

Inside was a timber-lined ante-room where a neatly dressed woman sat behind a typewriter. She glanced up as they entered.

'Commander Winthorpe. He is expecting you. Please go in,' she said, nodding in the direction of the inner door.

Johnny knocked then opened the door. Inside was a small office with little in the way of flamboyant decoration. There were several filing cabinets, a desk covered in files, three chairs and a rug. Otherwise the room possessed nothing superfluous to need.

'Sir, may I introduce the Reverend Clement Wisdom. Clement, this is Colonel Colin Gubbins DSO MC.'

Clement saw a battle-hardened Colonel with a serious face. He had a high forehead, prominent brows, deep set eyes and a full moustache. The Colonel gestured towards a chair opposite his desk and Clement sat down.

'I am supposing, Colonel, that you are not replacing His Grace Cosmo Lang?'

Gubbins laughed. 'No, I think the Archbishop of Canterbury can rest easy. His is the one job I am never likely to be called upon to do. I'll get straight to the point, Reverend Wisdom. Living in East Sussex, you will be more aware than most that the Royal Air Force has been keeping the Hun at bay for some weeks now.' The Colonel paused, shuffling some papers on his desk.

Clement thought of the air battles that had gone on almost daily in the skies above southern England and the lives it had impacted. Clive Wade and Ned Cooper who had lost his fourteen-year-old son from shrapnel wounds when a Stuka crashed into the man's south paddock while the lad was ploughing.

Gubbins opened a file and picked out a piece of paper. 'Before I continue, you should know that what we are about to discuss will require you to sign the Official Secrets Act. Are you willing to do so, Reverend?'

'Of course, if that is necessary,' Clement answered, his gaze on Johnny.

'It is,' said Gubbins. 'A little while ago, I was asked by the Prime Minister to set up a new group. Due to recent escalating enemy activity, we have decided to increase recruitment, and John here has put your name forward. This is strictly top secret and not to be shared with anyone not associated with the enterprise.' The Colonel slid a document across the desk for Clement to see. Before him was the Official Secrets Act. Clement wasn't sure if he should be flattered or concerned and for some inexplicable reason he visualised Mary's beans. He read the document - threatening him with death should he ever become talkative - before reaching for the proffered pen.

Clement handed the signed form to Gubbins who placed it in a file on his desk and leaned back in his chair. 'We have before us, Reverend, nothing short of a battle for survival. It appears we are entering a new phase. Intelligence informs us, that we can expect the Germans to step up their attack on us. This could be in the form of aerial bombardment and will probably be the precursor to an attempt at invasion. We don't know when it'll be exactly, but it will be soon.'

'Invasion?' Clement muttered. He felt a hollowness developing in his chest.

'Yes. We must expect it. But we must not be like the ostrich. Preparation is the key.' Gubbins stood and wandered over to the window, his back to them. 'We must be ready for them when they do come. To this end we are establishing Auxiliary Groups within the Home Guard. These special groups will be completely autonomous, answerable to me, but set up independently of each other. We are envisaging groups or cells of approximately six to eight men each, with a fifteen-mile radius of ground to patrol. Each cell will have a leader and an intelligence officer as liaison man between the group and us here at GHQ. You will have an underground Operational Base, which the Royal Engineers will build for you in some local woodland close to your village. It will be constructed so that you can live and plan underground, and patrol at night.'

Gubbins turned to face him. 'Reverend, these groups, which the Prime Minister somewhat euphemistically calls *Scallywags*, will only become operational on the broadcast of a word. That word is "Cromwell". If you receive a telegram or hear that word broadcast, invasion is imminent and you must leave everything and go to your designated Operational Base. As you already know, in the event of invasion all the church bells throughout the country will be ringing to alert the people. This would still happen. But what we are envisioning for certain selected men is more than Home Guard defence and raising the alarm. Kent and Sussex are our top priority and the likely places for a German amphibious invasion. We expect there to be a massive air support effort for the invasion, so lookouts and Observer Corps members will be on high alert. The closest observation post to you will be at Firle Beacon. This will give you some warning, but not a lot. Yours, and those further to the east, may be the only groups not to get much advanced notice.'

Clement heard the Colonel and he understood what the man was saying, but as Gubbins continued, Clement's brain was no longer taking it in. His mouth was dry and he could feel his heart beginning to pound in his chest. He licked his lips, trying to feel normal and look intelligent.

'Reverend, you may be wondering why you have been chosen. Your involvement and leadership of your local Home Guard makes you an obvious choice. Moreover, you have military experience from having served in the last war. Perhaps more importantly, through your vocation, you have had experience of death at close quarters.' Gubbins's bright blue eyes surveyed Clement closely. 'Your job would be to act behind enemy lines, targeting and killing high-ranking German officers, as well as blowing up bridges, railways, petrol depots… in fact anything the Germans could use to expedite their advance to the capital.'

Clement knew he was staring; he felt overwhelmed with all that Gubbins was saying, but he knew well enough what it meant. 'It's a suicide mission.'

'We prefer to think of it as guerrilla warfare, Reverend, but be that as it may, we do not believe you would survive long before being captured. They would, of course, shoot you. But you would be expected to take you own life, if captured. There is one other issue of importance, but we can discuss that tomorrow.'

Gubbins came around his desk and stood before him. 'Given the nature of the assignment I cannot force you to be involved, Clement, but I would ask it of you as one patriotic man to another. We are in the midst of what the Prime Minster is calling grievous times. We must anticipate the worst. It can only then get better.'

Gubbins paused. 'Think about it overnight. I would need your answer in the morning.'

Johnny waited by the door.

Clement reached for his gas mask and suitcase. He stared at Gubbins, his heart sinking. 'You think they are that close?'

'Yes.'

3

It was mid-afternoon when the car pulled up outside the rectory in Down Street, Mayfair. Johnny had taken him to St Martin-in-the-Fields for some lunch - a soup kitchen had been set up in the crypt - but there had been little conversation.

Clement's mind was spinning. Despite the wholesome meal, what he really needed was time and solitude to think and pray.

'Get some rest, Clement. I'll collect you tomorrow morning at half past nine,' Johnny said as Clement closed the car door. Standing on the pavement, he watched it drive away then climbed the steps to the rectory and rang the bell.

A man wearing a clerical collar opened the door. 'You must be Reverend Wisdom? I'm James Moore. We were expecting you. Please come in.' Moore closed the door behind Clement. 'You knew John from Oakhill, I understand?'

'Yes.'

Moore led the way to his study. 'John has told me not to ask you why you're in London. It must be marvellous to be so involved with all that is happening. Nothing so exciting about my work. I'm just a London vicar.'

Clement heard the disappointment. 'I'm just a country vicar myself, actually.' At least, I was yesterday, he thought.

'My wife, Helen will make the supper soon. I'm sorry it's so early. Little children. I'm sure you remember. Please do be seated.'

Clement nodded but didn't comment. Moore then told him about his parish work in Mayfair. While Clement wanted to be gracious, all he could think about was Gubbins and the Auxiliary Units.

Three hours later and pleading genuine tiredness, Clement retired to a bedroom to unpack and prepare for an early night. He closed the bedroom door and let out a long sigh. He was exhausted. He stared at his own reflection in the mirror above the washstand. Was he too old for such adventures? Gubbins and Johnny evidently didn't think so. Hanging his jacket on the hook behind the door, he lay down on the bed and, closing his eyes, tried to consider practical matters. He tried to imagine England ruled by the Nazis.

No one had succeeded in invading the island in almost a thousand years. Napoleon had tried but failed and Clement prayed Hitler would suffer the same fate. *Suffer*. It would be they who would suffer if the Germans succeeded. Despite his tiredness, he rose and knelt by the bed, his hands together, his fingers intertwined, and silently recited the Lord's Prayer. But his head was spinning and his prayers and thoughts jumbled. Overwhelming emotions of excitement juxtaposed with uncertainty and a degree of melancholy for what lay ahead for himself and the country. He opened his eyes.

He would need help at the church. He was already stretched with just routine church duties and the captaincy of the Home Guard. If the church bells rang...he stopped his thoughts. *When* the church bells ring, he corrected himself, the village will be in uproar. His villagers would look to him, and if they couldn't find him they would believe themselves abandoned.

He decided to arrange an Invasion Day exercise with the villagers on his return. He would place Mary in charge and he would act as observer. That way, his absence, if invasion did come, would not affect the proceedings. He paused, his eyes staring at the bedspread's floral pattern and contemplated how life would be when it was no longer an exercise. Gubbins had avoided the term "suicide mission", but that was what it was. Mary would be a widow.

Clement looked up through the window pane at the diminishing light outside. Evening was settling; the sky turning from grey-white to cool night. He checked his watch. He had been thinking and praying for over an hour, but he hadn't made any firm decisions. His mind returned to his wife. Mary was a capable and resourceful woman. She visited her sister in Windsor regularly and was not afraid of travelling alone to carry out what she saw as her duty. She had also spent some months the year before caring for an aged aunt in a remote house near Combe Martin in the West Country, until the old lady died. She was resilient and independent.

21

Perhaps involvement in the Auxiliary Units was his life's purpose. God raised up men like Gubbins in an hour of need, why not him? His mind went back to the meeting at The War Office. Gubbins had said it would involve killing. Killing the enemy, of course. But they were still men, made of flesh and blood. He had taken up the sword as a young man, but since his epiphany he had devoted himself to his calling. Killing was something he had not thought about since the mud-soaked days of France.

Clement reached for his Bible; he knew the words of Ecclesiastes about a time to kill and a time for war but he wanted more guidance. He held the Book and closed his eyes. The Germans were the aggressors. They had marched on Poland and Czechoslovakia. His mind rattled off all the countries that Hitler had invaded and conquered. All of Western Europe from Norway to the Spanish border was under the jackboot. And now it was their turn. Yet the sixth commandment resounded in his head.

He opened his Bible and found he was looking at St Paul's letter to The Ephesians. At the top of the page he read, "Put on the whole armour of God that ye may be able to stand against the wiles of the devil". He closed his Bible feeling the tension between his faith and his duty. And what of taking his own life? He had given his life to God and it was for the Almighty to determine the time of his death. Yet it was a part of the entrenched Christian ethic to give one's life for others. If the deaths of his team and even his own death by his own hand saved others, would that violate God's commandments? There was no tidy answer. He prayed for a sign. Around ten o'clock, he turned out the lamp.

A loud and violent noise woke Clement. He could hear Helen's frantic voice in the hallway. He jumped out of bed and opened the door to the corridor.

'Do you know what is happening, Clement?' James was shouting.

He knew it wasn't a thunderstorm but something much more serious. 'James, do you have a crypt under the church?'

'We do.'

'Take Helen and the children and get them into it, as fast as possible. Don't forget your gas masks.'

With each passing second the low droning increased until it roared in the darkness above them; the unstoppable barrage, so loud that it passed through one's very core. Then came the detonation.

Clement grabbed his dressing gown and wrapping it around himself, reached for his gas mask and then ran downstairs. Moore, back from the crypt, opened the door to the street. The sky was dark, less than a quarter moon. People were gathering on the street, struck with astonishment at what was happening. But the sight of the local vicar opening the church was enough for many to follow.

Above them, Clement saw a single beam from a nearby searchlight strobe across the night sky and cross with another some miles distant. Caught in its ferocious glare were the dark and ominous shapes of aeroplanes - hundreds of them - passing through the piercing shaft of light. The incessant noise thundered on, only punctuated by the long screeching sound of falling bombs as they wailed towards the earth. People stopped where they stood, rooted in fear, staring into the darkness. Explosions and flashing lights in rapid succession lit up the sky. It was raw and powerful; death was raining down. James opened the door to the church and people ran for its shelter.

'This way', James shouted as frightened people - women, children and the elderly - descended the dark stairs in complete silence.

'Clement, do you have any matches?' James asked.

He shook his head as a man beside him produced a match-box and James lit the lamp hanging on the wall beside the staircase.

'Is that the only lamp?' Clement asked.

James nodded. 'I have several on the bookcase in my study. Useless now.'

'I'll go back.'

'Are you sure, Clement?'

James handed him the keys to the rectory. Clement held no illusions about his own mortality. A line from his favourite Shakespeare play, *Henry V* popped into his head. *We are in God's hand, brother, not in theirs.* It was just as truthful for them this night in London as it had been for the English at Agincourt. He hurried up the stairs and into the night.

The noise was intense. Overhead the search lights still lit up the night sky and anti-aircraft fire streaked towards the bombers. Somewhere sirens were wailing. The long piercing sound of falling bombs increased, silent only for a heart-stopping second before detonation. Then the earth shuddered. He ran into the house and opened the door to James's study.

Walking straight to the bookcase, Clement felt for the lamps. Hanging them over his arm, he felt his way into the kitchen and hurried towards the tiled wall of the scullery in hope of finding some food. A blast roared in the night and even with his back turned to the blacked-out scullery window his eye caught the flash. He jumped with the fright of it. On the dresser shelf above him two large containers hurtled to the floor with a crash of metal on tile. Two bread bins disgorged their contents onto the floor. He stared at the five loaves. 'Alright, Lord,' he said. 'I hear you.' Gathering them, he piled the bread into the crook of his other arm.

Hurrying, Clement ran down the pitch-black corridor and out of the house. Sirens were shrieking. Standing on the top step he glanced up. A faint orange glow was starting to rise in the east. In the darkness, he heard the sound of a car moving slowly along the street. He waited as it pulled up beside him.

'Have you seen the vicar?' the Constable called.

'I am a vicar. Clement Wisdom. Reverend and Mrs Moore and about fifty others are in the crypt under the church. Do you need a priest?' he asked still clutching the bread and paraffin lamps.

The man nodded. 'Some houses in Trebeck Street have been hit. Is there room under the church for more?'

'Of course. Let me give these to the people underground and I will be with you directly,' he said.

Clement looked at the large dark form that was Christ Church. Flashes of reflected light from the incendiaries were bouncing off the stained-glass windows. He ran across Down Street and into the church. Inside, the great edifice was dark and cold. He hurried towards the narrow steps to the crypt and descended them like a child.

Within minutes he had returned. The car had barely turned the corner before Clement was confronted by another world. Whole buildings had been obliterated. The devastation shocked him. While Down Street looked exactly as it did yesterday, Trebeck Street was nothing but rubble.

The car stopped and Clement and the policeman got out. Shells of houses were all that remained in Shepherd Street and fire was taking hold in some of the gutted dwellings that only half an hour ago held sleeping families. In the flickering light of the flames he could see that complete walls were missing and upper floors had disappeared. A picture still hung on a wall thirty feet above him. A man of his own age stood shaking on the footpath, a woman was sitting on what was left of the front steps, the remains of their home behind them.

'Anyone else in the house?' Clement asked. The man looked up at him; the face devoid of reaction. He had seen that expression before. It came from shock. 'Anyone in the house?' he shouted.

The man stared back.

Clement ran up the steps to the non-existent front door. He saw the bottom stair tread and the first three balustrades of the staircase. Lifting his gaze he saw the night sky, the search beams still strobing above them.

'Reverend!' the policeman shouted.

Clement turned, more from instinct than any sense of self-preservation. He felt the shudder. It was more a groan than anything resembling impending doom. He ran back into the street as the side wall of the house collapsed. Falling bricks, cracking timber and shattering glass crashed around them. The clanging bells of an approaching fire brigade resounded in the dust-filled air. Reaching for his handkerchief, he held it over his mouth and nose.

'Come with me,' he said to the man and woman.

Behind him, the policeman was telling the ARP warden about the crypt in Christ Church.

'As soon as you hear the All-Clear, Vicar, we could use you up here,' the Warden called to him.

'Not before?' Clement asked.

'We have enough to worry about, without a missing Vicar. Besides, you're more use to us where you are,' the Warden shouted.

Turning the corner into Down Street was like seeing normality where there has been none. He looked at the group that had followed him out of no sense of purpose, like obedient children. Opening the church door, he ushered them in and down the stairs.

Helen Moore stood at the base of the stairs handing out slices of bread to the growing crowd. Clement glanced at James as the young man moved around the crypt checking on everyone. A woman was crying. 'We'll find him. I'll come with you,' James was reassuring her. 'As soon as it's light enough for us to see.'

'Our Father which art in Heaven, hallowed be Thy Name,' Clement began, his voice echoing around the stone walls.

A chorus of people joined him. But James' words about his unexciting life flashed into Clement's mind. Was this what James and Helen Moore had to look forward to every night until either victory or the Germans came to England? It was just as valid a ministry as any clergyman on the battlefield or any minister engaged in more covert activities.

He knew what he had to do.

4

Friday 6th September

A chill wind greeted them on surfacing from the safety of the crypt. Clement pulled his coat around him. The morning sky was overcast, but nothing would be the same. The rectory appeared undamaged except for a few broken window panes. James was busy dispatching those who still had homes to go to and assisting the ARP Warden with the rehousing of those who didn't.

Looking along Down Street, Clement could see an ambulance. Beside it, blankets covered low forms lined up along the pavement. A pair of lady's feet wearing high-heeled shoes protruded from under one blanket. 'Helen, do you think the people from the crypt could wait in the vicarage? James is needed,' Clement said, his head inclined towards the line of bodies.

'Dear Lord,' Helen whispered and fetching the remaining group ushered them into the house.

Clement checked his watch. If the plans made the day before were still to be followed, Johnny would be arriving within minutes. He wondered whether he should stay to help. While it was the right thing to do, the events of last night had convinced him that his war was now elsewhere.

James joined him.

'There will be people you know there, James,' Clement said pointing to the line of corpses. He saw the young vicar blench and realised how little experience he had to draw on. 'Have courage. Remember, the grieving need you to be strong.'

Moore took a deep breath.

'And James, if I may offer a suggestion?'

'Of course.'

'Prepare the crypt for other such raids. Blankets, food, a means of boiling water, beds if you have any spare, stretchers and some medical supplies.'

James Moore frowned. 'You think they will come again?'

'Yes,' he said, thinking of Gubbins.

Light rain began to fall as Johnny's car turned into Down Street. Clement pulled his coat collar up against the drizzle. Thanking James and Helen Moore, he ran towards the car.

'Quite a night, Clement!' Johnny said as Clement got into the vehicle. 'Everyone alright?'

'There are a number of dead. But Reverend Moore will manage. And he has a capable wife to assist him.'

'I'm surprised that this area was hit at all. Until now Jerry has been targeting the airfields and the North. Bombing London's residential streets is something new.'

'You think it was deliberate?'

'In the East End, yes. But around here?' Johnny shrugged. 'It was possibly a leftover bomb or two they dropped randomly on leaving.'

The image of the dead lined up along the footpath flashed in Clement's memory. Random or not, one couldn't escape the wickedness of the act, nor its devastating consequences. The car turned into Piccadilly heading for Whitehall and Clement told Johnny about the events of the previous night.

'Clement, I don't mean to sound harsh or uncaring. As you have observed, James Moore is a good man with a beautiful as well as capable wife. While the local vicar plays a huge role, especially if we see more of what we experienced last night, I think you can understand that what we are asking you to be involved in is part of the bigger picture. Church matters are important. And grass root support is vital for morale as well as for body and soul. But that is for others now. I do hope you understand that?'

Clement stared at the passing buildings until his eyes focused on small rivulets of rain meandering their way down the pane. He did understand what Johnny was saying, but he didn't answer. He felt as if he were on the edge of an abyss, turning his back on everything he believed to be the decent thing to do and about to consciously and willingly take a step into oblivion.

'I see you survived last night well enough, Reverend?' Gubbins said as Johnny closed the door to the inner office. 'Have you reached a decision?'

Clement took the seat Gubbins indicated. His gaze shifted from the grey skies beyond the window to the waiting Colonel. He felt his throat tighten. With his answer, there would be no turning back. 'Yes,' he said.

'Good man!' Gubbins replied.

'I may need help with my church duties. A retired minister or curate perhaps?'

'John will arrange it,' Gubbins said. 'There are just a few other issues I need to raise with you. We would like you to prepare a list of around twenty names of suitable men to be in your cell. From these you will need to short list about six to eight. Consider their abilities - physical and mental - also their characters and age. Ponder their circumstances as well. Remember you must be self-sufficient. Farmers are good choices and landowners or gamekeepers if you have them, also professional men. You should have a variety of skills but you should all be able to live off the land for some weeks.'

'Will there be any training?' asked Clement.

'Yes. Once you have chosen your cell, we will arrange for you to attend a course at Coleshill House in Wiltshire. They are usually weekend courses for people otherwise engaged in reserved occupations but after last night I have decided to step up the intake. Members of these Auxiliary Units would ideally already be in the Home Guard but this is not mandatory. Then on Monday morning you can travel to Wiltshire where you'll be supplied with weapons.'

Gubbins looked up and held Clement's gaze. 'You will be learning how to use explosives, Wisdom, and of course, how to kill. It is customary for you to have your local, senior police officer vet your chosen men.'

Clement stared at Gubbins. Inspector David Russell was not a man Clement cared for. And certainly not a man he trusted to interview men for such an enterprise. 'I have very great reservations, Colonel. Inspector Russell is not a man of character. I must protest about involving him. Is there not another way?'

Gubbins paused. Clement saw a silent exchange between the Colonel and Johnny. 'Perhaps Commander Winthorpe could visit you on Sunday,' Gubbins said. 'You and he could go over the final list of names and meet with the men. But your police chief must be informed. A sealed list would suffice.'

'With respect, Colonel, must Inspector Russell know at all?'

'The list is for your protection, Wisdom. Imagine if a local found your underground Operational Base, not to mention the weapons you would have at your disposal? They would surely notify your police and perhaps even Special Branch who would arrest you as a collaborator. How would you explain it?'

Clement didn't answer. He could see the Colonel's determined expression. But despite Gubbins's insistence, it did not change Clement's anxiety about David Russell having top secret information.

'However, we are getting ahead of ourselves,' Gubbins cleared his throat. 'When you receive the "Cromwell" alert - the signal to assemble - your senior policeman is your first victim, for the very reason that he can identify you. If your group is to be effective, and if any of you are to survive long enough to thwart the German advance, your inspector must be eliminated.'

Clement knew he was staring. He couldn't help it. He had wrestled with his conscience about killing the enemy. Now Gubbins was asking him to kill a man who, although Clement did not trust, he had known for years.

'Think of it this way, Wisdom; if your police chief was taken prisoner by the invading Germans, your cell would be compromised and your entire group rounded up and shot. The Germans would then know all they had to do was seize the senior police officer in every town and they would have every cell in every county in Britain; our entire guerrilla network taken out by just one man. Unthinkable. There is no alternative, Wisdom. However distasteful, it must be done.'

Clement felt sick, the nausea welling up and grabbing his throat. He swallowed hard. He had thought the Auxiliary Units a good idea. And during the previous night he had even been convinced of the need for such groups. Moreover, he believed that God was telling him to do it, but the knowledge that good and decent men cut the throats of others because they knew too much was something he could not countenance, let alone commit.

Gubbins leaned forward in his chair, his voice subdued. 'I know, Clement, that it is easier for our consciences to kill someone dressed in the enemy's uniform. But that enemy is still a man with a mother and father and possibly a wife and family. Pull the trigger or use a blade, the result will be the same. If it helps, Clement, your police chief is one man, but if he talks, his loose lips could kill thousands of brave and decent men and women up and down the country.'

It didn't help. Clement leaned back in the chair. He felt confused. He knew he was staring. Gubbins and Johnny were watching him. No one spoke. Only the clacking of the secretary's typewriter in the outer office disturbed the silence. Clement's mind hurtled. Murder was still murder. His friend Peter had told him about the supposed ghettos in Poland where they were forcibly congregating those of the Jewish faith. Such brutality astounded Clement. He felt his brow knit. There was no honour any more, the last war had seen to that. It reconfirmed his opinion about the second madness. He had killed soldiers in the last war, but never civilians. He thought of the family in Trebeck Street. What had they done to the Germans? The high moral ground is so easily taken in theory or in peacetime. He thought of the verses in Ecclesiastes and Ephesians, the five loaves in Helen Moore's kitchen and the glow in the east.

Gubbins and Johnny waited.

But no matter how dreadful or compromising, evil had to be repulsed and he knew Gubbins was right. It had to be done. He swallowed hard. 'Very well,' he whispered.

'A brave and patriotic decision,' Gubbins said. 'John will visit you on Sunday and you can go over the final list of names. You should invite your selected men to a special meeting of the Home Guard on Sunday afternoon. It doesn't give them much time to contemplate their decision and perhaps that is a good thing. Either way, Clement, you will be a different man when I see you next.'

'I fear you are correct, Colonel.'

Clement felt drained. The meeting with Gubbins had been relatively short yet, following that half hour, life for him would never be the same.

Outside there was a hurried tension about London. The bombing of the previous night showed on the faces of the passing crowds. Shopping bags were full of all kinds of rationed foodstuffs. Even small children carried string bags containing bread and tinned fruit. Clement breathed in the air, glad to be away from Gubbins's office. A red bus stopped near him. On the outside, written in gigantic letters, was the statement; *Loose Lips Sink*

Ships. People boarded the bus and it pulled away from the curb. He had seen the sign before but now it meant more. He felt his heart pounding. The period the newspapers had called the Phony War really was over. Europe had fallen. Now it was their turn. A profound sense of dread was settling in his chest.

'What about some lunch?' Johnny was saying. 'We could go to the Savoy. Special treat before the austerity begins in earnest.'

Special treats. For a fleeting second Clement wondered what the famous hotels did offer travellers. But it wasn't what he wanted. He felt hollow. The seriousness of it all had impacted hard. Above all, he wanted to see Mary. Not that he could discuss any of it with her. 'I just would like to go home, Johnny. While I have one. Could your driver drop me at Victoria Station?'

'Of course.' Johnny hailed the driver who was waiting on the opposite side of Whitehall and they drove past St James Park and the palace. Clement looked up at the Royal Standard fluttering high above Buckingham Palace. 'Will they leave London?'

'Unlikely. I can't tell you how relieved many of us are that we have the King and Queen we now do.'

'Divine intervention?'

'Indeed.' The cab pulled up outside the station. 'See you Sunday.'

They shook hands.

'And Clement, I am pleased to have you with us.'

The next train south was not for thirty minutes. Clement purchased a ticket and then went to the tea room. Names started filtering through his mind and he took a small note book from his pocket.

By the time Clement stepped down onto the platform at Lewes, two names were already on his list. He strode up the hill towards the bus stop, the bus for Fearnley Maughton not due for fifteen minutes. If the invasion took months, he and whoever he selected would have to work and survive through winter. Underground and bitterly cold. Not his favourite combination. And only two days training to transform law abiding men into saboteurs and assassins. But it was Gubbins's parting information that had shocked Clement even more than the necessity for eliminating Inspector Russell. Gubbins had told him that, once activated, the cell had a life expectancy of two weeks. That information had already affected his choice of men.

He stepped from the bus, the doors closing behind him. Clement looked around. Everything in Fearnley Maughton now looked different to him. He wanted to remember it just as it was, like a photograph for his memory and the hard times ahead. Across the village green was *The Crown Inn*, the face of a young Queen Bess on the placard swinging above the door of the black and white Elizabethan building. Further up the high street was the elegant, blue-painted Georgian building that was Peter Kempton's legal office. Beyond that, the red-brick doctor's home and surgery faced the old Victorian police station. And beside it was Church Lane that led to the vicarage and *All Saints*. As Clement walked through the village he smiled and was greeted by people he had known for years. One of the shop doors suddenly opened and young George Evans, the local postman, stepped out.

'Afternoon, Vicar,' George called.

Clement smiled at the boy who continued on his rounds. *Afternoon, vicar!* How many times had Clement heard that in twenty years? Village life; its familiar routine was like an old and cherished clock; a blessing when all its parts worked in harmony. And it had for the most part been a blessing.

He turned right into Church Lane.

He almost ran to his cottage. The last of the flowering shrubs by the fence and the hanging basket of brightly coloured annuals lifted his heart. Opening his front door he went straight into the kitchen. Holding Mary in his arms, he breathed in her scent. He hoped never to forget it.

'Well! Do tell me, Clement? Are you to be Archdeacon Wisdom?' Mary asked breaking free of his embrace.

Clement shook his head. 'It was Home Guard business, Mary. Johnny has been made a regional commander and they want to increase the role of the Home Guard. Nothing very exciting.'

He saw her face fall.

'Never mind. We're happy here, aren't we?'

She smiled and picked up the knife on the kitchen table. 'Well, we've had some excitement. And I was a bit concerned for you, Clement. The village is buzzing about German planes seen flying north.'

'German planes?'

'The men on duty last night with the Observer Corps reported hundreds of German planes flying overhead. Did you see them in London?'

'You wouldn't recognise London, Mary. Sandbags, barricades and windows boarded up everywhere. There is such confusion. Johnny will be coming down on Sunday. Says he would like to meet some of the men from the Home Guard.'

The bean stringing stopped. She was staring at him but said nothing.

He saw the slicing recommence. And the tight corners of her mouth.

'I will arrange sandwiches,' she said, the knife cutting a carrot.

He knew he had evaded her question about the German planes, and he'd heard the controlled disappointment but he couldn't talk about them for fear that he would let something slip about the Auxiliary Units. As the seconds ticked by, he couldn't think of what to say and the need for an answer faded.

'Well, I'll just go and unpack my bag,' he said leaving the kitchen.

He heard the distinctive sound of the tongue in the lock click as he closed his study door. Mary wouldn't disturb him until supper time. He needed to be alone to consider the men and the attributes each would bring to the group. He stared through the window at the evening sky. He felt guilty about evading her question. Secrecy. It divided. And he didn't want any enmity, especially with Mary. He pondered the role of women. Was it solely to care for others? Clement remembered all the women he had seen in London in uniform and wondered if it would be different in the future.

Swivelling in his chair, he turned to face his desk. He took his notebook from his jacket pocket and read the two names already on his list: Peter Kempton and Reginald Naylor.

Peter's calm analytical mind would be an asset to the group, and although his friend was now fifty-five years old, he had kept fit from walking the South Downs Way with Boadicea, his black Labrador. Reginald was a land-owner - not gentry, but he had made his money from selling American sewing machines to British house-wives. Unlike Peter, Reginald was not a member of the Home Guard. He was married, but other than his wife Geraldine and a grown son who had moved to Australia to run a sheep station, Reginald had no dependants.

Clement leaned back in the seat and, turning the chair, gazed out the window. The list was proving harder to compile than he'd imagined. He decided to make a start on his sermon. He hoped by doing so his subconscious mind would filter names. He reached for his lectionary and turned to Sunday the Eighth of September - the fifteenth Sunday after Trinity - and read the suggested Biblical texts. He decided to focus on divine help in adversity through faith. As he wrote, names flowed in and out of his mind.

By supper he had twenty names.

An hour later it was a dozen.

By bedtime he had a short list of nine men.

Peter and Reginald, Clive Wade the baker, young George Evans the postman, Ned Cooper - a widower who had a farm on the outskirts of the village - the village doctor, Phillip Haswell, Inspector Russell's son, Stanley, the local butcher and John Knowles, the bank manager.

Clement turned off the lights in his study and opened the curtains, staring through his study windows at the slice of moon which shone above them. The moonlight would increase each day from now on. He reached for his calendar and checked the moon's cycle. The full moon would be the sixteenth of September. That night and the nights either side of it, London would be lit up by the heavens. He stared up at the omnipresent moon, frowning. He hadn't heard the low drone of the bombers this evening and he began to wonder if the previous night had been a rehearsal for something far more catastrophic.

5

Saturday 7th September

Reginald and Geraldine Naylor were not exactly reclusive, but Clement had only occasionally been to their home. It was a large, two storey red-brick house, covered in Virginia creeper and the epitome of its owners; conservative, ordered, with evident Protestant frugality.

Clement and Reginald sat in the drawing room while Geraldine brought a tray of tea and fish paste sandwiches.

'Is that all we have?' Reginald looked up at his wife.

'And lucky to have anything, what with the convoys being targeted the way they are. Remember Mister Wade's boy?'

'Damn Germans!' Reginald Naylor added.

Clive Wade, the village baker, was on Clement's list for the very reason that Clive had lost both his sons during the year. The baker had, understandably, an entrenched and vocal dislike for the Germans. He also

41

drove a van for home deliveries and knew his way better than most around the 'un-signposted' country lanes.

'Well, Vicar? I am guessing your visit is not entirely social?' Reginald said.

Clement placed his cup and saucer on the low table before him and shot a glance at Geraldine then cleared his throat.

Reginald's teacup hit the edge of the saucer, spilling tea onto the rug.

'Reg!' Geraldine chided and ran from the room.

'Quickly, Vicar, you have about a minute.'

'I have been asked to form a sub group to the Home Guard which I would like you to be involved in. Can you come to a meeting in the vestry tomorrow after church?'

'I'll be there. Probably not the service. What time?'

'Midday.'

Reginald Naylor nodded as his wife returned with a towel and a fresh pot of the palest tea Clement had yet seen.

They talked mostly about the bird life of the Downs. Geraldine raised the German planes sighted the night before last but Clement said he knew nothing other than the rumours that everyone appeared to know. He drank his tea. Half an hour later, he left.

It surprised Clement to see the black car parked outside the vicarage. Standing in his opened doorway, he listened. He could hear Mary's voice. She was laughing. It was like a sudden burst of sunshine to his ears. He followed the sound of voices to the kitchen.

'Hello, Clement. Mary has asked me to stay. I do hope that's convenient with you also?'

'Johnny! We expected you tomorrow. Is everything alright?' Clement asked.

'Yes. I had some business in Brighton which concluded sooner than I'd expected. I hope you don't mind me showing up earlier than anticipated?'

'Of course not. But I do have two commitments today. A wedding later this morning and a baptism at half-past three. If you wouldn't mind waiting?'

'Not at all, Clement. We can continue our chat about old times when you're free,' Johnny said smiling. 'Besides, it gives me the opportunity to chat with your better half.'

Mary laughed. Sandwiches were being churned out. Fish paste. Clement made a mental note that if England won the war, he would never eat fish paste again.

'Now, you two go into Clement's study. I'll bring the tea as soon as it is ready,' Mary said.

'Every vicar should have a wife. In fact, I don't know how I've managed without one all these years!' Johnny told them.

Mary laughed. Clement and Johnny left the kitchen and walked along the corridor to Clement's study. Johnny's ability to charm had not changed in twenty years. It was a skill Clement had never acquired. Pity, he told himself; charming people got church roofs fixed and organs repaired. He closed the door to his study, the familiar click of the lock soothing his ear.

'Has anything happened, Johnny?'

Johnny smiled. 'Do you have your team, Clement?'

Johnny hadn't answered his question, but Clement ignored it. 'Nine. I've made a list. And my assistant with the church?'

Johnny reached into his coat and handed a slip of paper to Clement. 'Reverend Herbert Battersby, retired but lives in Lewes. A good man - knows how to be discreet but will only come when you call him. All he knows is that you have Home Guard duties which could call you away at a moment's notice.'

'Excellent,' Clement said, reading the name and telephone number. Placing the note on his desk, he opened his diary and took a small piece of paper from between the pages and handed it to Johnny. 'Everyone on that list has either a knowledge or skill which, I believe, will be useful.'

Johnny listened while Clement told him about the men. First was his friend Peter Kempton, the village solicitor, who had a way with leading people and carried authority in the village. 'I also play chess with Peter, so I know the way he thinks. Good man - thorough, plans ahead. Then there is Clive Wade. He lost both his sons earlier in the year. It has made him not so much bitter as determined to see our enemy defeated. For this reason I believe Clive would be an asset to the unit. I spoke with a local landowner, Reginald Naylor, earlier this morning. Of course, he can fire a rifle and, from what I've heard, is an excellent marksman. He will attend the meeting tomorrow after church. I have also selected our local postman, George Evans, a lad from Wales who is an accomplished Morse Code telegrapher. That and because he delivers the post, means George knows most of the goings-on in the village. However, George does have a heart condition so the army wouldn't take him, but I know he has a personal reason for doing his bit.'

'Which is?'

'I did say I wouldn't tell anyone, Johnny.'

'Sorry, Clement, no confessional privileges. Not for this. I must know everything about them. All our lives are in their hands.'

'He received a white feather. Don't know who sent it, but it was a beastly thing to do to the lad. He used to be so carefree but now, it's almost as if he has something to prove.'

'And the heart condition?' Johnny asked.

'Irregular rhythm, apparently. Considered minor but enough for the services to refuse him.'

Johnny nodded, his gaze returning to the list. 'Ned Cooper?'

'Ned is a farmer. He has been a widower for many years and his father, who assisted him with the farm, died last year. Then recently, Ned's only son, an awkward boy, was killed when a Stuka fell from the sky over their fields. Some of the shrapnel hit him. Cut the lad in two.'

'Who will be running the farm in his absence?'

'He has three Land Army girls who do wonderful work. I have included Ned for several reasons: he can use a gun, he is physically strong and a decent man, but there is a profound sadness about him. Due to his son's death, there's no one now to inherit the farm and, in my opinion, Ned is without purpose in life. I believe the Auxiliary Units could give him that, even if only for a short time.'

Clement went on. 'The sixth is Stanley Russell our butcher. He is single, and of course, can use a knife,' Clement stopped. Beans and carrots. Perhaps he should have asked every married woman of twenty years or more to join. 'Then there is Doctor Phillip Haswell. Phillip lost his wife in childbirth about three years ago. The child also died. He hasn't remarried and has no dependants. And finally John Knowles, our bank manager. A good man,' he paused. 'But I cannot decide if he should be included.'

'Why?'

'His wife, Margaret, is expecting a child. This alone should be a reason to exclude him. However, John is what Mary would describe as "highly strung".'

Johnny raised his eyebrow. 'Why do you wish to include him?'

'He speaks German.'

Johnny nodded. 'You said that Mrs Knowles's pregnancy alone should be reason to exclude the husband. Do you have other reservations?'

'Our police chief, David Russell, to whom I must give the list of names, is very charming. Too charming. David, apparently, enjoys spending time with other men's wives. Margaret Knowles appears to be a favourite. It is probably innocent, but this is a small village and people talk.'

Clement watched Johnny process the information.

'And lastly, me.'

There was a light tap on the door.

'That will be our tea,' Clement said, opening the door.

Mary stood in the hallway but there was no tray. 'John Knowles was just at the door, Clement,' Mary told him in a low voice. 'He is very agitated and wanted to speak to you but I said you were with someone and that you would call him later. I'll get the tea.'

He watched her walk back along the corridor before closing his door again. He heard the click.

'Anything you need to look after urgently, Clement?' Johnny asked.

'It can wait,' he replied. But something troubled him about John Knowles's visit. Clement hadn't heard the doorbell. He glanced at the window. It was ajar. Had John overheard their conversation? Clement chastised himself for being so suspicious. Why would anyone stand under a window amongst the flower beds eavesdropping anyway?

'We'll leave out the bank manager. Language skills aside, the man may not have the mental stamina. Imagine if he was interrogated by the Germans.'

Clement nodded. He could almost visualise Knowles telling the Germans anything they wanted to know.

'And the doctor,' Johnny continued, 'we will exclude also, because his skills will be required in the village. Are they both Home Guard?'

'John Knowles isn't. Phillip Haswell is, although due to his vocation, not in a position of authority - but he is a Church Warden. Whilst he is a quiet, unassuming man, I know he'd be disappointed not to be included, if he knew about the Auxiliary Units.'

'That can't be helped,' Johnny said. 'This butcher, Stanley, he's a stable character?'

'Yes, I think so. Although his father treats him rather badly.'

'Father?'

'Stanley is Inspector Russell's son. But he's a decent young man.' Unlike his father, Clement thought. 'I'm sure Stanley will be an asset to us. It could be the making of him.'

'And you don't foresee any problems when the time comes to eliminate the Inspector?'

'I know this will sound odd, Johnny, but I don't believe Stanley will be too upset at his father's passing.'

Johnny nodded. 'You have chosen some interesting people, Clement. So, what's your sermon for tomorrow about?'

They talked for an hour about everything and nothing; the old days at Oakhill, rationing, London. But the German planes, everyone's favourite subject, were not mentioned. Toward eleven o'clock Clement reached for his cassock and stole and dressed before leaving the vicarage to greet the bridal party at the church.

Johnny stood and walked with him to the doorway. 'Don't worry about me, Clement. I can amuse myself. Perhaps I can assist Mary with the sandwiches.'

'Sorry, it's such a busy day.' Clement said. 'In addition, I have a baptism at half past three. But I should be back well before supper time.' Gathering the wedding and birth registers, he left Johnny sitting in his study, reading theological tomes. Closing the garden gate, Clement walked up the hill towards the church.

It was just after four o'clock when he returned. Johnny was exactly where Clement had left him reading. He hung his clerical robes on the hook and placed the marriage and baptismal registers on his desk.

'All went well?'

Clement nodded.

'Mary says dinner will be at seven.'

'Can I interest you, Johnny, in a stroll on the Downs before dinner?'

As they walked down Church Lane, Clement told Johnny about his lunar observations.

'An interesting theory.'

Within the hour they stood on a ridge and surveyed the expansive valley before them transform from verdant green dotted with the rustic colours of autumn, to deep purple in the dwindling evening light. The sky turned a translucent blue and the occasional star twinkled above them. A crescent of golden moon was low in the sky. It was a breathtaking sight. But it made Clement think about the full moon and the nine days before the sixteenth. He glanced at Johnny who had followed his gaze to the heavenly realm.

'If your theory about the full moon and the rehearsal run is correct, Clement, then we have nine days before the sixteenth to ponder it. And it is true that last night there was no bombing in London. But...'

Clement reached out to grab Johnny's arm. 'Listen, Johnny.'

Silence.

'Listen,' he said again. Clement stared into the evening sky. Although the light was fading, it was not yet dark. He squinted, scanning the darkening sky. He couldn't yet see them but he knew they were there. 'Aeroplanes, Johnny. More than one and not fighters. I know the sound of fighters. We've heard little else for over a month.'

'Are you sure?' Johnny asked.

'No. But I'm certain the drone is different. It's lower.'

'There!' he pointed at the black specks in the sky which grew with every passing second. The low drone increased. Within minutes it was noise, too loud to ignore. As they passed overhead the sound was like thunder.

'I must get back to the vicarage,' Johnny said, running back along the path.

Clement was out of breath as he opened his front door. Johnny, who had run ahead was standing in the hallway, the telephone receiver in his hand.

'Bombers, aren't they?' Mary asked as Clement entered the house. 'Could you see them?'

'Yes.'

'London?' she asked.

'It would be my guess.'

Johnny was depressing the dial tone buttons on the telephone repeatedly and shouting for the operator, then replaced the receiver. 'I can't get through. The lines must be down.'

There were multiple possible reasons for that, none of them good.

'Should we go into the shelter?' Mary asked.

'They're too high for us,' Clement remarked.

'No such thing any more, Clement,' Johnny added. 'But it is unlikely they would target Fearnley Maughton. Have you drawn the blackout curtains? No point in giving them direction lights.'

'I'll check the bedrooms,' Mary said disappearing up the stairs.

Clement went into his study and drew the curtains. He could only imagine what must be happening in London.

They sat in the dimly lit sitting room eating a dinner of tinned lamb's tongue and vegetables. There was little conversation. They prayed for London and James and Helen Moore.

An hour later Clement opened the front door and peered out. Dusk had come and gone, and night had

50

descended. No bombs had fallen on the village and no sirens had wailed. Every ten minutes Johnny tried the telephone, but it was a further hour before he could contact The Admiralty. Only overhearing half the conversation did not make any of it intelligible, but Clement guessed what was being discussed. He listened for the word "Cromwell" but it hadn't been voiced.

'I should return to London,' Johnny said entering the sitting room. 'There are things I need to do. It was my great pleasure to meet you Mrs Wisdom. And thank you for the dinner.'

Clement walked with Johnny to his car. 'Is there anything you'd like me to do?'

'Just get your team, Clement. The training will take a minimum of two days. As soon as you and your men have returned to the village, be in a state of readiness.' Johnny lowered his voice, his eyes glancing around. 'Gubbins believes the invasion has begun.'

6

Sunday 8th September

He chose *O God, our Help in Ages Past* as the gradual hymn. Clement climbed the pulpit steps and gazed around those present. Every pew was filled; even the Naylors were present. He had tailored his sermon around Divine help in adversity. Despite being written before the two devastating air raids on London the previous night, its relevance could not have been missed. Three hundred German planes had pounded the city in two successive waves, especially the East End, causing massive destruction and hundreds of people were dead or homeless. Invasion was on everyone's mind.

Clement finished his sermon with a quote from the Prime Minister about preparation, duty and confidence. He even included his favourite line from Shakespeare.

'Excellent sermon, Clement,' Peter said as they stood in the church doorway.

Clement smiled as Peter wandered away, ambling towards the graveyard to wait away from the general congregation. Clement shifted his attention to the next parishioner. The well-proportioned Mrs Greenwood hovered in front of him. As the village postmistress and telephone exchange operator, the woman knew more than she should about village affairs.

'Good Morning, Mrs Greenwood.'

'Vicar. I think you should know,' she whispered, 'there are deeds afoot.'

'I'm sorry, Mrs Greenwood. I'm not sure I understand you.'

'Perhaps I shouldn't say but…'

'Then perhaps you shouldn't, Mrs Greenwood. The Bible has much to say about gossip.'

'Well, I just thought you should know that Margaret Knowles's bicycle has been seen...'

'Yes. Thank you, Mrs Greenwood. I mustn't keep you. I'm sure you have a great deal to do.' Clement turned his attention to the next person standing in the queue. Mrs Greenwood strode away.

Twenty minutes later he checked the church to see if anyone remained, then closed the main door and hurried to the vestry to remove his cassock and stole. He knew the men would be assembling outside and he didn't want their presence there to cause suspicion, especially with the eagle-eyed Mrs Greenwood.

On a pillar to his right was a small mirror in which he could see his clerical collar. His gaze rested on it. He always wore it - it symbolised everything his Christian faith meant to him. 'Not for this,' he muttered, pulling it from his shirt.

Clement opened the small door to the churchyard. Six men stood waiting, brief smiles the only communication between them.

'What would you like us to do, Vicar?' Stanley Russell asked as they filed in.

'If you give the man a chance you'll find out,' Peter chided.

Clement smiled. Leaders and followers. He had seen it during his training for the last war. Some would exhibit what his former commanding officer had called, "leader's legs". Others would follow. And some would fail. Only time could tell. But all had to make a decision and all had to know the worst.

Clement stood before them, his gaze shifting from one smiling face to the next. He had known them all for many years, but now it was different. He tugged on his lower lip; the seriousness of what he was about to ask of these men, almost intimidating. 'Commander Winthorpe should have been here today to meet you and tell you the reason for this meeting. However, with the bombing last night in London, he was needed there.' Clement glanced down at his notes. 'I have to tell you that what I am about to discuss with you, and ask of you, is both extremely serious and highly secret.' He looked up. He saw the smiles being replaced with frowns. There was total silence. Clement went on. 'I have been asked to form a top secret, special group. You have been selected specifically, by me, for your skills and character. This will not be for the faint-hearted. It will be tough, physically and mentally, and there will be no disgrace if you decide not to be involved. We have all witnessed the planes in the skies this last month, and now they are bombing our homes, not just our factories. Invasion is no longer probable, but imminent. If the Germans land along the Sussex coastline, it would be our job to stay behind enemy lines and do as much damage to their advance as possible.'

'Like guerrilla fighters?' George said.

'Yes,' Clement said aware of George's excitement.

'More than Home Guard duties, Clement?' Ned Cooper asked.

'Yes.' Clement looked into each face. 'I cannot force you to volunteer. It is dangerous, and you will most probably not survive. Should you agree to be part of this special group there will be some extra training involved and, of course, you will be required to sign the Official Secrets Act.'

A palpable silence settled.

'How much time do we have to think about it?' Reginald asked, breaking the silence.

'Not much. In fact, I need your answer before you leave here today,' Clement told them.

The men stared at him for what seemed like hours.

'Where is this training?' Clive asked.

'Wiltshire.'

'How long would we be away, Clement?' Peter asked.

'You'll be back on Thursday. As far as your family and anyone else are concerned, you are doing exercises with the Home Guard. I wish to stress that this is top secret and cannot be discussed with anyone. You should know that the penalty for breaching the Official Secrets Act is death by hanging.' Clement paused. 'The Official Secrets Act aside, our safety lies in our coherence as a group and our loyalty to each other.'

'I don't have anyone to stay alive for anymore, so count me in,' Ned Cooper said.

'Thank you, Ned.' Clement understood the man's reasoning.

'It doesn't give us much time to rearrange things. I've got meat that needs portioning for the rations,' Stanley said.

Clement stared at the young man. 'I'm sorry about that, Stanley but time isn't exactly on our side.' Clement had expected some degree of apprehension, or even excitement, but given what was happening around them, he had not anticipated that chopping up meat would usurp the Prime Minister's plans to thwart the invading enemy.

'No, we apologise, Clement,' Peter said, glaring at Stanley. 'I don't think any of us really believed the invasion would happen this quickly. Of course we will reschedule things.'

'I suppose Gladys can do it,' Stanley added in a low voice.

Clement saw the pink flushes in Stanley's pale cheeks. The man would feel silly enough without further comment. At least, Clement hoped so.

Courage is a curious human trait. It has no signs or symptoms until displayed. Every man among them joined the team without further hesitation. He almost thanked the Germans for the bombing of the previous evening, and Peter for his steadying influence.

'You need to be at Lewes Station tomorrow morning at six o'clock. Wear your Home Guard uniform, if you have one, and bring only your personal needs. Everything else, including weapons, will be provided. May I remind you that you are not permitted to discuss this with anyone. Is that clear?'

Heads nodded and it was most certainly a different group of men who left the vestry.

Clement closed the door behind them and locked it. Despite the sobering effect of what he had said, he felt an odd sense of pride in his selection. Every one of them had agreed. Clement wondered about Stanley's acceptance, hoping the man's decision was not solely due to embarrassment. Regardless, he had a few days before he needed to make the final selection. If Stanley, or any of them, proved unsatisfactory, they would be excluded. Clement checked his watch. His new assistant, Reverend Herbert Battersby was arriving on the three o'clock bus from Lewes, and Clement wanted to spend some time with Mary. Hurrying through the cemetery, he walked down Church Lane to the vicarage.

A meal of cottage pie and vegetables was already on the table when he arrived home. Mary had already begun her plans for Invasion Day. She had organised a central emergency assembly point at *The Crown,* where a roll of all the villagers' names had been drawn up. She had even asked Doctor Haswell to place some emergency medical supplies there.

A few minutes before three, Clement wandered down to the bus stop by the village green and sat in the shelter. The bus drew up and an elderly man alighted wearing a clerical collar.

'Reverend Battersby?' Clement asked.

'The same. Reverend Wisdom, I'm imagining.'

'Thank you for coming.'

They wandered towards the vicarage where Clement knew Mary would have some tea and cake waiting. Clement learned that Battersby was nearly eighty years of age and had been a vicar for fifty-five years. Clement decided there wasn't much about parish life that Battersby hadn't encountered. The man had a winning way about him that exuded calm efficiency, and Clement believed that Johnny couldn't have found a more perfect man for Fearnley Maughton.

Together they discussed the Invasion Day plans and parish business for some hours before Clement walked the elderly man back to the bus stop.

'Given the circumstances, it's been a most pleasant afternoon, Reverend Wisdom. Thank you.'

Clement smiled at Battersby as the bus door closed. With Battersby attending to the parish and Clement's team selected, he and the villagers were as prepared now as they could be for whatever eventuated.

7

Monday 9th September

Lewes Railway Station was cold and a lazy wind had accompanied the early light. Stamping his numb feet, Clement drew his overcoat around him and stared at the heavy, damp fog hanging like a shroud over the valley. Behind him, the towering barbican of Lewes Castle loomed above the High Street. His gaze settled on the parapet. A thousand years had passed since a foreign power had successfully invaded. It was a proud history and one to cling to when fear and hopelessness tried to conquer. He pushed the thought from his mind with a silent verse of *Onward Christian Soldiers*.

Peter joined him. 'Morning, Clement. All the men are here. Except one,' Peter said nodding towards the huddled group of men, chatting.

'Really? Who?' Clement said as the smoke of the approaching train became visible.

Within minutes people from the waiting rooms were gathering on the platform. Hurrying through the crowd ran Stanley Russell, his face florid.

'Sorry I'm late, Vicar.'

Clement felt a frown crease his forehead. 'Just get aboard, Stanley. Don't be late again.'

'Right you are,' Stanley grinned.

Clive Wade stood beside him. 'He'll be late for his own funeral, that one.'

Clement pursed his lips. He watched Stanley board the train, hoping his decision to include the boy wasn't a mistake. Clement took his seat, his mind still on Stanley. The next few days would sort the lad out, one way or the other.

Peter had already boarded and commandeered two compartments for them. Spirits were buoyant and excitement kept the men chatting. They stowed their few possessions and within minutes the train pulled away.

It was mid-afternoon when they walked down the road, away from Swindon Station. Clement scrutinised the waiting cars and lorries, searching for a military vehicle. Parked to one side of the station was a three-ton truck marked with the GHQ Home Forces insignia, a lion rampant and the unit identification number 490. Clement walked towards it as the driver's door opened and a man in a corporal's uniform jumped down.

'Captain Wisdom?' the man asked.

Clement nodded.

'I am to take you directly to Coleshill House, Sir. Major Bannon is expecting you,' the corporal said.

Clement opened the passenger door and climbed aboard as the men threw their packs into the rear of the lorry then climbed in. The engine roared and the lorry pulled away from the station precinct.

'Are there any activities planned for this evening, Corporal?' Clement asked recalling his military training prior to the last war. In his mind he could hear the gravelly voiced Drill Sergeant of long ago telling the new recruits to form a circle of equal sides. He smiled at the recollection.

'Major Bannon's the one to speak to, Captain.'

Clement had hoped to have forewarning about any activities planned for the remainder of the day but the corporal remained unforthcoming. The army had a habit of springing exercises on the unwary.

Coleshill village sat atop a long ridge with a commanding view over the surrounding countryside. At the top of the ridgeline the vehicle left the main road and entered the estate through a pair of tall ironwork gates. Clement glanced at the passing meadows. On both sides of the drive were fields with stands of mature trees. Off to the east was the dense foliage of a forest. A few minutes later Clement saw Coleshill House, a beautifully proportioned four-storey mansion.

'The big house is for the officers. And the two old girls who live there,' the corporal told him.

'The owners are still in residence?'

'Elderly sisters, Sir. And their dogs. All other ranks are in the stables. Major Bannon regrets that due to you coming mid-week, there is no room for you in the big house.'

'It suits me,' Clement said. 'Actually, I'm a vicar. My boss was born in a stable because his parents encountered the same fate.'

The corporal smiled. 'Let's hope the Lord didn't have to worry about rats.'

Clement shuddered; the furry little bodies and their smell were instant reminders of the trenches. As the truck pulled up in a courtyard at the side of the big house, a man in a major's uniform approached them.

'Sorry I wasn't there to meet you, Wisdom,' the major said. 'Bannon is my name. Corporal Davis will show your men where to put their things and where you can get a cup of tea. We'll assemble at nineteen hundred hours in the house.'

'I understand I am also in the stables, Major?'

'Sorry about that Wisdom. Full up this week,' Bannon said, but there was no additional reason provided.

'Will there be any training this evening, Major?'

'Dinner is at nineteen thirty hours,' Bannon said. 'And tonight there will be an address by the Colonel followed by a lecture on intercommunication. Tomorrow we begin in earnest. It's a full programme, Wisdom. Usually we see recruits on weekends, but your group is a bit of an exception. Colonel Gubbins has given your sector top priority. You're from East Sussex, I understand?'

Clement nodded. 'What will we be learning?'

'Explosives in the morning. Unarmed combat in the afternoon, then a lecture on guerrilla tactics and after supper a lecture on the Jerry army. Then it's a night patrol, I'm afraid.'

While the major spoke, Clement watched the corporal herd his men into the two-storey stable buildings.

'And Wednesday?'

Major Bannon turned to face him. 'On your second day we teach you about your Operational Bases, where you'll be living once Jerry arrives. And then it's putting the theory into practise. Normally the groups leave in the afternoon but Gubbins wants your group to learn a bit more about our clandestine enemy.'

'Is there a reason for that?' Clement asked.

'You're pretty close to the coast there, Wisdom. It could be that you will encounter enemy spies. Best to know how to recognise them. And what to do with them when you do. Your lecturer for that session is a civilian…and a woman. Comes from a family in your line of work, actually. Then there will be your assessments in the evening. So you'll be leaving us on Thursday morning.' The major smiled. 'Remember Wisdom, you never know who you're talking to. We have a slogan for that: *The Enemy is Always Listening*. Well, I'll leave you to settle in. See you in the house at nineteen hundred.'

'Sir,' he replied, saluting.

'We don't salute here, Wisdom. Not a habit we encourage in our line of work. Remember Nelson.'

Clement watched Major Bannon walk away then followed the team into the stables. Inside were rows of timber bunks. Each had a rolled-up mattress and between each structure were a small cabinet and shelf. No adornment of any kind graced the walls or floors. Peter had the men stowing their few possessions.

Clement told them what he had learned about the training. 'Doesn't appear as though there will be much time for sleep. And a word of warning. Expect the unexpected. The army has a habit of arranging surprises for the unwary. Especially after a large meal. You may also encounter rats.'

'I think they will be the least of our concerns,' Reginald said, stowing his razor and soap in a cup on the shelf.

Clement was inclined to agree but he didn't say so. Experience had taught him that the army tested men's resolve at every opportunity. And it was as much a test of the man as it was of the team.

A whistle cut through the silence. Clement swung his legs over the bunk and stood up. In the pre-dawn light, the corporal was standing in the stable doorway. 'What is it, Corporal?'

'You need to locate a lorry on the grounds. About a mile south of here. Once you find it, climb aboard and drive it back here. You have one hour.' The corporal vanished.

Clement checked his watch; half-past five. He pushed his feet into his boots and tied the laces then stepped outside. A grey-blue light filled the courtyard, but the corporal was nowhere to be seen. In fact, nothing whatever stirred. Peter and Reginald were beside him.

'How do you want to do this, Clement?' Reginald asked.

Clement pulled a compass from his pocket, a last minute inclusion as he left the vicarage. 'Due south is back down the drive we came in by,' he said. 'Peter will you make sure everyone is up and that their boots are comfortable. We leave in one minute.

'What do we bring with us?' Reginald asked.

'As we haven't yet been issued with weapons, I can only surmise that this is a fitness exercise,' he said as the men strolled out of the stable.

'Look lively. And form two lines. Hurry up, Stanley!' Peter shouted.

Clement stared at the group. Other than Peter and Reginald, Clement didn't see much enthusiasm for the task. From the corner of his eye he thought he saw a curtain move in an upstairs window, but while he couldn't see anyone, he felt sure Major Bannon's eyes were on them. They formed two lines and broke into a slow run, heading south.

Twenty minutes later Clement signalled for the group to squat in the long grass. He could see the parked lorry under a tree about fifty yards ahead. There was no one around it.

'Thank goodness for that,' Stanley said flopping down into the grass beside Clement.

'Quit your whingeing, Stanley or I'll put you on the bus for Lewes myself,' Reginald whispered between clenched teeth.

Stanley's face flushed.

Whilst Clement thought Reginald's comment harsh, it had achieved the desired result. Clement looked back at the lorry. He was about to speak when he heard the motor start. The vehicle drove onto the drive and disappeared among the trees on the right. It was an old trick; one used to test stamina - physical as well as mental.

'Gather round,' he whispered. 'They either saw us or heard us,' Clement said, his eyes flicking to Stanley. 'We know approximately where it is, but from now on we only use the hand signals we learned last night. No talking and keep low. We will divide into two groups and approach it from both sides. Clive, Stanley and Reginald, you come with me, George, you and Ned go with Peter. And stay off the road.'

Forty minutes later they drove into the courtyard. Bannon was there, waiting. 'Well done, Wisdom. You only fell into our trap once.'

'What would like us to do now, Major?' Clement asked.

'I'll hand you over to Corporal Davis. He has some intriguing little gadgets for you.' Bannon left and the team followed the corporal into a wooden hut. In the centre of the space was a long table and on it were a variety of objects some of which Clement recognised.

'This morning we will be handling explosives and learning how not to blow ourselves up,' Davis was saying. 'This is a detonator.' Davis picked up a short aluminium tube about two inches long. 'Open at one end, they contain a very high explosive used to trigger a main charge, using Safety or Orange Line. The fuse is inserted into the detonator and crimped in place. Orange Line contains more gunpowder and burns at a rate of ninety feet per second.'

Clement looked along the line of men. Every eye was on the corporal, including Stanley's.

'This makes sense to me, Clement,' Clive whispered. 'Not all that running around we did this morning. I understand why we did it, but it still annoyed me. But this!' Clive said grinning. 'This is how we'll kill bloody Germans. As long as I get just two of them I'll be happy.'

Clement knew revenge was a powerful motivator and Clive's face was alive with the emotion. His gaze shifted to Ned, who Clement believed had an equally strong reason for despising Germans. But if Ned hated Germans it wasn't evident in either his manner or speech. Clement watched Ned's face; the knitted brow. If Ned did harbour any anger, it was contained within his complete concentration for the task at hand. Clement gazed at the other two older men of the group, Peter and Reginald. He felt vindicated in his selection of these men. While Peter had a natural ability to lead men, Reginald brought a sense of discipline to the group and Ned had the steadying hand of a father. All three, Clement considered, were rational and thorough and would in time be real assets to the group. By lunchtime, George too had demonstrated his abilities. The boy's need to prove his bravery, even if only to himself, had brought out a dexterity with wires and plastic explosives.

The early afternoon was spent becoming familiar with their new weapons. Reg, as he now liked to be called, had confirmed his reputation as a marksman and handled the Sten gun as though he was holding a pedigree cat. But the one Clement was increasingly unsure about was Stanley. The lad was a little overweight, always had a flippant comment to make and was invariably the last one to join the group.

'Where's Stanley?' Clement whispered to Peter as they walked from the Mess to the unarmed combat lessons on the front lawn.

'Lavatory.'

'He is always last. It's just not good enough. His cavalier attitude will cause someone's death, if he's not careful.'

Clement heard the crunching of gravel under running feet as Stanley joined them. 'Stanley, you really must be more punctual.'

'Sorry, Vicar. It won't happen again,' Stanley said, his flushed pink face shiny with sweat.

Clement glanced at Peter. He had heard the empty apology before. 'You really shouldn't eat so much, Stanley.'

A whistle blew. Corporal Davis, who was taking the hand-to-hand combat lesson, was waiting for them. Beside him were several straw-filled dummies in German military uniform. After teaching them how to dispatch a victim silently from behind, the corporal issued them with their Fairbairn Sykes Commando Knives.

Clement watched each man holding the dagger, getting used to the feel. He grasped the round tapered handle of his own knife and felt the weight of it in his hand. Its double-sided blade was about eight inches in length. It was a formidable weapon with only one function; silent, immediate death. If the seriousness of what they were doing had not impacted before now, Clement could see the weapon's transforming effect on the faces of his team.

Each man then practised using it, swinging and thrusting the lethal blade. But the person who astounded Clement was Stanley. Clement knew that, as a butcher, Stanley could use a knife... but the force with which Stanley plunged the dagger shocked him. He couldn't take his eyes from the lad. Stanley stood with his feet spread wide, the double-edged blade clenched in a tight fist, stabbing and punching the dummies with incredible ferocity. A stab wound aside, no man would survive Stanley's powerful blows.

'Interesting, don't you think, Clement?' Peter whispered. 'I'm pleased Stanley is on our side.'

'I'm inclined to agree with you, Peter.'

Returning to the stables, each man fell into his allotted bunk. Perhaps it was the realization of the gravity of their task or just complete exhaustion, or the very real impact of the Auxiliary Unit motto: *Terror by Night*, but the group were unusually quiet. The evening lecture on Gubbins's training guide, entitled *Nine Points of Guerrilla Tactics*, had been short and Clement was grateful. Every muscle in his body ached. And he still had no idea where or what awaited them on the night patrol. He suspected he would learn of their mission during the evening meal.

At nineteen hundred hours, Clement roused the men, starting with Stanley. Dinner was at nineteen-thirty sharp and lateness or slovenliness were not well regarded. During dessert, Clement received a sealed envelope. He nudged Peter's arm as he opened the orders. Inside the envelope was a map and their objective. The aim of the night patrol was to locate a specific road and blow up a German vehicle which would be carrying high-ranking German officers. The vehicle was expected on the road between midnight and one o'clock. Clement showed it to Peter then folded the note and placed it and the map into his pocket. 'Peter, would you tell the men not to eat too much and very little alcohol. And Peter, tell Stanley first.'

Peter nodded and quietly left his seat to speak to the team.

Clement checked the time; nineteen-fifty hours. He gazed through the long windows. The sun had not long set and the forest would already be cold and dark. He calculated that it would take them about two hours to reach the designated road.

At twenty-one hundred hours they returned to the stables where Clement told them of the evening's assignment.

'I have a map and target for tonight's patrol,' he announced, and told them his plan for the exercise. 'Check your weapons and packs. Make sure you have enough water and ammunition as well as detonators and explosives and be ready to leave in forty minutes.'

Clement checked his own pack but he knew everything was in order. Sitting on his bunk, he closed his eyes and spent a few minutes in silent prayer. There had been no time for reflection during the day. His thoughts returned to the men and their suitability for the task as members of a team. He believed the session on silent killing and the use of the commando knife had been a turning point. The profound consequences of the weapon on victim and attacker had been shared and had brought them together. Clement put his hand to where his clerical collar should have been, feeling less and less like a vicar. But, he consoled himself, his men, no doubt, would be feeling the same about their vocations.

At the allotted time, Clement assembled the men. Lifting their packs onto their backs and, picking up their Sten guns, they headed out in silence.

They fell into a mute column with Clement in the lead, then Stanley, George, Reg, Ned, Clive and Peter. Leaving the house on their left, they headed east for the tree line. Clement had decided to wear his Fairbairn Sykes knife strapped to his inner left calf. As he walked, he could feel it rubbing against his flesh. He knew in time he'd get used to it.

They walked in total silence.

Just before midnight they arrived at the road. Clement selected a section with a long curve for the ambush. Adjacent to the road was a depression surrounded by fallen timbers. Checking the site, he squatted by a hollowed log and shielding the torch light, studied the map.

'George, run a tripwire at head height at this point,' he whispered.

'Stanley, you and Clive place the charges. Use pressure switches and put two on the road in the tyre tracks about five feet apart.'

George ran the wire across the road as Clive and Stanley attended to the explosives. Each man then took up a position around Clement in a circle to await the target. He and George occupied the middle ground. In front of Clement, Peter, as second-in-charge, sat beside Ned whose finger rested on the trigger of his Sten gun. Off to Clement's left was Stanley. To his right was Clive and behind him was Reg. Soon all was quiet. The temperature was decreasing. They waited.

Clement looked around as the cold seeped into his body, clouding his mind and making him sleepy. Wiping his hand over his face, he signalled to Peter to move silently between the men making sure everyone was awake and alert. One o'clock came and went and still no vehicles appeared on the road. Clement blew a long breath into the night and watched his condensed breath float away on the crisp air. He rubbed at his face, blinking sleep away, and blew hot air over his hands. He signalled again to Peter to do another solo patrol around the area. Ten minutes later, Peter emerged from the trees off to Clement's right.

They waited.

Grey light from the half-moon penetrated the forest floor at odd angles, casting deep shadows across the sector. Nothing moved except the occasional sound of rustling leaves. He had expected the forest to have more noise. Small animals, something. Badgers, at least. The silence was unsettling, but given the number and frequency of explosions at Coleshill, the wildlife had, no doubt, left long ago. Clement looked over a fallen log. He could see Peter and Ned in front of him, lying on the cold earth. Time passed. Nothing happened. He realised the timing had been deliberately wrong. Designed to catch them asleep or heighten the nerves and put them on edge.

'Hurry up and wait', he repeated the old army saying. He shivered. Behind him, he could hear Reg shifting position in the shallow dugout.

Two o'clock.

The sound of an approaching vehicle was unmistakable in the thin, night air. Clement sat up and signalled the men to take up their positions. Ned and George crossed the road and lay under the shrubs opposite, their Sten guns aimed at the point where any single motorcycle rider would encounter the tripwire. The sound grew louder but it troubled Clement. There were two motors; one a diesel - a lorry perhaps - the other, he thought, a car. Sending Reg and Peter further up the track to attend to any other vehicles, Clement lay in the foliage with Stanley. Clive lay off to his right, behind a fallen tree trunk, three grenades lined up beside him.

As the open-topped car approached, Clement saw a door open and a figure jumped out and ran into the bushes at the side of the road several yards back along the track. In that second, Clement saw Reg rush forward. In one movement Reg had the man on the ground, pinning him to the earth as the car with three straw-filled dummies dressed as German officers ran over the pressure switches. A small explosion, much less than any real targets would ever feel, lit up the dark forest floor. Ned and George strafed the upturned vehicle with machine gun fire as twenty feet away, Peter came out of the shrubs beside the road, his Sten in his grip and pointing the weapon at the driver of the stationary lorry.

A whistle blew and Major Bannon stepped from the lorry. 'Well done, everybody. Remove any unexploded devices, then make you way back to the house.' Collecting Corporal Davis from Reg's grasp, Bannon climbed back into the lorry and they drove away.

Clement looked around at the men. 'Well done, everyone.' He saw the elation on his team's faces. It was deserved.

'Collect any charges you laid. George, will you retrieve the trip wire? Again, well done, everyone. Please remember, no talking on our return.'

Ten minutes later, they headed off silently crossing the forest. Within the hour they were in the fields, the chimneys of Coleshill House visible above the hedgerows.

8

Thursday 12th September

When they saw Swindon Railway Station again, they were different men. What they had learned in three days could be condensed into one word: sabotage. What they had become was also one word: assassins. Clement wondered if any of them would ever be the same after Coleshill.

They climbed aboard the train and settled quickly into two of the compartments. There was little chatter. Clement took a corner seat and rested his head against the window. The train pulled away from the station and soon they were heading south through the countryside.

Clement opened his eyes and glanced at the men. Ned and George were asleep. Peter and Reg were reading Gubbins's rules on guerrilla warfare, while Clive and Stanley were playing cards. Clement had known these men for years but he saw them differently now. Living and training beside them had brought a level of familiarity but at the same time, he realised just how little he had ever really known about them. He smiled recalling the last lecture they had attended prior to leaving Coleshill. It had been about human psychology. Beverley, the woman who had given the lecture, had asked them to analyse what motivated them. Killing Germans had figured high on the men's list. But her lecture had made Clement think more deeply about his own life than he had done in years.

For himself, he had accepted the role Gubbins and Johnny had asked of him because he believed it was his duty. She had asked them to question more fundamental reasons. Clement closed his eyes reflecting on what she had said. Human behaviour was condensed into two prime motivators; approval and the need to be loved. Reg had led a chorus of contemptuous remarks saying that he was there to kill Germans, not understand them. But Clement wasn't so sure. If you understood what motivated a person, you could manipulate them. It was almost sinister.

Clement's mind drifted to his own childhood. He had always believed his father, also a vicar, had never wanted or loved him. The man had been habitually stern and disapproving, and after Clement's mother's death when he was only fourteen, his father had become remote. Thereafter, Clement saw little of him. Then in '14, while Clement was fighting in France, his father died. Now Clement wondered if his long-held belief about his father's lack of affection for him was, in fact, true. Many men he had known had had strained relationships with their fathers. Did it always manifest itself in bitterness, or even anger?

He opened his eyes and began to go through what he had learned about the men of his team during the past three enlightening days. Peter Kempton, although now a widower, had had a Jewish mother-in-law who had moved to Germany after Muriel's death. Peter had heard nothing from her in over a year and had reacted to photographs Beverley showed during her lecture that depicted German brutality. He said that the photographs were designed to arouse anger. Perhaps that was correct. Reg had certainly reacted with an angry outburst about German cruelty. But Peter's reaction differed from the other men. Peter, always a proud man, had become withdrawn, even sullen, saying that the photographs weren't true and that Beverley and her kind were using the team as guinea pigs. Clement realised that perhaps Peter's indignation was not so much hatred for the Germans, as anger towards himself for allowing Muriel to journey to Switzerland alone? Perhaps the photographs were faked. Clement knew the army used arousal to garner men's emotions. He frowned remembering what they had learned about the Nazi policy towards the Jewish people. He felt sure Peter's quite understandable reaction was fear for his mother-in-law's whereabouts. He had tried to engage him in conversation about it, but Peter would not be drawn on the subject.

Beverley's lecture had, however, made Clement appreciate one thing; resentment and anger, in all its various forms, was a powerful motivator, and in one way affected every member of the group. In addition to his own bitterness towards his late father and Peter's situation, Reg, so he had informed them, was also angry because he had received notification that his home could be compulsorily acquired for a hospital. Reg could do nothing to prevent it, if the government so wished. Clement hadn't known about this. In fact, none of them had. Then there was Ned who, with the tragic death of his son, had lost his reason for living. Clive's anger for his lost sons was well known and George who felt unjustly wronged, saw the unit as a way to redeem his honour. But the one who worried Clement the most was still Stanley. Clement recalled the wide-spread feet, the powerful lunge, the force of the knife as it ripped the straw soldiers. After Beverley's lecture and during one of the brief periods of respite, Stanley had confided to Clement about his abusive childhood. Stanley's anger towards his father was embedded and long established.

Clement had never liked David Russell, whom he regarded as rude and unfeeling and of low moral character. Now, after what Stanley had said, Clement despised the man. The thought of taking the list of his closely linked group to the Inspector appalled him. He had fought against it, but Gubbins had insisted. The envelope with the list would be sealed but Clement feared the temptation for Russell to open it would be too great.

An hour out of Lewes, and while the others slept, Clement compiled the final list and sealed it within the envelope Gubbins had supplied for the purpose. It bore the Ministry of Home Security official stamp on the top left corner. He placed it into his top pocket, his thoughts returning to Stanley. Should the lad be excluded? But Stanley's strength was an asset, and during the few days at Coleshill, Clement thought he discerned a change in Stanley for the better. The lad seemed to have matured. Clement's fingers tapped the envelope within his pocket, the names burning into his chest. Stanley's involvement aside, if the operation went ahead, every man on the list, including Stanley, would die. It was just a matter of when. Perhaps he was worrying unnecessarily.

Even though they all lived within a mile radius of each other, dispersing at Lewes station had a sense of finality about it; of lost naivety. Was it acceptance that with a German invasion, the peaceful life they had formerly enjoyed was gone, perhaps forever?

Clement watched Peter walk away, up the hill towards Lewes High Street. His friend had said he wanted to purchase some books from the antiquarian bookshop in town. Clement wasn't sure the reason was genuine. But during the journey, Peter's sullenness had softened to some extent. They had talked about the first aid class he and Peter, as second-in-charge, had had to attend. They had studied photographs of stab and gunshot wounds. They had even learned at Coleshill how to amputate a limb, if this proved necessary. No member of the team should ever be left behind, dead or alive, and all traces of their presence were to be removed in the event of an aborted mission. And the subject of Peter's deceased wife and her mother was not raised between them again.

Reg and his wife Geraldine, who had come into Lewes to meet the train, had gone into town to do some shopping. Ned, Clive, Stanley and George walked ahead of Clement towards the bus shelter. They were a mixed group, as different as any could be in age and background, yet they seemed to have found a common purpose and he was proud of them.

Thursday was usually Clement's day with Mary. And now he had missed two, he felt the cool wind of disappointment.

'Would you like to go to Brighton tomorrow?' he asked as he entered the kitchen.

The spoon stopped.

'We could take that Victoria sponge with us and have tea on the esplanade, if you would like?'

'What are you up to, Clement?'

'Nothing! I just thought that as I was away last week and for the best part of today, you may like a trip to the seaside tomorrow.'

'Friday is your chess morning with Peter? To say nothing of your sermon for Sunday?'

'It would be nice to see the sea birds and smell the salt air again.'

She was watching him; the hazel eyes missed little.

'A nice thought, Clement. But I think your war games have tired you out and you're not as young as you used to be. Tea in Lewes will suit me just as well. Besides, I need to pick up some flour there.'

It was a quiet evening. The radio was full of news about London and journalists speculating about invasion. It was a topic he did not wish to discuss.

The telephone rang.

'I'll go,' Clement said.

'Clement? It's Johnny. Can you talk?'

'A little.'

'No invasion as yet but your group is on high alert. How was Coleshill?'

'Exhausting.'

'Good. Clement, you will be contacted by the Royal Engineers who are to build your Operational Base starting tomorrow. Could you select an appropriate site?'

'Of course, Johnny.' He glanced along the hallway. 'But could they work with my second-in-command?'

'That should be alright.'

The line went dead.

Clement held the receiver in his hand then dialled Peter's number. He was about to hang up when Peter answered.

'Sorry to disturb you, Peter,' he whispered. 'I do hope you were not in bed already. I wanted to alert you to a call you will receive tomorrow from the Royal Engineers. I have suggested that they liaise with you about selecting the place for the Operational Base. If you have no objections, I could use the morning to spend some time with Mary.'

'Of course, Clement. Happy to help. And Clement, don't worry about me.'

Clement smiled. 'Thank you, Peter. Good night.'

An hour later they lay in bed. He knew Mary wasn't asleep but they didn't speak. He was weary. Yet despite this, it was the unknown that drained him most. Johnny had said they were on high alert. Any day. He felt a surge of nervous anticipation. His thoughts turned to the Operational Base. He was pleased Peter had agreed to liaise with the engineers. Whatever had triggered his friend's reaction to those photographs seemed to have abated. The building of the Operational Base was a blessing all around. He said a short prayer, asking the Lord for forgiveness for its brevity and turned on his side. In the darkness he heard another wave of droning increase and decrease overhead.

'London?' Mary whispered, turning over in the bed.

'Probably,' he replied.

He felt her nestle into his side and he drew her close.

9

Friday 13th September

The door closed behind them as they stepped from the bus. Mary slipped her arm through Clement's. As they walked the narrow footpath of Lewes High Street, one unfamiliar face followed another, but his mind was not on the people of Lewes. The men of his cell occupied his thoughts. Private lives. Secrets. Skeletons. Their lives had been changed, no doubt forever, but it couldn't be obvious to the casual observer.

While the outward behaviour of the older men of the group had not altered, it wasn't the case for the two young villagers, Stanley and George. While in the village waiting for the Lewes bus, Clement had seen how differently they looked at him. George had even winked. It was foolish. Nothing about their activities at Coleshill could even be hinted at in the village and he intended to raise it with them the next time they were all together.

His thoughts lingered over Stanley. The lad was a special case, and even now Clement felt ambivalent about his inclusion. He would never forget what Stanley had confided about his father, nor could he erase the image of Stanley's powerful swing. Swift and deadly. Stanley had thrust the blade with such force that it had shocked them all. But, as Clement had discovered, each one of them had their Achilles heel. Anger, in all its forms, lurked within the human breast.

Anger lies in the lap of fools, he thought, quoting Ecclesiastes and holding the grocer's door for Mary. He waited while she purchased their ration of flour. With the neat, brown paper bag in her basket, they made their way to the tea room.

'Tell me about the meeting Monday night, Mary. I'm keen to hear about it.'

'It went very well, Clement,' she said sitting beside him in the bay window of the tea shop. 'We have compiled a roll of villagers' names and a separate one for any evacuees. It was a unanimous decision to make *The Crown* the assembly point, with the roll kept there. Doctor Haswell is putting some basic medical supplies there also. I made sure to include the local ARP warden in the meeting.'

Clement patted her hand. 'Well done. Let's just pray all these arrangements won't be necessary.'

The waitress brought the tea and Victoria sponge. Forty minutes later they walked back to the bus stop.

'Do you ever think about all the people who have walked this High Street since the castle was first built?' he asked.

'You believe the invasion is imminent?' Mary asked.

He did not answer. Not that he intended to avoid her clairvoyant question this time, but they had reached the bus stop and a young woman was seated in the shelter.

'Are you going to Fearnley Maughton?' the young woman asked.

For a moment Clement was struck silent by her astounding beauty. He gathered his wits. 'Yes. I am Reverend Clement Wisdom and this is my wife, Mary,' he said and tipped his hat.

'Pleased to meet you, Reverend Wisdom. I'm Elizabeth Wainwright. But everyone calls me Elsie.'

'Do you have family in Fearnley Maughton?' Mary asked.

The girl shook her head. 'No. I'm the new nurse and midwife. I have to report to a Doctor Haswell tomorrow. Do you know him?'

'It's a small village, Elsie.' Mary's voice was sharp. 'We all know each other. Where are you staying?'

'At *The Crown*. Is it all right? Decent, I mean?'

'It will suit you well enough,' Mary said. 'I didn't know Doctor Haswell required a nurse?'

'I answered the advertisement in *The Times*,' the girl said.

'Where have you come from?' Clement asked.

'London,' Elsie said. 'Actually, I'm pleased to find employment outside London. What with the bombing since Thursday night.'

'Is your family still in London, Elsie?' Mary asked.

'My parents lived in Eastbourne but they died some years ago. They were quite old when they had me. But central London isn't the safest of places at present so I'm pleased to be out of it.'

'Where did you work?' Mary asked.

'Charing Cross Hospital. Its near...'

'I know where it is,' Mary said.

'You'll find it very quiet here in comparison, Elsie,' Clement put in.

'I do hope so and I am looking forward to meeting some of the people in the village. Who knows, perhaps I will meet someone special.'

The girl beamed her flawless, wide smile, her intense blue eyes sparkling.

The arrival of the bus halted the conversation and Clement watched as she reached for a battered, red tapestry valise. It wasn't much bigger than Mary's shopping basket and he wondered if the girl had lost everything in the raids.

Mary didn't chat on the return journey. That was unusual. And Clement knew the cause. Mary's eyes had not shifted from the disarming Elsie Wainwright and he saw the evidence of disapproval in the corners of his wife's mouth. As intrigued as he was to learn why the girl should be the object of such scrutiny, he knew better than to ask.

'There's *The Crown*,' he said, as they drew into the village. He bent to pick up the girl's odd, red bag.

'I can manage, really,' Elsie said grasping the tote.

'Will we see you in church on Sunday?' Mary asked.

'Yes,' the girl said. 'That is if there are no babies to deliver.' She walked away, carrying her limited possessions.

There was no conversation at the kitchen table as they listened to the Home Service broadcast on the wireless. London was ablaze, especially in the East End. Bombs and burning aircraft fell from the sky. People everywhere were homeless. Hundreds of previously evacuated children who had returned to London had died or been orphaned. The fire brigade worked around the clock battling the overwhelming flames from incendiary bombs. Even the Palace and St Paul's Cathedral had taken a hit, and there was no indication that the bombing would cease any time soon. Clement stood and switched off the radio. A gloomy pall descended.

'Clement, I think I should visit Gwen. She will be frightened,' Mary said.

'Do you think it wise?'

'Wise or not, she's my sister and Windsor is not that far away. I could catch this evening's train and be back tomorrow.'

He didn't like it but there was little use protesting. Once Mary had decided there was no stopping her. He glanced at his watch. It was not yet five o'clock. And even though he would worry about her safety, her absence would give him the opportunity he needed to see David Russell.

Clement went to his study to consider what he should say to Inspector Russell. He closed the door and listened for the click. Sitting at his desk he reached for the envelope. He carried it on his person at all times and never took it out anywhere but in his study. He ran his finger over the Ministry of Home Security crest and pondered the names on the list one more time. As much as he hated the idea of Inspector Russell's involvement, with the bombing London and other major cities were receiving, he knew Gubbins expected the German invasion very soon. Clement convinced himself that it would only be a matter of days that Russell had access to the list. Although, that led to another unsavoury duty.

Within the hour, he walked with Mary to the bus shelter.

'I've left some sandwiches in the meat safe for your supper. And don't worry about me, Clement. I'll be back tomorrow on the evening train.'

He kissed her goodbye and waited only long enough for the bus to leave the village.

Clement walked away from the village green. Tapping his fingers against his top pocket, he felt for the envelope and strode towards Fearnley Maughton Police Station. It was a building he passed daily, many times, but it was also a place he rarely frequented. Even though giving the list to Russell still didn't sit comfortably with Clement, visiting the Inspector did give Clement a chance to familiarise himself with the building's layout. He pushed open the door and walked towards the desk. 'Good evening, Constable Matthews.'

'Good evening, Reverend. How can we help you today?'

'I would like to see Inspector Russell, if he is still on duty.'

'You're lucky to catch him,' Constable Matthews said, glancing at the clock on the wall. He entered Clement's name in the daily log and noted the time; five forty-five pm. 'If you'll take a seat, I'll let him know you're here.'

Clement sat in one of the upright chairs that lined the walls of the public area and slipped the envelope from his pocket. The sealed list felt warm and it had developed a curvature from contact with his chest. He replaced the envelope, pushing it down into his inside coat pocket.

He heard the slow but deliberate stride of Constable Matthews and the man reappeared. 'If you would like to come this way, Reverend?'

Constable Matthews held open the glass partition door to the rear hallway. Clement had never been on the business side of that door. He looked around. Before him was a long corridor. To his right and left were glass panelled offices while directly in front of him, at the end of the hallway, was Inspector Russell's office. The door was ajar but Clement could see the name painted on it in large gold letters: *Inspector D Russell*.

'Just the Inspector and myself here at present, it being late.'

'This won't take long, Constable.'

Matthews smiled. 'I was just off home.'

Constable Matthews tapped on the door, pushing it wide. Clement stepped forward and the constable closed the door behind him. Clement heard the heavy footsteps disappear along the corridor.

David Russell was a small man in his mid-forties - red-faced, red-haired and with piercing blue eyes. Clement had never considered the man's age before, but now that he knew Stanley's exact age and about Stanley's young life, Clement realised that David Russell must have been in his mid-teenage years when Stanley was born. It explained a few things. Russell remained behind his desk, making no attempt to stand or greet Clement, he simply gestured towards a leather-covered chair before the desk. 'Well, Reverend, what can I do for you? I hope you haven't come begging for money?'

Clement furrowed his brow, visualizing the day, which could be soon, when he had to eliminate the man. 'I have come on the most secret of issues,' he said, his voice low.

The Inspector slouched into the chair. There was something condescending about Russell's posture,

Clement thought, as if he were saying, what could you possibly know that would be deemed secret? A derisive sneer spread over the man's lips.

'Last week I met with Colonel Colin Gubbins in London,' Clement began. 'I have been asked to form an elite sub-branch of the Home Guard known as the Auxiliary Units. These orders have come directly from the Prime Minister.' Clement reached into his coat and withdrew the letter, his fingers pinching the paper. 'This contains a list of names; men who have been trained to kill the enemy once they land on our shores. Until that happens, the envelope must remain in your safe and can only be opened if a member of the public were to report seeing any local men doing something they consider suspicious. Should this happen, you are to contact me immediately.

'These men have authority far beyond your own. You will not impede them in any way nor interfere with their decisions.

'Only you and I know of the existence of this list. And it is to stay that way.' Reaching across the desk, he handed the sealed envelope to Russell who leaned forward to take it.

Russell turned the envelope over in his hand, his eyes taking in the official crest of the Ministry of Home Security.

'You will notice that the letter is sealed. I cannot express to you enough the seriousness of this. This letter is both a protection and a death warrant for those men should it ever fall into the wrong hands,' he paused. 'When I receive notification that the invasion has occurred, I will come here directly and you can open the letter in my presence. Until then, it must remain sealed and locked in your safe, and I am to witness it being placed there.'

'What's all this about, Reverend?' Russell said, his pink lips curling at the corners.

'I have told you all you need to know. If you wish to confirm anything I have said, you should call Colonel Gubbins on this number for verification.' Clement handed a folded piece of paper with Gubbins's London telephone number on it to the inspector.

'You're serious, aren't you?'

'Very. And I will not leave until I see that envelope placed in your safe.'

Russell picked up the telephone receiver on his desk. 'Bring me the keys to my safe, Constable.'

A minute later there was a light tap at the door. Matthews entered and walked towards Russell's desk with a set of keys.

Clement noted that Russell had blocked his view of the safe while he opened it and placed the sealed envelope inside. He considered it a contemptible gesture. Young Stanley flashed into his mind. He would have liked to chide Russell about the abusive treatment the man had served up to his son over the years. As it was, he was pleased to see the man reset the locks. Now he could leave.

'Satisfied?' Russell asked, handing the keys back to the constable and dismissing him.

Clement stood. 'Call Gubbins. And safeguard that letter with your life,' he said, his eyes flicking to the safe.

He left Russell's office. Just being in the man's presence made him bristle. Standing on the front step of the police station, Clement looked along the street in both directions. Opposite, the door to Doctor Haswell's surgery opened and the doctor stepped out. 'Evening, Clement,' Haswell said, closing his surgery door.

Clement smiled and returned the greeting. 'What a contrast,' he muttered thinking of the two men he had just seen. With the letter now in the hands of a man he did not trust, Clement felt vulnerable for himself and his men. There was little he could do; Gubbins had insisted.

As Clement left the police station, the door to the doctor's surgery opened again and Elsie Wainwright came out. The girl descended the steps and reached for Doctor Haswell's old battered bicycle that was leaning against the wall adjacent to the surgery door. Clement smiled and lifted his hat in greeting.

'Hello Reverend,' she said.

The crisp light voice was a stark contrast to the growl of David Russell.

'How are you settling in?' he asked.

'Very well, thank you,' Elsie replied. 'Just one more to see, then I've finished my rounds in the village. It is hard with all the signposts removed. But I suppose I'll soon learn the way.' Elsie beamed her angelic smile. 'I expect it's because they want to confuse the Germans, if they come.'

'Well, I must not keep you. It's getting late.' Clement lifted his hat in farewell. His gaze followed her as she cycled down the street and past the police station, disappearing from view, her nurse's cape billowing behind her.

Clement walked back to the vicarage. Sitting at the kitchen table, he unwrapped his sandwiches.

10

Sunday 15th September

Clement reached for his cassock and placed his stole around his neck. His mind was troubled. He had worried all night and throughout the previous day about entrusting the list to David Russell. He had no wish to disobey orders, but his instinct told him it had been a mistake. At least Mary had returned safely and for that he was grateful. Collecting his Bible from his desk, he closed the front door to the vicarage and strode up the hill. By the time he reached the vestry, he had resolved to telephone Gubbins first thing tomorrow morning then visit Russell to retrieve the list. Gubbins would just have to understand.

There were more people in church this morning, even more than the previous week. Fear of invasion was the most likely cause, but the number of young single men led Clement to believe that there was another reason. Half way back on the left-hand side of the church sat Elsie Wainwright. On one side of the girl was George Evans and on the other was Stanley Russell. As Clement stepped into the pulpit, he cast his eyes along the rows of his parishioners. Behind Elsie were several other single men who seemed very keen to pass her a hymn book already open at the correct page.

His sermon was on trust and betrayal. Not that the one person he had in mind for his instruction was actually in the congregation. In the twenty years Clement had been at *All Saints*, he had never seen David Russell in church.

After the service he stood at the door and shook the hands of his parishioners as they left.

'I see you have met our new nurse, Stanley,' Clement said, shaking Elsie's hand.

Stanley blushed. 'Elsie told me she met you and Mrs Wisdom in Lewes.'

George joined the group. 'She's coming with me to Brighton next week. We're seeing the new flick at the Palace Theatre.'

Clement glanced at Stanley. Then George. He saw the rivalry. Beautiful girls, lovely though they were - and Elsie was lovelier than most - caused trouble. And trouble between his men he could not have.

'Have you found somewhere more permanent to live yet, Elsie?' he asked.

The girl shook her head. It seemed to sway side to side, the corn-blonde hair falling and floating over her shoulders. On duty, Clement knew she would have to wear her hair pinned up under her nurse's neat cap, but not today. It was loose and curled and it glittered in the morning sunshine.

'We mustn't keep you, Elsie,' Mary said, standing beside him. 'Mrs Faulkner! Good morning to you. And don't the flowers look lovely today.'

Elsie and her entourage wandered away.

Among the congregation was another new arrival. Not to the village, as with Elsie, but among his flock. Coleshill may have shifted things for Reg Naylor, but Clement didn't believe the man to have had an epiphany. Attending church, or so it appeared to Clement from where he stood in the pulpit, kept Reg involved and informed. The man had taken a seat in the back of the church. During his sermon, Clement could see Reg's eyes scanning the assembled group, waiting and watching for trouble. Clement found it unnerving. The penetrative gaze had even sent Mrs Greenwood hurrying from the church. He decided that back row dwellers fell into two camps: shy and retiring, or misfits and rebels. He remembered his school days and the boys who claimed the back row. Without fail that second group ended up in the headmaster's office every Friday morning.

'A word, Clement?' Reg demanded.

Reg's pragmatic voice brought Clement back from the past.

'That needs to be nipped in the bud,' Reg said, his eye shifting to Elsie flanked by George and Stanley. 'I'll do it. You'll be too soft. Besides they know not to mess with me.'

Clement watched Reg stride away. He hadn't actually said anything, yet Reg had taken it upon himself to sort out what the man evidently saw as a breach of discipline. It concerned Clement that the man was becoming obsessive about their clandestine mission. Major Bannon had said that Reg was a born sniper. Clement knew Bannon was not only referring to Reg's weapons handling.

It was the psychological profile that fitted and that worried Clement.

'Reverend?'

He heard the shrill voice coming to him from the lychgate.

Ilene Greenwood was calling. 'Do you know where Nurse Wainwright is?'

'I last saw her walking towards *The Crown*, Mrs Greenwood,' Clement said. 'Is something amiss?'

'No,' the woman replied. 'I have a message from Mister Knowles. His wife has gone into labour.'

'Well you best hurry, Mrs Greenwood,' he replied. Babies. He knew nothing about them.

Checking to see that no one was still at private prayer, he reached for his key and locked the door. He didn't like having to secure the church. There was something inherently wrong about closing a house of God. Yet he would never challenge a directive from the Archbishop of Canterbury who had sent out the circular requiring the closures. Apparently churches had been used by German spies as dead letter drops. Until his visit to Coleshill, Clement didn't know what a dead letter drop was.

He thought of George Evans. He had chosen the lad to be their runner because of his knowledge of all things to do with the post and telegraph and for his ease of mobility. George collected Clement's report for General Headquarters, which commented on happenings around Fearnley Maughton, and he took it to their dead letter drop for collection by persons unknown. Amateur radio operators then forwarded the messages to London. The reports should have been simple enough, except that Johnny had decided that their fifteen-mile radius sector should also include the country adjacent to the coastline from Eastbourne to Brighton. Cuckmere Haven, just west of Beachy Head, had been added to the list of possible German amphibious invasion sites, so his reports of the coastline had to be received and transmitted daily, without exception. Although, Johnny had been explicit that none of his team could actually go to any of the beaches, especially Cuckmere Haven. Clement didn't know why and he did not care to know. Besides the beaches were off-limits anyway and most were festooned in barbed wire and, reputedly, mined.

'You know what they are saying about Margaret Knowles?' Mary whispered into his ear.

The question jolted Clement back to village reality. 'Mary, I have never taken you for a gossip.'

'You need to be prepared if John Knowles comes back again. That's all I'm saying.'

Clement stopped, his heart sinking. 'Oh dear! In all that's happened I forgot about him.'

'You know that they're saying the baby's not his,' Mary went on. 'She never deserved a husband like John. And that David Russell, he's a predator of the worst kind. They also say he takes bribes. They deserve each other!'

'Mary, I have never asked you to remain silent in the twenty years we have been married but I must ask you, please, no more. John has enough to worry about, especially if what you say is true, without being the victim of village gossip.'

Clement pushed open the vicarage door and went straight to the telephone. Lifting the receiver, he dialled John Knowles's number.

Mary sat beside him eating her lunch. There was no conversation. That was unusual. John had refused to speak to him. Clement felt the icy silence. Mary's wouldn't last but his forgetfulness towards John Knowles made Clement profoundly anxious. As did the revelation that David Russell took bribes. If the Inspector was corrupt with his own, how quickly would he tell the Germans about the list, especially if the man thought it would save his life? Clement's mind was made up, but he needed to think about how he was going to convince Gubbins.

'I'm going for a walk, Mary. I'll be back in a couple of hours,' he said reaching for his coat and hat.

Closing the front gate, he walked down Church Lane. As he turned the corner into the High Street he hoped he may meet Peter walking Boadicea and they could chat about the Operational Base while walking the Downs. He hadn't yet seen it, but Peter said it was exactly the same as the one they'd used for training at Coleshill and that they had chosen a site adjacent to the old Roman ruins about half a mile into Maughton Forest from the western side of the woodland.

Clement walked towards the village green, intending to take the bridle path to the South Downs Way. Even from some distance he could hear the laughter. He paused. The front windows of *The Crown* were open and he could hear the jollity flowing into the street.

Laughter. It is a wonderful sound; full of fun and happy expectation. He smiled just listening to its joyous tones. The bombings and chaos of London seemed worlds away and for a moment the village had taken on the innocence of its pre-war isolation. He walked towards the inn and opening the door, stepped inside. The pungent aroma of tobacco smoke filled the small, low-beamed front room. As the men jostled about, Clement caught a glimpse of someone sitting on the bar itself. It was Elsie. He could see her clearly now. The slender, crossed legs were swinging, the skirt pulled high over her knees and one high-heeled shoe was dangling from her toes. She was holding their attention so completely that no one had even noticed him.

'You better drink up, gents,' the barmaid called. 'We'll be closing in fifteen minutes.'

There was a chorus of groans. 'Go on, Elsie. Don't mind her,' one man said.

'You should have heard him scream,' Elsie was saying. 'She is grunting like a stuck pig, the baby's head just visible between her legs and he starts yelling, "Whose is it, you whore!"'

'Well?' said one of the men. 'Is it his?'

'Unless he had red hair as a kid,' she said. 'I'm guessing you probably know who.'

All heads turned. As the noise settled the crowd hushed and Clement could see Stanley sitting beside the fireplace. Stanley placed the glass on the hearth, his movements slow and deliberate.

'You've got a brother, it seems, Stanley,' one said.

Stanley stood and moved through the crowd, stopping beside Elsie.

Clement wasn't sure what Stanley intended to do, but as he watched, the door to the street opened and John Knowles staggered in.

All heads turned.

'Have a drink, John,' someone said. 'To wet the baby's red head!'

Laughter ricocheted around the small room.

For a few seconds John stood shaking, his thick spectacles askew on his nose. Knowles was only a slightly built man but the facial tick that manifested under stress caused the man's whole body to twitch and an unsightly red skin rash flamed across the pale cheeks. For one second he seemed to be attempting to show bravado, even defiance, but he stumbled backwards into the bar.

The crowd laughed aloud.

Knowles' shoulders drooped in defeat. 'I want a whisky!' he demanded, turning and grasping the counter.

'You must be drunk. We haven't had whisky for over a month,' the barmaid scoffed and pulled a beer, placing the glass on the counter.

The man drank it back.

No one spoke. All eyes were on him.

'I'll kill that bastard! Do you want to help me, Stanley? Or perhaps one of your special army friends could do it?' John slurred.

Clement felt his eyes widen. He stared at Stanley. John's words sent alarm bells clanging. He glanced around the room. All eyes were on either John or Stanley who were staring at each other. Had it been a throwaway line? A derisive, even sarcastic remark about the Home Guard? Or did John know something? Clement frowned remembering the telephone conversation. Knowles had been dismissive of him and the church, because he felt forgotten. Had John overheard anything? He had come to the vicarage the day Clement and Johnny had selected the members of the team. He glanced again at the crowd. It seemed to Clement that they hadn't paid much heed to the remark. Their interest lay in knowing the paternity of the child. A few seconds later John slumped onto the bar, his head in his arms. He appeared to be sobbing.

Stanley moved towards John then stopped and put his arm around Elsie. As the big man swept the girl from the counter, Clement met Stanley's gaze. Everyone turned, the chatter abating.

'You want a drink, Vicar?' the barmaid asked. 'You'll have to hurry if you do. I got to close in a few minutes.'

'No, thank you.' Clement turned to leave. 'John, go home. You have had enough alcohol. That applies to you too, Stanley.' He paused. He wanted the whole room to hear. 'The child is innocent. Just remember that when you cast your judgement.' As Clement turned to leave he stared at Elsie. The wide blue eyes flared back. She had bewitched them all. Even him. Mary had had the girl's measure from the start.

Leaving the bar, Clement closed the door on all he had witnessed and stood on the opposite side of the street. He felt for John Knowles. He had let the man down when he was most needed. For that Clement would be eternally sorry. But John's remark about special army friends worried him. There was nothing to be done. In fact, investigating it further would only increase speculation. He no longer wanted to walk on the Downs. He just wanted to be with Mary.

The public house door opened and John staggered out ahead of the other patrons who, no doubt, would return to the pub when it reopened in the evening. There was no point remonstrating with John about his condition or anything he had said in the heat of the moment. Whatever the man may or may not have overheard, he knew nothing. His head and heart were consumed with bitterness and the lifelong consequences of the day's event. Such things were all pervading. Clement tried to imagine the public humiliation John must be suffering. Small villages are unforgiving places. Yet forgiveness was the price he had to pay; for his wife and for David Russell, and for his own sanity. Not easily done. Anger and its brooding by-products were the outcome if John could not or would not forgive.

Clement stood in the street and watched the inebriated Knowles stagger away from the public house. For one moment he wondered if he should make sure the man went home. He couldn't. John had too many issues to deal with. Home for him would never be the same again.

Clement walked back across the green, but after only a few paces he stopped. Overhead he heard it beginning. The unmistakable low drone. He looked up. He knew from the radio that planes had been dropping bombs all day in London. In the afternoon light and with his eyes lifted, he watched, mesmerised. Within minutes the skies were filled with aeroplanes. Wing tip to wing tip, in massive formations; bombers and fighters. As the minutes passed, hundreds and hundreds of aeroplanes passed above him. He felt his heart sinking. Planes of every size and type were heading for the capital. People came out of the buildings and were standing in the street, struck dumb by the clamorous noise and number of the aircraft. Clement looked around him and saw the young grocer's wife crying, the tears falling unrestrained from her eyes. He felt dizzy with the volume of aircraft.

'What do we do, Vicar?' the young woman sobbed.

He heard the panic in her voice.

'Stay calm. It is unlikely we will be affected, Mrs Clarke. Go home and make sure your blackout curtains are in place. And look after your little one,' he said. But Clement was praying as he turned and hurried back to the vicarage.

11

Monday 16th September

George was at the front door, ashen faced, an envelope in his hand.

Clement reached for it and tore it open. His heart was pounding as he read the word, *Cromwell*.

'Go directly home, George and collect your pack. I will meet you at the Operation Base in,' he checked his watch. 'Two hours.'

'I don't know where that is.'

'Stay calm and do as I ask. Take the western path into the forest as far as the Roman ruins. The opening to the base is beside the fallen stone arch. Peter will be there.'

The boy nodded and ran back down Church Lane.

Clement closed the door and rang Peter. 'It's come, Peter. I'll call Reverend Battersby now, and collect my kit. Would you call Reg and Ned and tell them how to find the base? They must be there by noon. And uniforms from now on. I'll bring my pack to you, if you don't mind taking it with you. Then go yourself. I'll visit the others and see you at the base.'

'Of course. You are sure about it, Clement?'

'Yes.'

He rang off then telephoned Battersby.

Ten minutes later he took the church keys from his desk drawer and left the house. Unlocking the door to the vestry, he walked into the quiet little room with its tall stone walls and ancient windows. He glanced at the stained glass. The familiar scene of St George stared down at him. He reached into the desk drawer and withdrew another set of keys. Opening the cabinet that held the altar vestments, he reached for his pack and changed into his uniform which hung alongside his robes. Lifting the bag onto the desk, he checked the contents. The Sten gun and its silencer sat on the top of the arsenal of weaponry beneath. He took the Fairbairn Sykes knife from the bag and strapped the scabbard to his inner left calf. Replacing his trousers over the blade, he glanced around the vestry. All looked exactly as it always had, except now Reverend Battersby's robes hung on the hook behind the door. Five minutes later Clement was standing in the front hall of his home, the pack in his right hand. He could hear the sounds of running water coming from the wash house at the rear of the house. He walked along the corridor and saw her standing at the tub.

'Mary.'

His wife turned around. Her eyes took in his uniform and pack.

'It's come then?' she whispered.

He didn't know how she did it. 'I want you to go to the West Country. To your Aunt's place in Combe Martin. Take Gwen, if she'll go.'

'You're sure?'

He nodded.

'I'll leave for Windsor this afternoon.'

He wrapped his arms around her.

'Be careful, please.'

He felt her trembling.

'I love you, Clement.'

'I love you too.'

He left her in the wash house promising to contact her when he could. Standing in the hallway of his home, Clement's gaze traced every corner. He breathed in its smell. Swallowing, he opened the front door then called out to her, 'May God be with you!'

The running water ceased.

Time stood still in that second. He paused on the front doorstep before closing the door. Walking the short garden path, he reached for his bicycle that rested against the fence. It was the habit of decades; so unconscious an action. He lifted the pack onto his shoulders and swung his leg over the bicycle. Passing Phillip Haswell's house and the police station, he headed for Peter's office.

'He told me to expect you, Reverend Wisdom. You may go straight in,' Peter's elderly secretary, Miss Forster said.

Clement smiled and followed her instructions.

Peter stood to greet him. 'I've called Reg and Ned, just as you asked, Clement.'

'Good. I'll be there as soon as I can,' Clement said handing his pack over.

Closing the door to Peter's office behind him, Clement walked towards his bicycle. The file on Peter's desk, with its neatly tied pink ribbon, occupied his thoughts. He had no knowledge of what it contained, but someone's affairs would have to wait. Perhaps everything would be different, if and when the Germans were in charge. Things that seem so important in everyday life take on a different perspective in the light of invasion. A child had been born not twenty-four hours ago and was now waking to a very different world.

He cycled through the village heading towards Clive Wade's shop on the far side of the village green. As Clement opened the door to the bakery he saw Clive look up, the grey eyes resting on him. He knew that look. The expression of something expected but dreaded.

Clive removed his apron and stepped into the rear of his shop.

Pushing back the dividing curtain Clement followed. 'Midday, Clive. In uniform from now on,' and he told Clive where to find the base.

'I'll be there.'

On leaving the bakery, he said good morning to two ladies he knew. He found that difficult, knowing that he may never see them again. Reaching for the bicycle's handles, he pedalled towards Stanley's butchery repeating his favourite line from *Henry V*.

The bells on the door announced his presence but it was Stanley's shop girl, Gladys who greeted him.

'Could I have a word with Stanley?' Clement asked.

'He isn't here, Reverend. Hasn't been in all morning. It's most unlike him. But,' the girl shrugged her shoulders, a coy, knowing expression on her face. 'I did see him leave *The Crown* last night with Elsie. They are sweet on each other, those two.'

It had not occurred to Clement that when the time came one or more of his team might be elsewhere. He left the butchery and cycled towards Stanley's thatched cottage on the outskirts of the village. He paused by the front gate. Upstairs, the curtains were still closed and he wondered if Stanley and the girl had allowed their physical desires to overtake their common sense.

Clement knocked at the door and waited.

A full minute passed and still no one opened the door.

Clenching his fist, Clement pounded on the door.

No one came.

Annoyed, he cycled away. If Stanley had not been in his shop and was not at home, Clement could only imagine that the silly boy would be at the public house. Didn't Fearnley Maughton have enough immoral behaviour? The pretty Elsie Wainwright, with the long slender legs and provocative ways, flashed into his mind. He pedalled as fast as he could without raising attention. Knocking on the rear door to the public house he waited until the barmaid opened it. The woman stood in the doorway, a towel over her shoulder.

'Is Stanley Russell here?' he asked before the woman could make any comment about the time.

'No, Reverend. Not here,' the barmaid told him.

Clement hated the smell of bars. Airless places of stale beer and even staler tobacco wafted through the half open door.

'What number room is Elsie Wainwright in?'

'Six.'

Without waiting he pushed past the woman and went straight to the staircase to the first floor.

'You can't just go up there!' the woman screamed behind him.

Clement climbed the uneven steps to the upper floor. The floorboards of the old inn creaked under his tread, but he had no time to waste. He knocked.

Again no answer.

'Do you have a key to this room?'

'You can't just barge in!'

'Give me the key!'

He almost closed his eyes as he burst into the room. What he found was nothing but a perfectly made bed. He threw open the wardrobe. Empty coat hangers swung on the rail.

He turned around staring at the deserted room, his mind racing.

'Why that little fiend!' the barmaid screeched behind him. 'She's done a runner. She owes five shillings!'

Clement didn't know if he was relieved or annoyed at not finding Stanley. There was only one other recourse. He needed to see David Russell anyway. The time had come. Now he needed to stay focused on his duty, no matter how unsavoury. But first he had to find Stanley. He moved his foot in his shoe and felt the hard blade of the Fairbairn Sykes knife dig into his left ankle. He left the room and bolted down the stairs. Leaving the public house by the rear lane, he returned to the village green and strode towards the police station.

Not four minutes later Clement entered the red brick, Victorian building. He glanced at the police station clock. It was just after eleven.

'Constable Matthews?' he shouted.

The constable wasn't at the front desk. Clement went to the glass-partitioned door and looked into the hallway beyond. He waited only a few seconds before he saw the constable walking along the corridor, a dust pan and brush in his hand.

'Reverend? And what can I do for you today?'

'Is the Inspector in?'

The man nodded. 'Once again it's just him and me. Skeleton staff, what with the pounding London copped last night. They say the invasion is imminent. What do you think, Reverend?'

Clement forced a smile. 'I just need to see the Inspector.'

'Of course, everyone's in a hurry today,' Constable Matthews said and glancing at the clock on the wall, entered the time of Clement's visit in the daily log. 'There was quite a to-do here this morning. I'm surprised you and your good lady didn't hear it in the vicarage.'

'What was that, Constable?'

'Mister Knowles, Sir. He came here earlier this morning. Nine thirty-five to be precise. Accusations were flying all over the place. Harsh words, Reverend. All kinds of threats,' the constable turned to face him. 'I shouldn't say it,' Constable Matthews whispered, 'but Inspector Russell is too fond of the ladies. I knew one day it would get him into trouble. Only from what I understand it is Mrs Knowles who is the one in trouble. Red hair. And a big baby I'm told. Just like young Stanley when he was a little one.'

'Have you seen Stanley, Constable?'

'He was here too this morning.' The constable shook his head. 'More shouting. Only this time about money. Stanley came for his late mother's inheritance saying he wanted to start afresh but his father was having none of it. In my opinion, and I suppose I shouldn't say this either, but I don't believe there is any money left.'

'Well perhaps you should keep that to yourself, Constable. Do you know where Stanley is now?'

'Left here about half an hour ago threatening all sorts of violence against his father.'

'Could I just see the Inspector? It is urgent.'

'Of course.' The constable moved to the partitioning door and held it open.

They walked along the corridor to the rear office. He could see that Russell's door was slightly ajar. Constable Matthews knocked at the door and pushed it wide then turned and walked away.

From the doorway Clement could see the empty chair behind the desk. The window to the rear lane was open and a light breeze was lifting the loose weave curtain. Through the window he saw the dark shape of the Inspector's car in its usual place.

Clement frowned as he scanned the room. He was about to call out to Constable Matthews, to say that the Inspector was not in his office when he saw the shoe. He ran around the desk. 'Dear Lord!' Clement drew in his breath as he stared at the body. Inspector Russell was lying face up on the floor, the eyes open and wide, the head tilted to the left. Congealed blood surrounded the man's head like a macabre halo. It had poured from the long, gaping cut to the neck that extended from one ear to the other.

From the corner of his eye Clement saw the safe. The door was open. He could hear the constable's tread on the hard, tiled corridor heading for the front desk. Standing, Clement stared into the safe searching for the sealed envelope. There wasn't much in there, some papers and a few five pound notes, but no envelope.

'Constable Matthews!' Clement shouted.

He heard the tread stop, then return with haste along the corridor. Matthews rushed through the open door.

'Call Doctor Haswell, Matthews! Hurry!'

The constable came around the desk and looked at the dead man. 'Dear God!'

'The doctor, Constable!'

Constable Matthews turned and ran from the room.

For one second Clement prayed the doctor was in his surgery. He went to the window and peered out, looking further along the rear lane to where Doctor Haswell parked his car. It was there! Relieved, Clement returned to the body. He stared at the congealed blood. It sat like a thick maroon scarf around Russell's neck. A dark curtain of the stuff ran from the man's throat to the floor. It had been more than twenty years since Clement had seen such a sight. He stood and checked the corridor. Constable Matthews had still not returned. Crouching beside the corpse, Clement ran his hand over Russell's trouser pockets, and checked the inside of the man's coat, waistcoat and shirt pockets. He found a long, unmarked key but no envelope. He pushed the key back into Russell's pocket.

Clement stood and checked the Inspector's desk. Using his elbows, he pushed the papers around in case the envelope was beneath the chaos. Nothing. He heard the running feet on the tiled corridor.

The Doctor ran into the room, dropped his medical bag on one side of the body and knelt down beside the man's head. Haswell remained hunched over Inspector Russell for a few seconds before leaning back on his haunches. 'Nothing I can do for him. He's yours now, Clement,' Haswell said, then opened his medical bag and withdrew a large rectal thermometer.

'How long has he been dead, do you think?' Clement asked.

'Not long at all,' Phillip said, staring at the thermometer. 'There is no sign of rigor mortis yet. But his temperature has dropped a little.' Haswell studied the room. 'Was the window open when you came in?'

'Yes.'

'I put it at about an hour.'

Clement watched the Doctor turn Russell's head. The cut extended almost from one ear to the other and had severed the windpipe. The pictures he'd seen of such injuries at Coleshill flashed in his memory.

Haswell glanced up at him. 'It was a knife of some size. It was pushed into the neck just under the right ear, then forward across the neck. You see the bruise here; the force of entry caused that. It was done by a strong person by the look of it and one who knew what they were doing. No hesitation, Clement. Swift and lethal.' Haswell closed his bag. 'I could take him to my surgery, but I have no way of keeping him cool. They'll want a post-mortem.'

'We should call Lewes for an ambulance,' Clement added.

'I expect they'll have been seconded to London, given the bombing up there. I could take him, if you'd give me a hand to get him into my car?'

'Yes, of course. Thank you, Phillip, if you don't mind?'

'Not at all. Perhaps a report should be made about this room and how you found it?'

Clement nodded. 'Of course. Constable Matthews can you make sure nothing is disturbed in Inspector Russell's office? You had better close that window, but you should note in your report that we found it open. Then we should notify Lewes Police. No disrespect, Constable but it will need a senior officer.'

Constable Matthews hadn't taken his gaze from the Inspector's body. Clement knew Matthews had little respect for Russell, but as the constable was the only other person in the police station at the time, and held the keys of Russell's safe, he would, at the very least, be called upon to give evidence at the inquest.

'Constable, can you get a blanket from one of the cells? We don't want to frighten anybody who may be in the rear lane,' Haswell asked.

Matthews nodded and left the room.

Clement stared at Russell's corpse, then checked his watch, but the list dominated his thoughts. He needed to be with his team and it was already half-past eleven. While he was pleased he had been spared the duty of taking Russell's life, his murder raised so many questions. There was no time to think now. It would be many hours before he could speak with Johnny. And even that was dependent on the speed of the German advance.

Matthews returned and together they rolled the dead Inspector onto the blanket. They carried him out of the police station, up Church Lane to the rear laneway and Doctor Haswell's car.

'If you don't mind, Clement, I'll put him on the back seat. Rigor mortis will start to set in soon and it will be impossible to straighten him out if he's in the boot.'

While Clement found Phillip Haswell's pragmatism rather unsettling, he was glad of it. There was nothing Haswell could do for Russell now. And he had been correct not to call on the already over-stretched ambulance personnel. Clement wished he had included the Doctor and not Stanley.

Clement closed the rear door of Haswell's car, his hands gently pushing the fold of the blanket that encompassed Russell's feet. The Inspector was not a tall man but Clement would not have described him as especially short either. Yet wrapped in a police cell blanket on the rear seat of the Doctor's car, Russell had become small, even pathetic. Did one man's life amount to so little? The words of the order of service for the Burial of the Dead flashed into his mind. "We brought nothing into this world, and it is certain we can carry nothing out."

'I'll go now, if you don't mind, Clement,' Phillip said. 'I'll get him to the mortuary as soon as possible.'

'Of course. And thank you for all your assistance, Phillip.'

Clement stood back on the pavement and watched the car drive away. He and Constable Matthews returned to the station. From the duty desk Clement called the police station in Lewes. 'Could I speak with Chief Inspector Arthur Morris?'

Clement explained the situation then hung up. 'They said they would be here in about an hour.'

'I am grateful to you, Reverend. I know it will look bad for me. I was the only one here at the time, but I never heard anything. I'm a bit hard of hearing. And I have no idea how the thief got into the safe. You need both sets of keys to do it.'

Clement saw the constable's eyes glance at the safe keys hanging on the hook on the wall opposite the desk.

'Perhaps we should find Stanley. If for no other reason than that he is Russell's next of kin.'

'Of course. Good idea, Reverend.' Matthews reached for his policeman's hat. 'Doctor Haswell put the time of death about an hour ago. That'd make it half past ten. About the same time Stanley came to see his father. Doesn't look good for him either, does it?'

Locking the police station door, they walked towards Stanley's cottage on the edge of the village. But it was the list that occupied Clement's thoughts. Was that why Inspector Russell had been murdered? Perhaps he had disturbed someone opening the safe? That implicated the man walking beside Clement and he couldn't imagine that. Besides, no one knew about the list, except himself and the Inspector. Clement considered whether Russell had told anyone about it. Or even opened it. Had the murderer just killed in cold blood once the safe had been opened? Clement quickened his pace. He needed to get to the Operational Base without further delay. But the Chief Inspector from Lewes Police station would be suspicious if he went missing as well as Stanley, especially as he couldn't prove his involvement with the Auxiliary Units without the list. Clement understood now why Gubbins had been so insistent. But he also wondered if any of it now mattered. The Germans were invading, and he was looking for Stanley. He was annoyed with Stanley. And he was annoyed with himself for including the silly boy in the first place.

He opened the gate and strode towards the front door of Stanley's cottage.

Constable Matthews knocked.

No answer.

Without waiting Clement marched around the cottage to the rear, his anxiety and his temper rising. The back door was ajar. 'Stanley?' he shouted entering the small scullery. Bending, he made his way into the house. Stanley was standing in the living room by the fireplace, a suitcase at his feet and his Fairbairn Sykes knife in his hand. Despite Stanley's tight grip on the blade, Clement could see the red fluid oozing between the chubby fingers.

'Stanley?'

'Reverend?'

'What's happened?' Clement asked, his eyes fixed on the blood-stained knife.

'I'm sorry, Vicar. I can't be involved any more. You'd better take my kit. It's upstairs.'

There was another knock on the door.

'Oh! She's come to the front,' Stanley said.

12

Clement sat in the police station waiting area and watched Constable Matthews remove the handcuffs from Stanley's thick wrists. A few minutes later, Stanley disappeared along the corridor escorted by the constable. Clement could hear doors being opened and closed.

Constable Matthews reappeared. 'Chief Inspector Morris says you can see Stanley now, Reverend. But just for ten minutes.'

'Thank you.' Following Matthews along the increasingly familiar corridor, Clement entered one of the previously closed doors that led to the two cells at the rear of the building. He stood in front of the cell door and peered through the tiny hatch. Stanley was sitting on the bunk bed, his tie, shoe laces and belt removed. Clement sighed. He thought Stanley looked a tragic figure. Physically large, with pale skin, light blue eyes and red hair, the lad had been the butt of many porcine jests during his youth. He watched as Stanley stood then paced the confined space, his loose shoes scuffing over the brick floor. But while Clement saw Stanley's agitation, it didn't appear to have much to do with his current situation. He seemed distracted, almost joyous. There was a grin on his face like a child at Christmas. Clement turned and walked back to the second office where Chief Inspector Morris sat reading the constable's report.

'Excuse me, Chief Inspector, could I speak with Stanley Russell inside his cell?' he asked.

Chief Inspector Morris lifted his gaze from the papers. 'You are in Military attire today because…?'

'Home Guard exercises.'

Morris nodded. 'Would you be carrying a weapon under that jacket?' Morris asked, his gaze on Clement's uniform.

Clement shook his head, thinking of his knife that was concealed under his trousers.

'I will have to lock you in, so just a few minutes, Reverend Wisdom.'

'Thank you.'

Morris stood and together they walked to the duty desk to retrieve the cell keys. The Chief Inspector seemed to Clement to be the antithesis of Inspector Russell. Morris was evidently careful and thorough but entirely without bombast. In fact, a quiet, almost sedate manner was the first impression. Intentional or not, it was reassuring. But it concerned Clement that Morris may think it an open and shut case. Although Stanley had, for now, only been detained, and not yet formally arrested for the murder of his father, he was obviously the main and probably the only suspect. And being caught with a blood-smeared knife in his grasp was bound to lead to his conviction.

The heavy cell door swung open and shut behind him. The lock rotated. Clement sat on the bunk. 'Listen to me, Stanley. We only have a few minutes. Who did you think was at your door? Who were you waiting for?' He remembered the suitcase. 'Where were you going?'

Stanley tapped his nose with his index finger. 'I'm sorry, Vicar. I can't be in the group anymore.'

'Stanley! Do you realise how serious this is?'

'I have to go. How long is this going to take? I have to get back to the house.'

'Stanley, you do know that you have been detained, pending investigation, for the murder of your father?'

Stanley stopped his pacing and stared at him.

Clement could see the confusion on the lad's face. 'Your father was found murdered this morning. By me. Here. In his office. His throat was cut. Guerrilla style, Stanley. Done by someone who knew what they were doing. With a large knife. Doctor Haswell says it happened about the time you came to see your father. You were overheard arguing.'

Stanley sat down on the bunk and leaned his head on the brick wall behind him. 'We're getting married. We're leaving Fearnley Maughton, Vicar. She just left to pack her bag. But I need to go soon as she'll be back at the cottage.'

'Why were you holding the knife, Stanley?' Clement pressed.

'I thought while she was getting her things, I should return my kit to you. But I couldn't find the knife.' Stanley leaned forward. 'When I did, it was covered in blood. I thought she must have found it and been playing with it. She could be hurt. That's it. She's hurt. That's why she's taking so long. I need to find her.'

'Where did you find it, Stanley?'

'In the scullery drawer, with the other knives.'

'Do you always have the back door unlocked?'

'Yes,' Stanley said shrugging. 'I got nothing worth stealing.'

Clement's mind was reeling. It would be easy to enter the house unobserved and drop the knife into the drawer. He sat back on the bunk bed, his mind processing the facts as he knew them. He glanced at Stanley. He didn't believe Stanley had killed his father. But whoever did wanted Stanley to take the blame. And what of the girl? Had she just taken fright at the idea of eloping with Stanley and run away, or had she committed murder? Either way, what the girl had done was contemptible. But why would Elsie Wainwright kill David Russell?

'Stanley, there's something I must tell you,' he said and told Stanley about Elsie's empty room.

'Of course the room's empty, Vicar,' Stanley said. 'She went to pack her things.'

'But she didn't return to the cottage, Stanley. That was the arrangement, wasn't it?'

'She's hurt, I tell you. We're going to be married. She loves me.'

In that moment, Clement despised Elsie Wainwright.

'I will only ask once, Stanley, because I want to hear it from you,' Clement said. 'Did you kill your father?'

'No, Vicar! But if I'm going to swing for it, then I wish I had. But I wouldn't have killed him like that.'

'Why do you say that?'

'Now that I know how to kill, if I'd killed him, I would have bashed the bastard's head in. Not cut his

119

throat. He wouldn't have suffered for more than a second. Not enough for what he did to me and my mother.'

Clement stared at Stanley, the image of the wide spread legs and ferocious swing of the blade Clement had witnessed at Coleshill bursting from his memory. Physical and mental abuse. Both mother and son. Hatred. Years of it. Hatred didn't make precision cuts, no matter how gory the end result. When a man killed with anger, the attack was...how did Major Bannon describe it? Frenzied. There would have been blood all over the room. Clement frowned for regardless of whether the attack was frenzied or premeditated, there just wasn't enough blood. Such a violent injury would have sent blood spurting forward. In his mind's eye, Clement could see the grotesque windpipe surrounded by raw flesh. Such an attack not only cut the windpipe but also the main arteries of the neck. Why was the blood confined to Russell's neck and not all over the office? He pondered the girl. Could Stanley be protecting Elsie? Even if he asked, Clement knew Stanley wouldn't say. Stanley was in love and he would swing for the girl if he believed she'd done it. 'I believe you,' Clement said. 'But I have to go, Stanley. I'll be back as soon as I can. I'll pray for you.' He stood and went to the cell door.

'I didn't do it, Vicar. And I know Elsie will be here for me,' Stanley said. But already Clement could hear the doubt creeping into Stanley's voice.

Constable Matthews unlocked the cell door. Clement stood in the doorway. He nodded and smiled at Stanley, but his heart was sinking. He wanted to share his thoughts with Chief Inspector Morris. There was so little time. Everything now was dependent upon the speed of the German advance.

Clement knocked on the door to the Chief Inspector's office. 'Thank you for allowing me to see Stanley.' He glanced at the clock on Morris's desk. The men would be assembled now and wondering where he was. 'I have something I must attend to now, but could I speak with you further about Stanley?'

Morris stood. 'Could I trouble you, Reverend, to show me exactly where you found the body?'

Clement glanced again at the clock; he was already late, but Morris would be suspicious if he failed to assist. 'Of course.'

'I won't keep you long.'

They walked into Russell's office and Clement told Morris what he had seen and done. The Chief Inspector said little as Clement retold his account of events. But he felt certain the man would check it all against the constable's statement.

'Is Constable Matthews alright?'

'Why do you ask?'

'This is a small village, Chief Inspector. We all know each other, and our Constable has had quite a shock. And he is elderly and a bit deaf.'

They walked back along the corridor to the glass partition door and Morris held it open. 'So I understand. Constable Matthews is too close to this investigation, so I have arranged for Constable Newson from Lewes to assist me with Inspector Russell's death. We'll be in Fearnley Maughton for the duration.'

Clement shook hands with Morris but he could see the man's attention was on a set of keys hanging on the wall opposite the duty desk.

'Do you know what those keys open,' Morris asked.

Clement nodded. 'I suppose anyone who has asked Inspector Russell to keep anything in the safe in his office would have seen those keys. But to open the safe, two keys are required. At least, that's what Constable Matthews told me.'

Morris tilted his head. 'Where is the second key kept?'

'I don't know. It's just what Constable Matthews told me.' Clement thought of the key he had seen in David Russell's pocket but he didn't know what it opened, so he hadn't actually lied.

Morris nodded. 'Why were you here this morning?'

'I came to ask the Inspector if he knew where Stanley was.'

'You needed Stanley because?'

'He's a member of the Home Guard of which, as you can see, I am group leader. I am organising exercises, in view of the recent increase in German bombardment.'

Clement turned to leave. Morris remained staring at the keys on the wall.

13

Even though it was now after one o'clock, Clement needed to retrieve Stanley's pack. Striding to the end of the street, he entered Stanley's cottage from the rear. He glanced around the scullery, looking for the cutlery drawer. The utensil drawers were under the bench right beside the back door. He stared at it realizing that as long as the door was unlocked - and it always was - anyone could have placed the blood-smeared knife there. They didn't even need to enter the house to do it.

He went upstairs to Stanley's bedroom. The bed occupied almost all the space. It was roughly made, the blanket askew and creased. In his mind's eye Clement saw the neat bed at *The Crown*. Wedged against the wall was the pack. He pursed his lips. Their packs were to be hidden away from prying eyes and Stanley had left his kit where anyone in the room could not only see it, but have access to it. Reaching for it, Clement swung it over his shoulder and returning downstairs, left by the rear door.

It was just after two o'clock when he approached the location of the Operational Base in Maughton Forest. Off to his left he heard a rustle in the bushes. He stopped, falling to the ground. He had no weapon immediately available to him other than his knife. Stanley's Sten Gun was in the pack, but it would take him too long to open it, assemble and load the weapon. Beside which, the noise would give away his position. He lay, motionless, in the first of the autumn leaves. With his nose pressed to the decaying leaf matter, he moved his left leg, bending his knee, his left hand feeling for the blade. Without a sound, he grasped the dagger and lifted his head, his eyes scanning the woodland. Up ahead the early afternoon sun shone through the trees, the gentle light flickering on the foliage. Squinting, he scanned the forest ahead. His ears strained for any noise. A falling leaf caught the dappled sunlight as it fluttered earthwards. He saw it bounce then fall. Screwing his eyes tight, he focused on the spot. He could just make out the trip-wire stretched across the forest floor at about ankle height. It crossed the path and went off into the bushes on the right side of the track near a remnant of Roman stonework half-concealed in the foliage. Grasping the knife to his chest he rolled sideways off the path and into the bushes at its edge and waited. Nothing stirred. He stood and hunching low, ran through the trees before falling again to the ground about ten feet away from the ruin. He could see the wire. It was wrapped around the base of a tree but he couldn't see any explosive. Staying in the low shrubs, he skirted the site, approaching it from higher in the woodlands. Crouching beside the remains of the moss-covered ancient wall his eye followed the wire. It was secured to an explosive device at the base of the tree on the high side making it invisible from the forest path. Waiting he listened, the Fairbairn Sykes blade still in his grasp.

'Clement!'

It was Peter's voice; quiet and sharp.

Peter Kempton stood there, his Sten gun in his hands. The man had twigs and branches all over his clothes. Peter made a sweeping gesture. Clement heard the movement behind him. Reg Naylor stood. The man had been hiding in a copse higher up the slope. The disguise had been perfect. Clement had crawled right by Peter yet had not seen him. And Reg would have had Clement in his sights since he arrived in the woods. He only hoped the Germans were as distracted as he was.

They walked in silence, about ten feet apart, further along the hillside then higher to the trees and the Operational Base. Peter placed a hand on a tree stump and pulled it sideways. Beneath it was the small trapdoor opening to their underground bunker and one by one they descended the stairs into the subterranean base.

The long, narrow, arched tunnel was sectioned into a living area with a table and chairs and a sleeping area with several bunk beds. Near the entry steps, sectioned off and behind the blast door, were the latrine on one side and the stove on the other. The flu rose from the stove, through a bunker and into a hollowed out tree trunk above ground to disperse the smoke and cooking fumes. Beyond the living space was the supply and weapons store and at the far end was the emergency escape door. Numerous lamps hung from wooden beams along the narrow tunnel. Clement put Stanley's pack down and sat at the table.

'What news?' Peter asked. 'We assumed something had gone wrong.'

Clement told them about Stanley.

'I thought he would pop that bastard one day,' Clive said.

'I don't think he did it,' Clement said. 'I think he's covering for the girl.'

'That slip of a girl couldn't have done it. Besides, why would she?' Clive replied.

'I've been asking myself the same question,' Clement said.

'And the invasion?' Peter asked.

Clement shook his head. 'I know nothing more than you do. So we maintain a watch and patrol tonight. We could be here for a while, so we better settle in,' he said, his mind still on Stanley. But right now there was little he could do. The group had been activated. Killing the invading enemy came first and Stanley would have to wait.

'He no longer matters to us,' Reg added, voicing what Clement believed the others may be thinking. Reg removed his camouflaged suit then, grasping his Sten Gun, sat at a distance from the others, the weapon on his knees, rubbing an oiled cloth over the barrel.

'What's to report here,' Clement asked.

'Nothing, other than an unwary vicar,' Reg answered.

Clement nodded. He wasn't proud of his inattention, even if he had good cause. If the Germans had landed, his absent-mindedness would have cost all their lives.

'With one man down I'll rework the watch,' Peter said.

The men dispersed and Clement watched them go about the routine tasks of life in the Operational Base.

But there was little conversation. Stanley aside, he had another problem: the whereabouts of the list. So many questions flooded his mind, and yet he couldn't share any of them, not even with his second-in-command.

Reaching for the ordnance survey maps of the area, he unrolled them and, spreading them on the table, plotted the evening's patrol routes. Had the Germans penetrated their wood? Was the invasion even now moving towards Fearnley Maughton? He told himself their village was not on the road to London, but he had to fight a feeling of dread. They had received the universal invasion code word to assemble. The Germans must at the very least be approaching their shores. Plus they would surely be parachuting troops in. But even as such questions invaded his mind, Stanley was never far from his thoughts. He wondered if Clive was correct about Stanley - was the motive anger? If so, Stanley had the most to gain from his father's death. And Stanley had no alibi other than Elsie, who had disappeared. Had the lad thought that now he knew how to kill, and had protection because of his membership of an elite group, he could get away with murder? Yet if Stanley had opened the safe, it would be for the money, not the list; a list the man didn't know existed.

Clement thought of the five pound notes he had seen in the safe. Why would Stanley leave a stack of five pound notes if he had come for his inheritance? Clement shook his head. Stanley did not kill his father. He believed it. So who other than him and Russell knew about the existence of the list? Not his men and certainly not the illusive Elsie. He began to wonder if Elsie were entirely innocent and had also met with foul play. Only he, David Russell, Gubbins and Johnny knew about the list. But they all, except Russell, already knew the groups' identities. A squeezing knot was forming in his stomach.

Clement focused on the maps laid out before him and devised the route. 'We should get some rest. Tonight we need to be on high alert. George, you and Reg take the first watch. We'll change again in two hours. At midnight we'll patrol the area east and south of Firle Beacon. And we'll check Firle Place on our way back.'

Clement lay back on his bunk, his head on the hard pillow. His team had been a cohesive unit after Coleshill, but now, with Stanley's imprisonment and the confined space of the Operational Base, tempers would be quickly raised. Clement glanced at his men from time to time. They were occupied tending their own areas of expertise, but the tension was palpable. He imagined that with each passing night the routine would become more familiar, and the dynamics of the personalities would in time, sort themselves out. Closing his eyes, he recited the Lord's Prayer and asked God for guidance and strength.

As the afternoon became evening there had been no sightings of any enemy activity within the forest. In fact, each returning watch had reported that there had been no one sighted in the forest at all. It was as if all England knew the Germans were on the foreshores and had stayed at home, waiting.

As night descended and the patrol time approached, their nerves were only just under control. It was to be expected. Despite the uniforms, none of them were guerrilla fighters. They were bakers and clergymen and solicitors. Ordinary people waiting to do extraordinary things. Clement wanted and needed to stay focused, as much for himself as the team. He swung his legs over the bunk and went to the table and stared again at the maps, going over every detail. What he found most frustrating was that he didn't even know where the invasion was taking place. He checked his watch. In five minutes, Peter and Ned would be returning from their watch. He glanced at the men. Reg and George were preparing for their watch and Clive was sorting explosives. Time passed slowly, and no one spoke.

At midnight they lifted their packs, and with Sten guns in hand, left the Operational Base in single file, heading south.

14

Tuesday 17ᵗʰ September

With morning, long shards of sunlight penetrated the forest. They had seen nothing unusual and encountered no one. It was always possible they had skirted advancing troops, but Clement didn't believe so. Invasions required armoured vehicles and tanks that can be heard and felt miles away. From Firle Beacon, and with the aid of the early dawn light, he had scrutinised the coast but hadn't sighted any shipping that would indicate an amphibious invasion.

Clement watched his men remove their packs and stow their weapons before collapsing on the bunks. They had walked for over six hours and covered more than the forecasted eight miles. Full moons are a night patrol's worst enemy. He thought of his theory about full moons and bombing. He had been right about that. But for them, the strong moonlight had meant staying away from open fields and ridge tops, where their silhouetted forms would make them like ducks at a seaside shooting gallery. Being forced to stay in the valleys and criss-cross fields behind hedges and clusters of trees had turned eight miles into twelve.

'What now, Clement?' Reg asked.

'Well, just because we didn't see the enemy doesn't mean they haven't landed. I need to contact Commander Winthorpe,' Clement told them. 'He needs to know about Stanley and I want to hear about the invasion. I'll be as quick as I can but if I'm delayed I'll let you know by a reverse dead letter drop. George, make sure you visit the bus shelter during the day. Get some rest. All of you. And well done last night.' He turned to go. 'Remain vigilant. In my absence Peter is in charge.'

'Clement. Perhaps you should have a gun on you,' Peter said.

Clement shook his head. 'If I was caught either coming or going from here, the Germans may come looking for you. Stanley is in enough trouble, I don't need to worry about all of you too.'

Clement walked back through the woodland, alert to the sounds of the forest. Sometimes in the summer, if the weather was fine, instead of playing chess, he and Peter would walk the forest with Boadicea, discussing theology. Then the woodland paths were happy places, an escape from the routine pressures of life. Now Clement saw them as places of concealed death.

He skirted the village and let himself into the vestry to change his clothes. Ten minutes later he walked down Church Lane and let himself into the vicarage. Closing the door, he walked along the hallway towards the kitchen. It was still early, not yet seven o'clock and possibly too early for Johnny to be in his office at The Admiralty. Even though Mary was not there, her fragrance lingered and Clement breathed it in. Filling the kettle, he placed it on the stove then went to his study. Reverend Battersby had left some correspondence on Clement's desk. He dealt with church matters until he heard the clock in the hall chime nine. He dialled Johnny's number.

'Nothing to report in our sector. Any news?' Clement asked.

'Nothing as yet,' Johnny answered. 'It's a waiting game, Clement.'

Clement could hear the strain in Johnny's voice.

'We have a problem, Johnny, that you should know about.'

'Not on the phone. Come. Same day, same place.'

The phone rang off.

Clement replaced the receiver and returned to his study. In the stillness he heard the droning. As it increased, he stood and went to draw the curtains. They were early today. Even though it was daylight he decided to check the house and close all the blackout curtains. He stood in the middle of the hallway, listening. There was something different about the noise. The sound was higher pitched, more like fighters. And they were low. Dorniers, possibly. Within seconds the noise was fierce. It seemed as though an aeroplane was above the house. He waited, hardly moving. Then the unmistakable squeal.

He ran into the scullery and sat on the floor in the corner, his head between his arms. He stared at the locked scullery door, the Anderson Shelter only yards away. But there was no time to reach it. Then the detonation. The whole house shook and several windows shattered, the sound of the breaking glass sudden and intense. His mind flashed to the scullery at the vicarage in Mayfair. A second later, another explosion. Smaller. Standing, he ran to the front door and opened it.

Flames were rising from the roofs of the buildings and shops in the High Street. He ran outside into the lane. The noise, though terrifyingly loud, was different now. Short bursts of exploding cracks shattered the morning. Hearing the high-pitched squeal he looked up. A German Stuka was descending out of the sky. Clement stared at it, not sure if it was crashing into the village or strafing it. He could hear people screaming. He ran down Church Lane then leaned against the red-brick wall of the police station and looked up.

The plane pulled high and circled and once again came in low, the noise thunderous, the destruction deliberate. Its presence in the village was not just a stray encounter designed to intimidate then fly away; it was intentionally mowing down anyone in the streets. Clement watched, horrified, as the plane once more strafed the village. The bullets cracked the air in bursts of two or three seconds before the plane rose into the sky. Circling, the aircraft lined up for a third run then thundered over the village, the terrifying sound of rapid spraying bullets mingling with screaming. It turned, pulling high, this time disappearing into the sky.

Clement ran into the High Street. Some of the buildings and the shops around the village green were partially destroyed and fire was already taking hold. The scene was something unimaginable. Windows and shop fronts had been blown out into the streets, and flames now leapt high into the sky. Peter Kempton's large Georgian office building was nothing more than rubble. People were lying on the footpaths and in the roadway. Others were staggering around in aimless circles, their clothes ripped into shreds. Clement's gaze fell on a pram, standing alone in the middle of the street, a woman prostrate beside it. His chest felt hollow. Looking up he saw *The Crown*. It appeared to be undamaged. He remembered it was the emergency assembly point, and thanks to Mary and Phillip Haswell, there were medical supplies there. 'Go to *The Crown*,' he bellowed.

Clement ran towards the woman lying beside the pram. He recognised the young mother immediately. Mrs Clarke had been shot through the chest and would have died instantly. His eye turned to the baby. He placed his hand on the infant and felt its tiny breaths. Looking up he saw two older women comforting each other nearby.

'Can you take care of this child?'

'Dear Lord! Is Mrs Clarke dead?' one asked.

'Please take the child to *The Crown*, I must find Doctor Haswell.'

Clement ran back up the hill. The buildings at the top end of the High Street appeared not to have been so badly damaged. Without knocking, he opened the doctor's door and ran in.

The front hallway was filled with dust. Covering his mouth with his hand, Clement looked into the front room that was the surgery. It seemed to be undamaged except for debris and dust from shattered brickwork. He walked further into the house. 'Phillip?' he shouted. Daylight filtered through the dust haze. There was nothing left of the kitchen or scullery. Clement stood at the edge of the brickwork, the rear wall of the house completely missing. Phillip Haswell was standing in what was left of his garden. His Anderson shelter had taken a direct hit and had been completely destroyed. A crater ten feet deep was where the shelter had once stood.

'Phillip? Are you unharmed?'

The man was coughing and blinking dust and dirt from his eyes. 'I was in the shed, Clement,' he said staring at the flattened brick and wooden structure a few feet away. 'I decided while I was outside to cut a few vegetables for my dinner. If I hadn't been on my haunches pulling up carrots at the end of my garden...' Phillip's voice trailed off. 'A few seconds earlier...' Phillip stopped again.

'Many of the villagers are injured. There are several already dead. If you could come. Now?'

'Of course, Clement. I'll just get my bag.' They ran into the house going straight into the surgery. 'Is Elsie in attendance?'

'You didn't know Elsie has left Fearnley Maughton?'

Phillip stopped filling his medical bag and stared at Clement. 'What? Why?'

'I was hoping you could tell me.'

'Can't be helped. We must make do with what we have. Thank the Lord for Mary's foresight and planning. Where are most of the wounded?'

'*The Crown.*'

'Clement, would you call Lewes Ambulance station? Ask them to send all they can. And Clement,' Haswell paused. 'I think the villagers will need you, but before you go, can you open the church? We'll need somewhere to put the bodies. It's best the dead are not with the living for too long. Bad for morale.'

'Of course.'

Leaving the surgery, Clement watched Phillip run down the street towards the devastation, then he ran to

135

the vicarage. Why had the Stuka targeted Fearnley Maughton? There were no industries, no railheads or munitions factories. Had it just been a random release of left-over bombs? But the strafing runs had been deliberate. That was sheer wickedness. Clement ran into his house and telephoned Lewes Ambulance, then went to his study. Taking the keys from the drawer in his desk, he ran up the hill and opened the church.

One of the long, stained glass windows had been blasted inwards. He paused for a moment. The windows at *All Saints* had survived the Reformation but not Herr Hitler's henchmen. 'Such vandalism,' he muttered and hurried back into the village.

Rounding the corner from Church Lane into the High Street he passed the police station. He suddenly remembered Stanley and turning back, decided to check on him. Glass from the shattered front windows lay like snow over the waiting room floor. Picking his way through the debris, Clement looked around but no one was behind the duty desk. Surmising Constable Newson was helping with the injured, Clement went straight to the partition door and pushed it open. The body of a man in a constable's uniform was lying, face down on the floor in the corridor.

'Constable Newson,' he called, and bending down, shook the man's shoulder.

Clement reeled back. The man was dead. But not from blast damage. A bullet hole, the size of a sixpence, glared back at him from the bloodless visage. It had entered the man's head through the left temple. But there was no exit wound. Clement swallowed hard. The man's brains would be nothing but slush, the bullet still within the skull. Most likely subsonic. Special. He stood and ran towards the cells where he knew Stanley was imprisoned. The cell door was open.

15

Clement stared at the empty cell for what seemed like a full minute. His mind was reeling. He ran from the cells. 'Chief Inspector Morris?' he shouted, hoping the man was somewhere in the building. But no one responded. Stanley's whereabouts would have to wait. The dead and dying people of Fearnley Maughton needed him. As Clement ran along the corridor to leave, he passed an open door. It was a large cupboard with several labelled items sitting on the shelves. Stopping, he realised it was the police evidence cupboard. His eye scanned the contents for Stanley's blood-stained Fairbairn Sykes knife. It wasn't there. Clement licked his dry lips. There was no time for finding the commando knife. Leaving the police station, Clement hurried towards the village green.

In the distance he could hear the siren of the local fire brigade. ARP wardens from Lewes were already on the scene and appeared to be directing the chaos. Along the street in both directions, Clement saw people lying on the ground. Fearnley Maughton, his pretty village, was almost unrecognisable. He ran towards the public house.

The main bar had been transformed into an infirmary. Tables had been placed side by side and upon each lay an injured person. Phillip Haswell was running between the tables, enlisting the help of anyone who could wrap a bandage or pack a wound. The barmaid was fetching and emptying buckets filled with blood-stained cloths and blood dripped from the edges of the tables to the floor. Behind the bar, Ilene Greenwood was shredding sheets from the linen store into long strips.

Haswell looked up as Clement entered.

'They're on their way,' Clement said, staring at the doctor's blood-soaked clothes and hands.

Haswell nodded. 'Keep the hot water coming,' he shouted to the barmaid. 'Wet all the surfaces, we have to keep the dust levels down. And could someone get the ARP to put a sheet or a blanket over that open window, please!'

Clement backed away. Haswell, although clearly finding the makeshift surgery stressful, was managing well enough. And the village women had swung into action. With all the deaths, Clement was going to need assistance organizing the funerals. He should call Battersby, but for now his role was to pray with the dying and take the deceased to the church. His mind went to the team still dug in at the Operational Base. With the Germans not yet on their shores, the men would be alright. His place was here in the village, with his flock, but he made a mental note that if things returned to something close to normal he would telephone Mary and ask her to return.

Outside, Clement found the ARP warden. 'Lewes Ambulance is sending all three of their ambulances.'

'I'll go to the main road and direct them,' the Warden replied. 'Can you find a stretcher, Vicar. I understand from Doctor Haswell you are using the church as a temporary mortuary?'

'Yes. There're two stretchers in *The Crown*.' His mind went to Mary and he thanked God for her foresight.

'I'll leave you to it then, Vicar.'

All around him, Clement saw carnage. He saw a line of bodies, evacuees from London. The ARP Warden wanted them kept separate for identification purposes. Returning to the inn, Clement brought a stretcher outside and laid it on the ground beside the body of Emma Clarke. Looking around for able men to help him carry the deceased, he saw John Knowles standing, staring open mouthed at the scene.

'John!' he called.

The man seemed dazed.

Clement called again.

'She's dead,' Knowles muttered. 'She came looking for me.'

Clement realised with horror what the man was saying. Looking up he could see the body of Margaret Knowles lying face down on the footpath outside what was left of Peter Kempton's office. Clement felt utterly ashamed. He had failed John. By forgetting him, even though only temporarily, the man had sought comfort from the church but found it in *The Crown*. And John's wife had died because of his forgetfulness. 'The child?'

'At home with a neighbour,' Knowles responded.

'Can you help me carry stretchers, John?'

The man nodded. 'But we take her first,' John said pointing to his wife.

Together they placed Margaret's body on a stretcher. Beside Clement a lengthening queue awaiting treatment was forming outside *The Crown*. Gladys, the girl from Stanley's shop, was sitting by the door to the inn, bandaging the less injured and checking names against Mary's roll.

For several hours Clement alternated between carrying the dead to *All Saints* and praying with the dying and injured. Battersby arrived in the village, although Clement wasn't sure how or when the man had arrived, but he had gone straight to his task of comforting the wounded.

By late afternoon all the injured had been taken to Lewes Hospital and a silence had descended over the village. Fearnley Maughton was shattered. Thin plumes of smoke rose from the destroyed rubble. Buildings could be repaired but nothing would eradicate the memory. In his mind's eye Clement could see their faces. People he had known for years. Gunshot wounds wreaked such devastation. He closed his eyes remembering the jagged and bloody, raw and gaping wounds of brutality. The burns victims had impacted his mind most; the hideous charred blackness of burnt flesh. For those who survived, theirs was the long and silent suffering of enduring pain and disfigurement.

He sat with Battersby in the dining room at *The Crown*. He could see the elderly man's exhaustion. Clement learned he had come from Lewes in one of the ambulances and he was grateful for the practical and spiritual assistance.

'There is a bed for you at the vicarage,' Clement said. 'I cannot thank you enough for all your help. With Mary away, I couldn't have done it without you.'

'Thank you, but no. One of the ARP wardens is giving me a lift back to Lewes. It's a sad day for the village and for our nation,' Battersby said sipping some tea. The old cleric sighed. 'Should I come tomorrow?'

Clement nodded. 'I will telephone my wife and ask her to return. As you know I have some Home Guard business that cannot be ignored, and I may have to be away for a few days. I'm sorry to put so much on your shoulders, Battersby.'

'I know you have other duties. You do what you need to, Clement.'

It was just on sunset when he scribbled a note for the team telling them that he would not be back before Thursday night. It was longer than he'd anticipated but he knew Peter would follow the routines they had learned while at Coleshill. Placing the note into the dead letter drop collection point, Clement then returned to the vicarage.

For over ten hours he had ferried the dead, prayed with the dying and the living and done whatever he could to assist. But he knew that, as their vicar, his greatest use to them was in the future. Dealing with trauma, both physical and mental, always led to anger and seeking someone to blame. And the first one they held responsible was God. But that would only be, if they, as a village, and a nation, had the luxury of time to apportion blame. If the Germans were invading…Clement didn't want to think of what horrors lay in store for them. He, presumably, would be dead.

As he closed the door to the vicarage, Clement realised that he had been awake for thirty-six hours. He felt physically and emotionally numb. Nineteen bodies lay on the stone floor in his church, six of them evacuees. He felt the tragic irony; they had come to Fearnley Maughton to escape dying in London. He slumped into the chair in his study.

During the time he had spent with John Knowles, Clement had ascertained that John, despite his cryptic comment to Stanley in *The Crown* about his "special army friends", really didn't know anything about the Auxiliary Units. Clement closed his eyes, the image of Margaret Knowles lying dead on the street etched in his mind. His thoughts went to the infant. The child would need John now. Clement hoped his words at the public house about judging the child would find resonance with John. During their repeated trips into the church he had offered to baptise the infant. Although if the Germans occupied England Clement wasn't sure what he would be baptising the child into. Would the Church of England survive?

He pulled himself from the chair and trudged along the corridor to the kitchen. Filling the kettle, he told himself he was too exhausted to philosophise tonight. He put a heaped scoop of tea in the pot. It was extravagant but this night he needed it. He poured the milk into a jug as the faces of the dead, people he knew, flashed in his memory. What did small children know of the Nazis? When the Germans did invade and drove into Fearnley Maughton, he'd seek revenge for the little children. He closed his eyes. He was tired. Was he right to think such thoughts? He remembered Gubbins's words about killing. But killing the enemy because they were the enemy was one thing. Killing for revenge went against everything his vocation represented.

The front door bell sounded hard, interrupting his thoughts. He made the tea and reached for another cup. 'Coming!' he shouted.

Putting the tray in his study, he turned out the hallway light and went to open the front door. There stood Chief Inspector Morris.

'Reverend Wisdom. Could I have a word?'

'Of course,' he said. In all that had happened he had forgotten Stanley and the dead constable.

'Please,' Clement said gesturing towards one of the winged armchairs in his study. 'I'm sorry the room is so cold. My wife is away at present seeing to her elderly sister. But at least I can offer you a cup of tea.'

'Thank you.' The policeman sat down. 'Reverend Wisdom, could I ask you a direct question? Are you involved in anything other than clerical duties?'

Clement's mind raced as he poured the tea. He couldn't answer directly. Handing the cup to Morris, he poured his own tea and sat in the other chair. 'I am group leader of the Home Guard here in Fearnley Maughton.'

Morris sipped the tea. 'Is Stanley Russell also involved?'

'He was in the Home Guard.'

'Was, Reverend Wisdom?'

The silence was as cold as the room. 'I'm sorry but I cannot discuss it.'

Morris nodded. 'Constable Newson was killed with a nine-millimetre bullet at close range. Would you like to tell me what you know about it?'

Clement had nothing to hide but he wondered how Morris knew he had been there.

'I did go into the police station,' Clement began, and he told Morris what he had seen. The man listened as Clement told him about the dead constable and that Stanley was not in his cell.

'And you left the police station exactly as you found it?'

Clement nodded.

'Did you retrieve the Fairbairn Sykes knife from the evidence cupboard?'

There was another silence.

If his activities had been so easily spotted by the outsider from Lewes, Clement wondered if Gubbins should dissolve the group and elect a new leader. 'No,' he replied.

Another minute passed without comment. He watched Morris sip his tea.

'My father was a Vicar,' Morris said, eventually.

'Really?'

'Could you have gone to the police station during the raid and arranged for Stanley Russell's escape?'

'Despite what I, or anyone else for that matter, may be called upon to do to defend our nation, Chief Inspector, our country's enemy is Germany, not English police constables.'

Clement bit his tongue as he thought about what he had been asked to do to Inspector Russell. For one second he pondered Morris's fate. But Chief Inspector Morris was in Fearnley Maughton, not Lewes. Perhaps the investigation into Russell's death had prevented Morris from suffering the same fate.

Morris took another sip of tea but Clement noted the man's expression had not changed. 'I grew up on the Wellington Estates in Stratfield Saye, in Hampshire. I was named after Arthur Wellesley, a man of extraordinary insight. And a nose, a large one as it happens, for predicting future needs. Reverend Wisdom, I do not want to know what you and Stanley Russell were or are involved in. But Stanley Russell is in very serious trouble. Especially if the man had access to special and unusual weapons. If you have any idea where he could be, I must insist you inform me without delay. If Stanley Russell, or you for that matter, is relying on classified wartime activities to pervert the course of justice, I would have to arrest you both pending investigation. Or until ordered otherwise.'

Morris's intense, authoritative brown eyes were staring at Clement.

'Whilst I cannot discuss any other role I may or may not have, Chief Inspector, I must tell you that I do not believe Stanley Russell killed his father.'

'Why?'

Clement told Morris about Stanley's childhood. 'Such anger once unleashed would be violent. Emotion, not reason, takes control and hatred would make for a frenzied attack.' David Russell's office flashed into his mind. 'But I will tell you something I thought was odd.'

Morris tilted his head, the eyebrow slightly raised.

'I know this will sound strange, especially from a man of the cloth, but there was just not enough blood. I served in The Great War, and I have seen what bayonet wounds do to necks.'

Morris nodded. 'I think you're right.'

Clement waited but Morris didn't add anything to his remark. Clement knew that everything pointed to Stanley's guilt. He felt sorry for the gullible lad, especially when it came to Elsie Wainwright. And Clement felt responsible for getting Stanley involved in the first place. 'Perhaps you should know, Chief Inspector, that Elsie Wainwright, our recently arrived district nurse, has also disappeared from the village. We could have done with her nursing skills today. She may be completely innocent. She may even be dead herself, either from German dive bombers or some other foul play. But in the light of what I told you about the relationship between Stanley and Elsie, it would appear that they have vanished together as Stanley had originally intended. It could also explain the empty room and the open safe.'

He watched Morris process the information.

'Why would that be?' Morris asked.

'Constable Matthews heard Stanley and his father arguing about money. Inspector Russell did keep money in the safe. I saw some. But if Stanley wanted his inheritance, why did he leave more than a few five pound notes in the safe? It must have been a tidy sum.'

'Did you see anything else in the safe, Reverend?'

Clement shook his head. 'There were some papers, but I don't know what they were.'

Morris placed his cup on the nearby table but said nothing.

Clement wondered about Morris's silences. They were palpable. 'I saw that the safe was open, but I swear before Almighty God, that I did not take anything from it. And I'm sorry I didn't mention Elsie's disappearance sooner. But with all that happened today, I forgot about it. What will you do now, Chief Inspector?'

'Arthur, Reverend. We'll be seeing quite a lot of each other over the next few weeks, I have no doubt.'

'Then you should call me Clement.'

Morris smiled but remained silent.

'You think Stanley did it, with the assistance of the girl?'

'It certainly looks that way.' Morris made to stand. 'Well, it's been a long day. Thank you for the tea.'

Morris reached for his hat and moved towards the study door. 'I'll be staying in Fearnley Maughton for a few days at *The Crown*. If Stanley should contact you or you have any further information, no matter how insignificant you may think it, please tell me as soon as possible.' He paused. 'If Stanley Russell is innocent, Clement, then we have a very cunning murderer who could still be here in Fearnley Maughton.'

Morris must have seen his expression of alarm. 'If Stanley Russell did have an accomplice who shot Constable Newson, that person, whether male or female, would have to have access to a weapon which uses a nine-millimetre bullet.'

Clement's mind raced to Stanley's pack. He hadn't checked to see if the Sten gun was actually in the kit bag.

Morris went on, 'Furthermore, if Stanley Russell had such a weapon and if Elsie and he were planning an elopement, it's possible the girl was waiting for just such an opportunity to stage a rescue. But did that rescue include premeditated murder? Either way, given what was happening outside today, no one would have paid much heed to two young people running through the streets. Well, I'll say good night.'

Clement switched off the hall light and opened his front door. The strong moonlight flooded into the front hall, the pale grey-blue glow lighting up his front garden and the gate to Church Lane.

They shook hands. There was an honesty about Morris that Clement very much liked. He was pleased for Stanley that Morris was investigating the business. If Stanley was innocent there was a greater chance of proving it with a man like Arthur Morris on the case. Clement stepped back to close the door but Morris held his gaze.

'It may not surprise you, Clement, that while Fearnley Maughton was being bombed today, I was in Lewes at the hospital. I attended the post-mortem of Inspector Russell. He was shot with a gun using a nine-millimetre bullet.'

16

Wednesday 18th September

Despite his exhaustion, Clement found it difficult to sleep. Eventually he rose and opened the curtains wondering about his men, and whether the Germans had landed during the night. A pale blue sky greeted him; the early morning sun was highlighting the changing leaves of the trees in the churchyard. He checked his watch. It wasn't quite seven o'clock, but despite his anxiety about the invasion, he couldn't stop thinking about what Chief Inspector Morris had told him last night. All the evidence pointed to Stanley's guilt. And to Elsie as his accomplice. Yet, Clement really didn't believe that Stanley had murdered his father. Clement was, however, now convinced that whoever had killed David Russell wanted Stanley to take the blame.

Clement's thoughts turned to Constable Newson. His death had not been due to a shot fired at random from an enemy aeroplane; it was cold-blooded murder. And at close range. That took either terrifying courage or psychopathic insanity. Could Elsie have done such a thing? Could Stanley? Clement visualised the hole in the constable's head. Subsonic bullets. Special. Such specialised ammunition was not available to farmers or gamekeepers. Clement thought again about his team. But he knew these men. He had known them for years and had hand-picked them. He trusted them with his life. Although Reg Naylor had been a big revelation with his skill and aptitude for sniping. Young George had set up the trip wires and Clive the explosives. Even Peter, who had an aptitude for disguise and stealth, could have returned to the village at any time. All of them had the skill to move in and out of the village without being seen. But why would any of them kill David Russell, a man they had all known for years? There was no motive. And what of Constable Newson who none of them knew?

Clement stared through his window feeling wretched. How could he doubt his team? Good and decent men who had put duty ahead of personal safety.

He wanted to speak with Johnny, although, Clement didn't know what Johnny could do. He believed just sharing his thoughts would be helpful then, perhaps, he should tender his resignation, if such action was permitted. But above all, he wanted to hear Mary's voice.

Walking into the front hall, he dialled Gwen's number, forgetting the earliness of the hour.

'Hello?' a man's voice said.

'Oh! Sorry. I must have telephoned the wrong number,' he said and rang off. Still holding the receiver in his right hand, he depressed the dial tone buttons and redialled the number. He had phoned that number so many times he knew it by heart. The lines were evidently crossed. He rang again.

'Hello?'

'Mary?'

'Is that you Clement? Hello?'

'Mary, it's Clement,' he shouted. 'I'm sorry to call so early, I hope I haven't woken Gwen.'

'Clement? The line is so bad at this end.'

Clement stepped down from the bus and looked along Lewes High Street. Everything here looked normal to him. Why had the Stuka strafed Fearnley Maughton and not Lewes, that was so much bigger and more economically important? He looked up at Lewes Castle. Perhaps the proximity of the high Keep to the roadways had prevented the plane from flying low over the town. He walked towards the town centre and purchased a newspaper, turning it over and scanning each page. There was no mention of invasion and no pictures of high-ranking German officers standing on the steps of the Houses of Parliament. He felt utter relief.

He strode down the hill towards the railway station, the newspaper under his arm. As he passed Lewes Police Station he thought of Stanley. He knew a nationwide alert had been posted for him and the girl. Had she led him astray? Had war or love driven Stanley to dishonesty? Did his actions include murder?

Clement stood on the platform as the train pulled into the station. The slender ankles stepped from the train and he embraced her.

'I heard about the village. What a terrible thing. I can hardly believe it,' Mary said.

'I'm so pleased you're back. It has been hectic since the bombing and it is taking its toll on poor old Battersby. There are twenty-two funerals to arrange. Three of the burns victims died in Lewes Hospital. I still can't believe it. And this business with Stanley. I think you could well have been right about the girl, Mary.'

Mary handed him her suitcase and they walked together up the hill towards the bus stop. Fifteen minutes later they were in Fearnley Maughton. They walked through the village.

'What a sight!' Mary said.

'People are being stoic but I fear it'll take some time before the village looks and feels the way it was.'

Clement opened the front door to the vicarage.

'I'll make some tea,' Mary said, leaving her hat and coat on the stand in the hall.

'Put a third cup on the tray would you, Mary. I'm expecting Reverend Battersby to call by soon.'

The doorbell rang.

'I'll go,' Mary said. 'You both look exhausted.'

Clement saw the appreciative smile on Battersby's face. It had been a busy morning. Before going to Lewes to meet Mary, Clement and Reverend Battersby had visited many injured in their homes. And this afternoon, Battersby was taking the first of the funerals. Clement felt guilty that he wouldn't be there. But in a way, his presence in the village yesterday had been by divine intervention; if the Germans had invaded their sector, he wouldn't have been in the village at all. He heard the familiar voice from the hall and went to the front door. 'Chief Inspector, I see you've met my wife, Mary. What can I do for you?'

'How do you do?' Morris said raising his hat.

Mary smiled. 'I'll get the tea, Clement.'

'That won't be necessary, Mrs Wisdom,' Morris said. 'I was wondering if your husband would come with me to the police station. Not to detain him, I assure you, but as he was the first to find the late Inspector Russell, I was wondering if he would go over one more time what he remembers?'

'Of course, if it'll help.' Clement reached for his hat and coat.

'How long have you been in Fearnley Maughton, Clement?' Morris asked as they walked down Church Lane.

'Twenty years. Mary and I moved here just after we were married.'

'I won't keep you long. I know you must be in great demand after yesterday's events.'

'I've been out all morning. It'll take the villagers some time to get over this attack. I suppose we have been lucky until now. Unlike so many other places. Hastings, for example, has been hit almost repeatedly by random bombings. They say the Germans drop any leftover bombs as they leave England. I think we just happened to be in someone's way yesterday.'

'I've heard that too,' Morris added.

They rounded the corner onto the High Street.

'I don't know that I can add anything to what I have already told you, Arthur.'

'You may well be right. But sometimes just being in the same place will jog the memory.'

Chief Inspector Morris opened the door to the police station and they walked in.

'Good morning, Sir, Reverend,' Constable Matthews said as they entered.

'I thought you put Matthews off-duty for the investigation?'

'I did. But in view of Constable Newson's death, I need him. And he can handle other things.'

Morris pushed open the repaired partition door and they walked towards David Russell's office. The room was cold, the office furniture still as it was the day Clement found Russell's body.

'You say you found Inspector Russell on the floor?' Morris asked.

'Yes. In fact, I couldn't see him from the doorway. I entered the room and found him lying on the floor beside the desk and a little behind it. His foot was the only visible part of him from the doorway.'

'The window was open, I understand.'

'Yes. I remember the curtains moving in the breeze.'

'Did you see anyone outside?'

'No. But the Inspector's car was in the rear lane. You can see it from the window,' Clement said pointing through the taped glass panes.

'And the safe was open?'

'Yes,' he said hoping that Morris wouldn't pursue the safe and its contents.

'Just for now let's assume that the murderer is not Stanley Russell.'

Clement felt a wave of relief, but before he could say anything Morris continued.

'Nor Constable Matthews. Then the murderer came in through the window.'

'But surely Inspector Russell would see someone entering his office through the window. Unless he was already on the floor?'

Morris shook his head. 'No. I believe Russell was seated in his chair.'

'Which means he knew the person?' Clement said thinking again of Stanley.

'Perhaps. Would you like to see the Coroner's Report?'

Clement had never been involved in a police investigation, much less a murder enquiry. He wondered why Morris was including him, but he reached forward and took the proffered file.

'The relevant part is marked,' Morris said.

'There are three wounds to the head,' Clement read aloud. That surprised him. He looked up at Morris then continued. 'The first injury is a contusion to the back of the head caused by a blunt instrument but not occasioning death. The second and fatal injury was caused by a gunshot wound to the neck fired at point blank range. The third wound is a deep incision to the throat which severed the trachea and carotid arteries. The third injury was sustained after death.' He looked at Morris. 'Why would anyone hit him over the head then kill him twice?'

'Good question.' Morris said, walking around the room.

He watched as Morris' eyes scrutinised every surface. 'Clement, would you mind sitting in Inspector Russell's chair?'

Clement sat in the chair behind the desk.

'Someone comes in through the window and hits the Inspector over the head,' Morris began.

'Perhaps Russell has his head down. Perhaps the safe is already open when he's hit,' Clement added.

'It is possible, but he falls or rather slumps in the chair. If he were leaning forward, as he would if he was

156

head down in the safe, he would fall forward off the chair hitting his forehead on the floor or the edge of the safe. No. I think he knew who came through the window. And given that the window was open, he may have even been expecting them. And I think he was seated in his chair when he was hit. Now, Clement, take a look at the edge of the chair. Do you see dark staining on the armrest? Where it joins the seat?'

Clement swivelled around to see the armrest. Caught between the tight folds of the leather upholstery was a thin, blackish smear. 'Is it dried blood? It isn't very much, is it?'

'I agree. But it is my opinion that the wound to the back of Russell's head was either not intended to kill or the attacker was not strong enough for the blow to cause death.'

'A woman?' he asked. He could only think of one.

Morris lifted his eyebrows in response. 'Russell's body is slumped in the chair. The murderer turns the chair to face the side wall then Russell is pulled onto the floor where he is shot. The blood in the leather is from the wound on Inspector Russell's head as he is pulled to the floor.'

'Then to disguise the shot, his throat is cut.'

'So it would seem.'

'Surely even Constable Matthews would have heard a shot.'

'Perhaps.'

Clement watched Morris. The Chief Inspector had stopped speaking and was staring at the floor, his brow deeply furrowed.

'Clement, would you mind lying on the floor exactly in the position you found Inspector Russell?'

He lay down half-twisting his body to replicate the supine Russell. Morris came and stood beside him extending his arm, fingers pointed like a pistol and knelt down beside his head. Clement could feel Morris' index finger on his neck.

'The throat wound covered the entry and exit points of the shot. Which means that the murderer was kneeling or lying beside Russell's body on the floor.'

Clement sat up. 'But, if the murderer shot Russell and it killed him why would he or even she bother to cover it by cutting the man's throat?'

'If I was to fire a pistol at such close range then there would be powder and burn marks on the skin,' Morris went on. 'The knife wound would cover the burn marks and the entry and exit wounds.'

'Forgive me for questioning your judgement, Arthur, but it doesn't make sense.'

'It would if the killer wanted the murder to resemble a knife attack. Lie back again, Clement, if you would?'

Morris stood, and stepping over him, looked on the other side of his neck. 'As no bullet was found on post-mortem, the bullet would have exited the neck and travelled...' Morris stopped speaking.

Clement turned his head and stared to where Morris's finger was drawing an imaginary line from his neck outwards. 'I can see something,' Clement said. He pointed to the wall.

Morris lifted a curtain and they stared at a neat round hole in the skirting board.

'Would you mind not mentioning this to anyone?' Morris said. 'I want to play this as if we think Stanley is guilty.'

'You think he is innocent?' Clement said, standing.

'I didn't say that. I have an open mind on it for now. But I think it is more complex than it appears.' Morris went to the door and called to Constable Matthews. 'Constable, when Inspector Russell was in his office was it his habit to have his office door open or closed?'

'It was usually ajar, sir. The Inspector didn't welcome unexpected interruptions. But he always wanted to hear what was going on outside.'

'And he could see if anyone was standing at his doorway?'

'That'd be difficult, Sir. But he had good hearing,' Matthews said, pointing to his policeman's boots. 'And he kept a close eye on the supply cupboard. What with the rationing, Sir.'

Morris paused. 'When Stanley Russell was in his father's office, where were you, Constable?'

'At the front desk, Sir.'

'But you heard them arguing?' Morris asked.

'I'm surprised the whole village didn't, Sir.'

'Did you leave your desk at any time after Stanley Russell left his father's office?'

Matthews paused. 'I did visit the supply cupboard. I have the requisition form, if you'd like to see it, Sir?'

'That won't be necessary. It is just outside this door, isn't it, Constable?'

'Yes, sir.'

'Did you see Inspector Russell?'

'No, Sir. But I did feel the breeze. I knew the window must have been open.'

'Was that unusual?'

'Most unusual, Sir. Inspector Russell was not the outdoor type.'

'Could you stand in the corridor, Constable, just outside the supply cupboard door? Reverend Wisdom will say something and I would like you to tell me what he says. Can you do that? And leave the door to this office as it would have been that morning.'

'Of course, Sir.'

Matthews left the office, placing the door in its customary position.

'Clement would you cough, just the once?' Morris whispered.

Clement nodded then emitted a short, forced cough.

'Well, Constable?' Morris shouted.

The constable pushed open the door and stood in the doorway. 'I'm sorry, Sir. I was listening hard. But I didn't hear the Reverend say anything. Actually I thought I heard him cough.' Matthews paused, the man's face a study in concentration.

'What is it, Constable?' Morris asked.

'I heard him cough, Sir. Inspector Russell that is. He had a loud cough and a very loud sneeze. But this was...'

'Go on,' Morris said.

Matthews shook his head. 'Different, Sir. Shorter. And hard. Just the cough. Nothing else. Then the door closed.'

'The door closed?' Morris asked.

'Yes, Sir.'

'Thank you, Constable. You may return to your desk now.'

Clement watched the bemused Constable Matthews walk back along the corridor to the duty desk.

Clement looked at Morris. 'A silenced weapon?'

'It would be my guess.'

17

Thursday 19th September

Four o'clock. The coldest hour of the night. Clement wanted to see the men before going to London. He also wanted to check the contents of Stanley's pack. Rising, he hurriedly dressed in a clean Home Guard uniform and let himself out of the vicarage.

It had rained at some time during the night and the ground was damp. Clouds scudded across the moon, the strong light coming and going in uneven flashes. Clement pulled the collar up on his jacket. Nothing stirred. Not that he expected there to be anyone around at that hour. The blackish-blue moonlight lengthened the shadows and heightened the nerves. Standing at the front gate of his home he looked up and down Church Lane before hurrying away through the churchyard.

His men had only been at the Operational Base for forty hours, but it seemed like a week. Half a lifetime. He opened the church, the last of the corpses from the raid on the village now gone. The door creaked closed behind him and he went straight to the church office. In the pre-dawn hours, everything seemed silent and alien. Shadows concealed imagined beings, and what sounds could be heard were intensified, juxtaposed with crisp silence.

Unlocking the filing cabinet drawer, Clement took out his knife and strapped it to his inner left calf. It was becoming second nature to him. He pulled his trouser leg over the weapon and glanced at the neat piles of paperwork Reverend Battersby had left on the table in the vestry. He thought of Mary, who was still asleep in their bed. With her return another anxiety had arisen. If Stanley was innocent, as Clement believed, then a murderer was on the loose in Fearnley Maughton. The neat hole in the skirting board flashed into his mind. He understood why the murderer would not want to leave the bullet, but whoever this killer was, the person was cool-headed enough to remove it. They also had the time to do it. Those two facts ricocheted around his brain.

Calm, rational thinking was dictating the murderer's actions. Were they following a plan, a well-constructed and thought-out strategy? Clement felt the unemotional, detachment of a ruthless killer where personal issues played no part. Yet, the murder of David Russell confused the personal with the impersonal. Was that the murderer's intent? What was the motive? Whichever way Clement thought about it, he felt confused. He thought of Elsie Wainwright. There was little he could do there. Finding Stanley and Elsie was in the hands of the police now, and while Clement had his reservations about the girl, he was almost sure that Stanley had been framed.

What had precipitated the murder of David Russell? Clement thought of John Knowles's threat the day the child was born. But Clement couldn't imagine John calmly killing David Russell. John's threat had been made in the heat of the moment, and as Clement already knew, the killing of Inspector Russell and Constable Newson had not been frenzied. Besides, Knowles's threat had not extended to killing Constable Newson or assisting Stanley to escape.

Clement looked up as a flash of moonlight lit up the church yard. Reaching for his keys, he closed the door to the church and hurried into the darkness, crossing the fields, heading for the woodland. The dawn light was tingeing the sky as he approached the forest. He was about fifty yards from the Operational Base when he heard them. Bird song filled the woodland and he dropped to the leafy floor. Pausing, he responded with the raucous warble of the Jay. Within seconds Ned and Clive were around him.

As Clement crawled through the narrow opening to the Operational Base, he saw Reg in the low light of a lamp. The man was sitting with his Sten gun over his knees, the oil rag in his hand. Reg looked up as Clement sat down at the table.

'What's happening, Clement?' Peter asked as the men gathered around the table.

'You heard the Stuka?'

'George went into the village through the night and collected your note. He told us about the destruction.'

'Twenty-two dead,' Clement said. He saw their wide-eyed horror and told them what had happened. 'It could have been more had we not had our Invasion Day plans, but twenty-two is too many for our small village. I checked on Geraldine yesterday morning, Reg. She knows you're doing your bit and while she is worried, she is unharmed and the house is undamaged. I also saw one of your Land Army girls, Ned. She told me that they were not hit. But the village has been damaged quite badly. I am sorry to tell you Peter that your office took a direct hit.' He remembered Doctor Haswell's garden. 'So did Phillip Haswell's Anderson Shelter.'

'So George said,' Peter answered. 'Is it completely flattened?'

'A direct hit. Peter, if you had been there you would have been killed.'

'I suppose I should be grateful for that,' Peter replied. 'What about Miss Forster?'

'She's uninjured. She heard the plane and went straight to *The Crown*.'

Clement could only imagine what it would be like to lose, at a single blow, one's life's work. But his friend was alive, at least for now. 'Anything to report here?'

'Only one incident, which occurred during my watch,' Peter said. 'I tracked a young man in the forest between two and three this morning. He must have slept here overnight but he left just after three o'clock. He was heading south. He didn't meet anyone and he didn't stay long. He appeared to be foraging for forest food.'

'What did he look like?' Clement asked.

'He wasn't wearing a German uniform,' Reg said. 'Apparently.'

Clement glanced at Reg who continued to polish his weapon. 'Who was on watch with you, Peter?'

Clement saw Peter shoot a glance at Reg.

'I didn't recognise him, Clement,' Peter told him. 'About thirty, rather unkempt. Dark hair and whiskers. He was wearing a coat, but it was old and quite worn. Put it this way - he was dressed like he should be if he is that hard up for food he needs to forage in woodlands in the early hours of the morning.'

'He could be a deserter,' Reg added.

'Did you see this man, Reg?' Clement asked.

Reg shook his head. 'The coat. Peter said it had epaulettes. And there is some sort of underground naval installation near Cuckmere Haven.'

Clement felt the frown crease his forehead. Johnny had not mentioned any Royal Navy bases within or near their sector. Besides Cuckmere Haven was specifically off-limits. He turned his attention from Reg to Peter. 'I thought you said you were on watch together, Peter?'

'Reg did a solo patrol to the coast during our watch this morning,' Peter told Clement.

'That was never what we are about, Reg! We patrol in groups of no less than two. You could have got yourself and the others killed,' Clement said, his anger evident.

'In this moonlight a patrol is too obvious. We learned that the night before. Sitting ducks! Besides, Peter and I became separated. And I work better alone,' Reg added.

Clement looked around the faces. He could see disapproval in the eyes of Clive and Ned. From the way the three men had seated themselves, Clement guessed there had been heated words. Living in the confined Operational Base was taking its toll and they had been there less than two days.

'So where is this invasion, Clement? Because it isn't here nor, apparently, is it at Cuckmere Haven,' Peter asked.

'I'm seeing Commander Winthorpe this morning at ten. I've been helping Chief Inspector Morris from

Lewes.' Clement leaned back in the chair. 'It doesn't look good for Stanley. The police have issued a warrant for his immediate arrest and sent a description of him and the girl up and down the country.'

'How do you issue an arrest warrant for someone already in custody?' Clive asked.

'I'm sorry, of course, you don't know. Stanley has escaped. And someone else has been murdered; the constable from Lewes who was at the police station at the time. It happened during the raid. Did any of you come into the village during the attack?'

'Except for watch duty, none of us left the base during daylight hours. And during last night we patrolled to the south and east,' Peter said. 'Anyway, from what you've told us, it is just as well none of us were there, especially me.'

'Of course. I'm sorry,' he said.

'You think we freed Stanley?' George asked.

Clement stared at the boy. Something was different about the lad. For the first time since Clement had known George, the boy looked alive. The young face had transformed into that of a warrior and the pale visage of cardiac arrhythmia was nowhere to be seen.'

'So, once you are back from London are you here to stay?' Reg asked.

Clement heard the barb. 'I'm sorry. It was my decision to include Stanley and I feel responsible. I also believe he is not guilty.'

'You may want to revise that, Clement,' Reg added, throwing Stanley's pack onto the floor. It landed with a thud in front of him.

'You mean the Sten isn't there?'

'That's exactly what I mean,' Reg said.

166

'And a magazine of ammunition is missing, Clement,' Peter added.

Clement allowed a long sigh to escape his lips. He felt tired. His legs and head ached. He wanted to believe Stanley innocent. And the girl.

'People have been hanged for less,' Reg said, breaking the silence.

'If Stanley is guilty, I for one wouldn't blame him,' Clive added. 'That father of his was a sadistic bastard. If anyone deserved to die it was David Russell. Pity there has to be any investigation. If he had been killed during the raid, no one would be any the wiser.'

'This Chief Inspector from Lewes, is he likely to cause us trouble?' Reg asked.

Clement shook his head.

'You haven't told him anything, I hope, Clement,' Peter said. 'We are trusting you not to give us away.'

'Of course your identity is safe. I would never tell anyone,' he said, which he knew to be correct. But with the list gone, he couldn't speak for others.

'What do you want us to do?' Peter asked.

Clement thought for a moment. He glanced at the faces staring at him, waiting for him to make a decision. Even though the alert had been issued, he believed the greater danger was from Arthur Morris, especially as, according to Johnny and *The Evening Argus*, no invasion had yet taken place. The Chief Inspector would be asking questions, and if the town solicitor, the baker, the postman, a local farmer and a landowner couldn't be found, Clement would have to invent an excuse. 'Other than the vagrant, you saw no enemy activity of any kind last night?'

'None! And not a ship in sight,' Reg answered.

'Perhaps you should go home. Peter would you compile the report and George, will you drop it as usual? Make sure to include a description of the vagrant. Then go home. But please be careful. With Lewes Police in the village, it would be wise to conceal your packs. All of you would be suspects if Chief Inspector Morris discovers you have a weapon which uses nine-millimetre bullets and Fairbairn Sykes knives. I should only be in London today. We'll meet at Peter's place tomorrow night at eight, if that is alright with you, Peter?'

Clement left the Operational Base and walked back through the woodland towards the village. He wondered about his team. The level of tension in the underground base was unnerving and he was glad to be away from them. Had they divided because of Reg's actions? It had been risky to patrol alone and specifically against General Headquarters' orders. Reg should have been disciplined for his breach of procedure, but his actions had also confirmed that no enemy amphibious invasion had occurred in their sector. Regardless, dissension was always corrosive and spawned the bane of any team; mistrust. Standing them down, Clement hoped, would give them breathing space.

It was daylight now. He checked his watch. Ten minutes past six. Mary would be awake within the hour. He wanted to return home via the church, firstly to return his knife but also to fetch a book in case Mary was already awake. He was tired but he could sleep on the train.

He broke into a slow run. As his feet fell into a rhythmic pounding, he contemplated the person who had stolen the list. If it had been taken by a local, what would they do with the information? Perhaps it was thrown away as meaningless. Perhaps the theft had always been about money. 'No,' he muttered. Ordinary people do not know how to break into safes. Neither did they remove bullets from skirting boards. Besides, if it had been about money why would the thieves leave some?

His thoughts returned to the list. It contained only names. There was no indication of their mission. He quickened his pace, his eye on the brown mulching leaves beneath his feet. If the murderer had intended to get the list, then they had to have known its location and its content. Clement slowed and stopped. The morning birdsong had quietened. He had previously wondered whether the murder of David Russell had always been personal or was it a means to get the list, but perhaps that was not the right question. Who would want the list? The enemy, of course. But that would mean there had to be a local contact. Clement thought of the vagrant. An outsider would have been seen. Especially one shabbily dressed. Besides, everyone in the village had lived there for years. Except one. Elsie.

Clement was back on the platform at Lewes station at nine o'clock. Mary had been more than usually quiet during breakfast and he wondered if she had awoken through the night and found him missing from their bed. Secrets. Whether during a war or between husband and wife, secrets divided.

Two hours later the train slowed and entered the familiar railway terminus of London Victoria. A Dornier bomber had crashed into the station the previous Sunday during heavy bombing. Twisted wreckage still lay in piles around the old building, but whilst the damage had rendered the railway station inoperable for a few days, people now hurried about as though nothing unusual had happened. He stared at the faces. What he saw made him oddly proud. It was as if the mighty city and its people were thumbing their collective noses at Hitler and his Luftwaffe.

Clement turned, his eye scrutinizing the waiting crowd in the street, searching for the naval commander's uniform. But Johnny wasn't there. Clement felt his heart sink. He didn't like being a disappointment to anyone, especially Johnny who had shown such faith in him.

Looking along the street, he saw the car. It was parked outside the public house on the corner where he'd seen it before. A few seconds later the car left the curb and joined the main stream of traffic. Turning, the vehicle pulled up beside him and the driver got out. Clement recognised the man who opened the door for him, but there was no conversation.

Johnny met him in the entrance foyer of Number Seven, Whitehall. They shook hands but Clement thought it was not the eager greeting he had previously been shown. Following Johnny up the familiar staircase, Clement smiled at the secretary before being shown straight into Gubbins's office.

'Winthorpe tells me, Wisdom, that you are having problems?' Gubbins said. 'I could do with some good news, especially now.'

Clement thought Gubbins looked exhausted. 'I'm not sure I can provide that, Colonel.'

Gubbins remained silent while Clement told them about the strafing, the murder of Inspector Russell and Constable Newson, the subsequence disappearance of Stanley and Elsie and, of course, the list.

Gubbins's face clouded. The man remained silent for a few minutes. Without, the clacking of the secretary's typewriter was the only sound.

'The vagrant is interesting. John will you have some of your people look into that.'

'And Elsie Wainwright?' Clement asked.

'You say she answered an advertisement placed in *The Times*?'

Clement nodded. 'She said her parents were from Eastbourne, although now deceased. I don't know anything else about her. She did say she had come from London.' He paused. 'She had very little luggage.'

Clement looked at Gubbins who was scribbling notes in a file.

'Many people don't have much to show for their lives nowadays,' Gubbins said. 'But perhaps you're right to be suspicious.' Gubbins pressed a button on a wooden box to the right of his desk. A woman's voice responded. 'Miss Bradwynn, would you look into an Elizabeth Wainwright? John will give you the details.' Gubbins released the button. 'We need to find your runaways, Clement.'

'And the invasion, colonel?'

'It appears that the war in the air is not abating. But there have been no signs of any landing craft on our shores that would indicate an amphibious invasion. Hitler may well have planned his invasion to follow their control of the air. Fortunately, as yet, they have failed to achieve this.' Gubbins stood and walked to his window. The man was staring at a barrage balloon framed in the centre of his cross-hatched window. 'Where are your men at present, Clement?'

'As we haven't found any sign of the German invasion, I have stood them down, Colonel, pending your orders. What with the raid on the village and the murders and Stanley's disappearance, emotions are running high and the Operational Base is a confined space for volatile spirits.'

'I agree. Have your meeting with them tomorrow evening but it would be a good idea if they were to have a refresher course at Coleshill. Arrange it for this weekend would you, John?'

Clement saw Johnny's surprised glance at Gubbins but didn't question the Colonel's request. Or was it an order? Either way it would be obeyed.

Clement frowned. Was Gubbins not including him in the exercise at Coleshill? He glanced at Johnny who seemed equally perplexed.

'Well, I won't keep you,' Gubbins went on. 'Clement, stay in touch with this Chief Inspector Morris. The runaways must be found. For now we must assume that Stanley Russell has confided in Miss Wainwright. We can't have them talking.'

Gubbins sat down and picked up some papers. The interview was over. Johnny went to the door and held it open.

What Gubbins had said about Stanley worried Clement and he wondered if he would ever see the young man again. Whether hanged for murder or killed in secret, Clement felt sure that Stanley Russell was a dead man. Stanley aside, why were his men returning to Coleshill? A shudder ran through Clement's body. Johnny's surprised reaction also worried him. Clement left Gubbins's office more confused than when he had entered it.

Neither he nor Johnny spoke as they left the third floor. Clement wondered whether he should mention that Reg had been to Cuckmere Haven. In view of all that had happened with his cell, and that Johnny had told them to stay away from the place, Clement decided it would be best left for another time. 'How will Miss Bradwynn find out about Elsie Wainwright?'

'It's quite an ask given that we know so little about her. But we'll see what Miss Bradwynn can unearth. By the time we've had lunch, I expect she'll have something for us.'

'As tempting as that sounds, Johnny, what I really need is sleep.'

'Food first. Then after we've read what Miss Bradwynn has for us, I'll drop you at the station. You can sleep on the train.'

'I should call my second-in-command and confirm the stand down.'

'Food first,' Johnny repeated and leaving Number Seven, they walked towards Trafalgar Square and entered St Martin-in-the-Fields.

An hour later they returned to Gubbins's office. Miss Bradwynn handed an envelope to Johnny. Gubbins wasn't there so they went up another two floors to the smallest office Clement had ever seen.

'This is my cupboard,' Johnny said, squeezing past the desk to sit in the chair. 'Not for much longer, I'm happy to say.'

Clement looked at the tiny round window set high in the wall. Even if Johnny could stand behind his desk, it was impossible to see out. Not even the barrage balloon disturbed the visible whitish-grey sky.

Johnny gestured towards the phone on the desk. 'You can use this phone to call your second-in-command, Clement.'

Clement dialled Peter's number.

'Is everything alright, Clement?' Peter asked.

'Yes. I'm a little tired that's all. Not as young any more, you know how it is. I should be home late tonight, but I will see you and the team tomorrow night at eight. And Gubbins has confirmed the stand-down.'

'Any news of Stanley?'

'None.'

Clement rang off. He glanced at Johnny.

Johnny opened the envelope and pulled out the papers and began to read aloud. "Eastbourne has a population of forty-five thousand, three hundred and fifty two at the last census of 1931. There are one hundred and two women with the name Elizabeth Wainwright living in the Eastbourne area. Of these, thirty-four would currently be aged between twenty and thirty. Removing the ten who have died in the intervening years since the census, there are twenty-four possible matches. Correlating these against the father's profession, there are six women whose fathers were medical practitioners in the Eastbourne area. The search would be further advanced if the Christian names of the parents were known."

Johnny handed the paper to Clement. 'Not bad for an hour's work. And Miss Bradwynn has included a copy of *The Times* advertisement,' Johnny said handing him the newspaper cutting. 'I'll ask Miss Bradwynn to keep digging.'

Clement sat alone in the tea room at Victoria Station. All he could see in his mind's eye was Elsie Wainwright sitting on the counter in *The Crown*. He could hear her voice now. Gone was the genteel lilt he had heard in the bus shelter in Lewes. It had been replaced with the hard-edged sound of vulgarity. As far as Clement was concerned, she had the manners of a bar-room harlot. He suddenly felt sorry for the girl's deceased parents. He had seen it before, older parents who indulged the child they had so long waited to have.

The police would find Stanley and Elsie, and when they did, they or Gubbins would deal with the pair.

18

Clement opened the door to his home. He could hear Mary in the kitchen singing her little ditties. He smiled and put down his satchel. At that moment the telephone rang.

'Hello?'

'Reverend Wisdom?'

'Speaking.'

'Please be in the graveyard in ten minutes. You'll be contacted.'

The line went dead.

'Hello?' Clement said again. Looking along the corridor, he could still hear Mary singing in the scullery. He stared at the geometric pattern on the hall runner in the corridor, wondering whether he should go or not. The caller had been insistent. Clement felt weary, but he couldn't ignore the call. He searched his memory for anything in the caller's voice that sounded familiar. He wondered if it were Stanley disguising his voice. For that reason alone Clement needed to go.

'Clement?' Mary called, appearing at the door to the kitchen.

He looked up and smiled and reached for the hat that he had only moments before placed on the stand.

'Are you going out again?' Mary asked, her head tilting in the direction of the telephone.

'Wrong number,' he lied. He bit his tongue. 'I just remembered I wanted a book from the church office. I'll fetch it before I get too settled.'

'Don't be too long. I'll be serving supper in ten minutes. How was London?'

'I'll be right back,' he called avoiding her question, at least for now.

Closing the door, he trudged in the semi-darkness towards *All Saints*. It was a path he had trodden so many times that he almost never thought about it. He stopped and listened. Had he complied too willingly? In the decreasing light his eyes scanned the path ahead. And behind. Perhaps he should have been carrying a pistol. He put his hands into the pockets of his coat searching for anything he could use as a weapon but he found nothing. The unarmed combat lessons at Coleshill flashed into his mind. Coleshill. Why did Gubbins want the men to go back there so soon? Clement recalled Johnny's surprised expression. Was it Gubbins's way of permanently removing a troublesome team? Did death await his men at Coleshill because they knew too much about Gubbins and the Auxiliary Units? Their bodies would never be found. A story would be concocted for the families. But he would know. Or would he? Perhaps the same fate awaited him. He began to recite *The Lord's Prayer*.

As Clement approached the old cemetery at the side of the church, he could see a figure standing behind one of the graves. A man he didn't recognise stepped forward from behind a headstone. The stranger wore a long black overcoat, dark hat and plaid scarf.

'Reverend Wisdom?'

'Yes,' he said drawing in his breath in preparation.

'It is vital that your reports are submitted every day. But I cannot transmit what I do not receive. Your failure to drop your report is a serious breach of the trust which has been placed in you.'

'I can assure you the reports are attended to and dropped every day,' Clement replied.

'Perhaps you have another escapee. See to it immediately. It is never to happen again.'

Clement stared after the stranger as he walked away. The confrontation made little sense to Clement. Was he Gubbins's man? Or Johnny's? Clement didn't even know if the man was English. Yet he had an educated accent. Johnny had told Clement to expect German spies, especially along the coastal counties. Even Major Bannon had said that the enemy had so many spies in England, that they should be suspicious of everyone. 'What is the world coming to?' Clement muttered. Regardless, the plaid-wearing man knew about the dead letter drop. And if Stanley's disappearance wasn't enough, now George was letting him down.

Clement returned to the vicarage deciding that after supper he would cycle out to Peter's house and find out why the report had not been done.

Two hours later Clement collected his bicycle from the side of the house. Night had settled and cycling through the devastated village and out to Peter's cottage in the dark was not Clement's idea of enjoyment. He couldn't imagine that Peter had let him down. So why had George? As Clement passed the rear lane behind the police station he caught sight of Doctor Haswell pulling into his usual parking space. Clement had been so annoyed with George about the missing report that he had not seen the car until the last moment. What with the vehicle headlights covered by the strange downward deflecting shades all cars were required to install, Clement was surprised he had seen Phillip's car at all. That he might have been run over by the over-worked Doctor made Clement even more determined to chastise George for his cavalier attitude.

Clement hadn't seen much of Phillip lately and he was sorry for that. Between Stanley, the Auxiliary Unit and the dead and injured, they both had been kept busy. Clement reflected on Phillip Haswell and the amazing work the man had done in *The Crown*. No doubt more than a few owed their lives to the Doctor's skill. Clement felt a twinge of guilt for not yet spending time with the wounded in Lewes Hospital. He pedalled on. In the silence he heard the low drone. It was high and distant. Twenty minutes later he swung his leg over the bicycle and leaned it against the front fence of Peter's cottage.

He knocked at the door. A minute later he heard Peter's step and the tinkle of Boadicea's collar. He could hear the dog's agitation. The door opened.

'Clement? I have already rescheduled the meeting for tomorrow night,' Peter said, standing in the doorway.

'I haven't come about that.'

Peter stood back and gestured for Clement to enter then closed the door behind him. They went into the sitting room where Boadicea sat on a rug before the fire. 'Will you have some tea?'

'No thank you, Peter. Is there anyone else in the house at present?'

'No. But I don't imagine you have cycled here at this hour to check on my moral well-being.'

'Quite. Sorry. As I said, Gubbins has agreed with the stand down. His view is that the Germans are waiting to win aerial supremacy before invading. But he wants us to keep meeting and training.' Clement swallowed. 'The reason I have come, Peter is to check that you handed in the report this morning?'

'Of course, Clement. Just as you asked. I gave them a description of the vagrant and said that we had patrolled to the coast. I didn't say that it was a solo patrol. And I didn't mention what Reg told us about the activity at Cuckmere Haven. My guess is that they already know about it anyway, which is why we were asked to stay away. I also stated that they, whoever they are, should check on the vagrant who we believed could be a Royal Navy deserter. Is there a problem?'

Clement leaned back in the chair. 'I was contacted by whoever it is who transmits the reports. Well, that may not be true. The voice on the phone told me to go to the cemetery to meet a man who chastised me for not submitting my report.'

'The report was done, Clement, and given to George as usual.'

'I never doubted it. But something is amiss. What happened in the village today?'

'Nothing much. Most people are still sombre and I have been all day at what was my office. Years of records have been destroyed. Peoples' wills, personal papers, accounts, all gone. What I could salvage is in my garage. I think I am getting too old for it all anyway. And now faceless men harassing you over some perceived delay in submitting a report that contains nothing of any real value. Have you spoken with George?'

'Not yet. I'll go now and see him. I just hope he is at home.' Clement turned to leave as Peter pulled the blackout curtain over the doorway. 'Good night, Clement. Take care in the dark.'

Clement heard the door close behind him. It was late and he wasn't sure he would find George at home. The lad had a liking for the night life and the picture theatres in Brighton in particular. Clement couldn't blame him. There was little for the young to do in Fearnley Maughton.

He cycled back to the village and went straight to the post office where George rented an upstairs room. Clement was tired now and just wanted to be at home with Mary. Knocking at the door, he prayed George would be in. It was several minutes before Ilene Greenwood appeared.

'Hasn't been in all evening, Reverend Wisdom,' Ilene Greenwood told him.

'But you saw him today?'

'No! Until recently George has been such a good boy. A real blessing to me. But lately he's been away all day and all night. Breezes in then breezes out. And he won't tell me where.'

'When you do see him, Mrs Greenwood would you please ask him to come and see me?'

'Of course. I hope he isn't in any sort of trouble.'

Clement lifted his hat in farewell. He had stood the unit down, but that did not include trips to the seaside.

19

Friday 20th September

The heavy rain had continued to fall throughout the night and scudding, grey clouds promised a bleak day. Collecting his bicycle, Clement pedalled down Church Lane. He hadn't slept well. Although it wasn't the weather that had kept him awake. Just after nine o'clock, he leaned his bicycle against the wall of the post office and stuck his head around the door. Ilene Greenwood was on the switchboard. He raised his eyebrows enquiringly, but she shook her head.

Closing the door, Clement collected his bicycle and cycled out of the village towards Peter's house, a worrying seed taking root in his mind.

Peter was standing in the doorway to his cottage when Clement arrived.

'What did George have to say for himself?' Peter called.

Clement leaned his bicycle against the fence. 'Peter, will you come with me to the Operational Base?'

'Of course, Clement. You look concerned. You found George alright then?'

'That's just it, Peter. I haven't. Of course, he could have forgotten to drop the report and has gone off to Brighton or Eastbourne. You know how he likes the night life.'

'I do know. But that is unlike George. He takes his duties very seriously. Too seriously at times.'

'I can only think that if he's not enjoying himself on the coast he's returned for some reason to the base. Perhaps he left something there. Or he may have stepped into a trap. Perhaps there are more vagrants coming into the woods to trap and forage what with the tightening of rationing. He could be injured. Would you mind coming with me?'

'Of course, I'll bring Boadicea but wouldn't Doctor Haswell be better?'

'I'd sooner keep it in the family until we know where he is.'

Peter nodded and attached the lead to Boadicea's collar.

At the edge of the woodland, Peter unclipped the leash and the Labrador ran off, her nose to the forest floor.

'We haven't laid any traps in the area, have we?' Clement asked.

'No. But when we have to take to the base again, it could be a good idea.'

They walked in silence but Clement kept his eye on the damp path looking for any sign of recent activity.

Boadicea was barking some way ahead. An uneasy and palpable silence wrapped around them.

'Should I whistle for Boadicea to return?' Peter whispered.

Clement nodded, his heart pounding. 'Don't want to walk into an enemy trap.'

Peter whistled, the insistent yelping continued, magnified in the moist, woodland air.

Clement looked at his friend. 'I think Boadicea is at the base. You didn't leave any cooking refuse did you?'

'Of course not, Clement. All ship shape and Bristol fashion.'

Peter whistled again. Within minutes Boadicea reappeared beside them in the bushes. The dog was excited and ran off again.

Clement stared after the dog. A sense of dread had gripped the back of his throat. In the forest stillness everything around him seemed to have intensified. 'Do you have any weapons on you?'

'No. Do we go on or go back?' Peter asked in a low voice.

Clement looked down at the ground, his eye fixed on a leaf stuck to Peter's shoe. 'You circle around. Take the right side of the path. I'll take the left. If we see no one, we meet on the path below the base. If there's someone there, go straight back to your house and I'll meet you later.'

Crouching low, Clement ran into the trees and fell to the ground. He could see Peter higher up the hillside but within a minute he had lost sight of his friend in the undergrowth. Rising to his knees, Clement scanned the forest around him. The only movement was the leaves rustling in the wind. He listened hard. He could hear the scratching sounds of foraging birds.

Although the base was only half a mile inside the forest, it took him over an hour to criss-cross the forest and arrive at the path below it.

Peter stepped out from behind the dilapidated Roman arch and joined him on the path.

'Anything?' he whispered.

'Nothing.'

Together they walked in silence up the hill towards the Operational Base, their eyes and ears straining for any movement, their senses on high alert. Ten feet from the tree stump opening to the underground bunker, George lay on the ground amongst the fallen autumn leaves. The boy's intense blue eyes stared out from an ashen face gazing up at the forest trees, his mouth open. A hole, the diameter of a sixpence, between his eyes.

Neither of them spoke. Staring at the boy, minutes passed before Clement's gaze turned to the forest around them.

'Dear Lord, Clement. The Germans?' Peter whispered.

'I don't think it can be. If George was killed by the enemy; where are they? They would surely have entered the village by now.'

'You're saying it was someone local?'

Clement swallowed. 'I think the murderer is English.' He looked out across the slope, then scrutinised the moss-covered ruins before scanning the trees and dense foliage below them.

'Poor George. What could have happened? Why was he here?'

'I wish I knew, Peter. We should look for the bullet.'

'It would be difficult to find here, Clement. Why do you want it?'

'Constable Newson was killed with a bullet fired from a gun that uses nine millimetre rounds.'

'Like a Sten Gun? You're not thinking that Stanley killed George?'

Clement shook his head. 'No. But it could be the same weapon as the one that killed Constable Newson.'

'Is there something you're not mentioning, Clement?'

Clement swallowed. 'It is possible David Russell was also killed with a nine millimetre bullet.'

'I thought his throat was cut?'

Clement nodded. 'Both.'

He heard Peter's long exhaled breath.

'Someone is sending us a message, Clement. That much is clear,' Peter said. He squatted and reached forward to close George's eyes.

'Don't touch him, Peter. George may be lying on a grenade.'

'Dear God! What do we do? The bullet is probably in the ground under him. And besides, we can't leave him here, so close to the base.'

'I agree.'

'There is some rope in the store cupboard in the bunker. We could drag him further down the slope,' Peter suggested.

'We must assume that whoever killed George has left him here for a reason. The Operational Base may be booby-trapped. It's a risk only I can take. Stand well away, Peter.'

'Clement?'

'Life expectancy two weeks, Peter. It may be less for me. Tell Mary I loved her, if it blows.' He shook Peter's hand. Peter and Boadicea walked away, down the hillside.

Clement grasped the tree stump and pushed it sideways exposing the tunnel then immediately jumped backwards, falling and rolling down the hillside. He waited. But there was no detonation. Walking back up the hill, he stared into the narrow, dark entry. Placing one foot onto the top step of the descending ladder, then his other foot onto the next rung, he descended into the bunker. Several minutes went by before he reached the floor. By then his eyesight had grown accustomed to the diminished light. His eyes scanned the air in front of him. Then the ground. Slowly, he stepped forward. His skin prickled and he could feel the perspiration building on his upper lip. Almost without breathing, he crept past the stove and the doorway to the latrine, into the living areas, past the bunks and into the rear of the base, nearly the entire length until he stood beside the storage cupboard. Taking several deep breaths, he placed his hand on the doorknob and squeezed the handle. The cabinet opened. He reached in and withdrew a length of rope.

Retracing his steps, he climbed back up the ladder and pulled himself through the trapdoor to the forest. Peter was staring at him from the pathway lower down the hillside.

Unravelling the rope, Clement tied one end to George's feet and backed away down the hillside to the forest path.

Peter joined him and together they pulled George's body down the slope away from its resting place.

Nothing happened. They waited in case of a delayed detonation.

Still nothing.

'I should go this time, Clement.'

'No, Peter.'

Clement walked back up the hill. He had expected to find the bullet where George's body had been, not what he did see. The canvas shoulder bag George used to carry the daily reports lay in the autumn leaves.

Clement squatted down and palmed away the leaf litter around the canvas pouch. He couldn't see any wires. Moving it to one side, he checked the damp soil for the bullet, but he didn't see anything. His gaze returned to the sack. Running his fingers along every edge, he checked the flap before lifting it and looking inside.

Empty.

20

Clement! Mr Kempton. Come in,' Chief Inspector Morris said. 'Won't you sit down? How can I help you?'

Clement glanced around the small office as they took the indicated seats before Arthur's desk. As Inspector Russell's office was a crime scene, Arthur had chosen to use the second office. Clement had already noted the newly hung photograph of the Prime Minister in the waiting area. And his eye had caught the other changes. They were, he considered, indicative of the man now in charge. A large framed picture of the King hung on the wall in the office of Arthur's choosing and freshly painted fire buckets filled with sand had been placed around the public areas and rear hall. It was the epitome of order.

Clement gazed at the neat stacks of files on Morris's desk, then at the man. 'Arthur, Peter Kempton and I have just returned from walking in the forest. We have found the body of young George Evans, the village post-man. He's been shot.'

Morris leaned back in his chair, frowning. 'I am assuming, Clement, by your reaction that you do not believe Mr Evans's death to be accidental?'

'No. He was killed at point-blank range, between the eyes.' Clement felt the utter futility of the boy's death and the sight of George lying dead in the forest flashed into his mind.

'You can positively identify the deceased?'

'Yes.'

'How long ago did you find him?'

'No more than forty minutes.'

'Was the body cold to touch?'

'Yes.'

'And rigid?'

Clement shook his head.

'Have you told anyone else about this?'

'No. I did try to find the bullet but in the thick leaf litter, I couldn't.'

'We should go to the scene now. And Mr Kempton?'

'Of course I will come.'

'We'll go in my car.'

Twenty minutes later they were standing beside George.

Clement had seen many corpses in his lifetime, but in death the young man seemed a mere child. Too young to die. Clement frowned at the thought. That was not true. George had gallantly volunteered; his death inevitable. But not like this.

Clement and Peter stood to one side as Arthur Morris walked around George. Without touching the lad, Morris's stern gaze scrutinised the body and Clement could see that he carefully looked along both legs and arms before settling on the hole in George's forehead. A minute later, he turned around and gazed up the hillside. 'Is this where you found him?'

'Yes,' Clement said, biting his lip.

Morris turned to face him. 'You say you didn't find the bullet?'

'That's right.'

'Well, I don't believe you would find it here. Because I don't believe George Evans was killed here and it may be that he wasn't killed where you actually found him either. Would you like to tell me where that was?'

Clement swallowed before glancing at Peter. 'Higher up the hillside,' he said feeling like a small boy who had taken sweets from the counter.

'Thank you. And you moved him because?'

'I was afraid there may have been a grenade under him.'

Morris pursed his lips. 'Clement, I said I didn't want to know what you were involved in, but I think the time has come for me to speak to your Commanding Officer.'

'Perhaps it's best. I will telephone him and ask if you can see him.'

'His name is?'

'Commander Winthorpe.'

'And I am assuming Mr Kempton also knows about this?'

Peter nodded.

'Thank you,' Morris said and walked up the hillside. He squatted down where George had lain, the Chief Inspector's hand smoothing away some leaves and exposing the moist, soft soil. He then took a tool, like a hand trowel, from his coat pocket and dug the ground. Within minutes Clement saw Morris put something into a white handkerchief.

'Must have found the bullet,' Peter said.

Clement nodded but his gaze was on Morris. Finding the bullet would help, although, if it was nine millimetre calibre, it wouldn't be good for Stanley. Morris stood and looked towards the tree stump over the entrance to the Operational Base before walking towards it. A minute later the Chief Inspector joined them on the path.

'You think George was killed elsewhere and brought here?' Clement asked as Morris joined them.

'I don't anymore.'

Morris took his handkerchief from his coat pocket and opened it. Two bullets lay in the Chief Inspector's palm. 'Did you and Mr Kempton drive a car here this morning?'

'No,' Clement answered, his eyes staring at the two bullets.

Peter shook his head.

'And you didn't notice the recent tyre tracks where I parked the police car?' Morris said.

'No,' Clement replied.

'Sorry,' Peter added.

'And there are several sets of footprints at the entrance to the woodland and around the ruins. Too many, perhaps?' Morris paused. 'It's my opinion that whoever killed George Evans didn't want his body found by just anyone.' Morris turned again to look back up the hill. 'But did our killer bring Mr Evans here, then shoot him, or did he happen upon Mr Evans? Or did Mr Evans happen unexpectedly upon him? Or her? Or was it a rendezvous?'

Clement felt himself nodding. That would explain the close proximity. And if it was "her", why George had been so close to his killer. But why had the killer fired twice? Had there been a struggle of some kind and the weapon had fired prematurely before the second bullet found its mark?

'Moreover,' Morris continued, 'would it not seem logical to bury the body? A forest, surely, is the ideal place to bury a corpse, especially when there's little likelihood of being disturbed while doing it. Most murderers do not want their victim's body discovered. So I must ask myself, why does the murderer want Mr Evans to be found?'

Clement knew Morris was speaking rhetorically. There were no answers. At least, not yet. They walked back along the track to the parked car in silence but until Clement could speak with Johnny there was nothing he could tell Morris. At the stile, Clement saw the profusion of footprints on the pathway in the friable soil. They were all large; not the size or shape of a woman's shoe.

He and Peter waited beside the police car while Morris lingered over the recent tyre tracks.

Morris rejoined them. 'I'll arrange for the police from Lewes to remove Mr Evans's body.'

They drove away from the forest and pulled into the road heading for Fearnley Maughton.

'Do you think it was a car or a van?' Clement asked.

Morris glanced at him. 'The tracks are more likely to be those of a car.'

'Can you be so decided?'

'I believe the killer wanted George Evans found, Clement. However, he or she does not want to be caught. A van with a name emblazoned on the side is far too memorable. Even if that van had been stolen. I've been a detective for over twenty years, and in almost every case of murder that I have ever been associated with, there is always a witness. Someone will have seen something. Unfortunately, usually that something is so routine that no one questions it.'

Ten minutes later they were back at Fearnley Maughton police station. While Morris arranged for Lewes Police to collect George's body, Clement telephoned Johnny from Morris's office.

'Something else has happened,' Clement said. There was silence at the other end of the line for a few seconds. 'You may remember that I mentioned a man from Lewes. He'd like to speak with you.'

'Usual place, Clement. Tomorrow. Bring your new friend. As for all your other friends, they are expected at holiday camp this weekend.' Johnny rang off.

Clement replaced the receiver. He had never felt so wretched in his life. First Stanley, now George and to make matters worse, Clement believed that Johnny was regretting involving him with the Auxiliary Units. Clement glanced at his friend of many years. Did death await Peter and the others of his team at Coleshill? His head was pounding.

Morris came in and sat in the chair behind the desk.

'I was wondering, Arthur, if you've had any news of Stanley or the girl?'

'They haven't been sighted.'

Clement closed his eyes. With Stanley the prime suspect for the murder of his own father and now with George dead, Clement could only imagine the effect it would have on the others, especially Reg. The man was already a loner and since joining the Auxiliary Unit, Clement believed he'd become distant, almost reclusive. The lone-wolf type was always unpredictable. If Coleshill was really for a refresher, Clement was glad of it. The team needed it, especially Reg. But if Coleshill was for another purpose; Clement screwed his eyes shut. He didn't want to think about it.

While Morris took Peter's statement about the morning's events, Clement stood up and stared out the window at David Russell's black car still parked in its usual place. On the other side of the lane Phillip Haswell was getting into his. Clement waved, trying to catch the Doctor's attention. He wanted to ask about the injured in hospital. Phillip's car backed up and drove away. The Doctor had not seen him. Clement turned around and watched as Peter read over the statement he had given to Arthur, but Clement's mind was still on Phillip Haswell. The odd thing about a view from a window is that there is, potentially, one hundred and eighty degree visibility. But it isn't the same from the outside. Seeing in is like looking down a tunnel; restricted and dark. He felt the frown cross his forehead.

Arthur was staring at him. 'Clement?'

'David Russell had to have been expecting the person who murdered him.'

'What makes you say that?' Morris said.

Clement pointed to the window at his back. 'I can see out clearly, especially in daylight. But seeing in, especially from a distance, is well-nigh impossible. Whoever entered through the window knew that Inspector Russell was in his office. Russell probably let them in, which means David Russell knew his attacker.'

Clement glanced again at the window. He felt what he had just realised was important, but something still evaded him, and he couldn't make any sense out of it. Peter was staring at him. His friend's raised eyebrows expressing the bewilderment that Clement could see on both men's faces. 'It was just a thought,' he said, sitting down again.

Arthur nodded and smiled.

But seeing Phillip again had also reminded Clement of the villagers in Lewes Hospital. He should have visited them before now and he felt guilty that he hadn't.

'If you are finished with me, I'll get back to the debris that was my office,' Peter said, standing.

Morris accompanied them both to the front door of the police station.

'You are redecorating, Arthur?' Clement said, his eye on the newly-painted front door.

'Someone smashed a bottle on the front step and it damaged the paintwork. It seems rather odd to me, in light of the damage to other buildings in the village, but Constable Matthews has found a renewed sense of pride in the place recently and insisted on doing it.'

Clement remembered seeing John Knowles stagger past the police station on his way home the previous Sunday night. Despite the man's inebriation, it would be a night John was unlikely to forget. 'When did that happen?'

'Monday morning. But it could have been Sunday night.'

'No, Sir,' Constable Mathews said behind them. He approached holding a piece of board. 'It wasn't there when I arrived at the station first thing Monday. Someone did it during the morning. I heard them and came running to catch the culprit, but they had vanished. Kids, probably. No respect.'

Constable Matthews hung the "wet paint" sign on the door and returned to his desk.

Clement said goodbye to Peter and watched his friend walk away. There was a droop in his shoulders and Clement wasn't surprised. Everything was complicated. Arthur Morris stood beside him. 'You are to come with me tomorrow, Arthur, to London.'

'Very good. I can drive us to Lewes tomorrow. What time do you suggest?'

'If we catch the nine o'clock train we'll be in London at about the right time.'

'I'll meet you here then just after eight?'

Clement shook hands with Morris. Walking away, he looked down the High Street towards the village green. Most of the shops were in the process of being repaired; all except Peter's lovely Georgian building that was gone forever. Nothing of it remained, except rubble. Clement could see Peter standing amongst the broken stone and shattered timber. Gazing along the row of familiar buildings, Clement watched as the people he knew went about their business. People stopped and chatted, life was slow and somehow, in the midst of German bomb damage, ordered. But perhaps life was never really as it seemed. He thought of John and Margaret Knowles; people he thought he knew, and realised you never really knew anyone that well.

He turned to walk back to the vicarage, but his gaze fell on the bus shelter. It was the dead letter drop where George secreted the reports. Clement stared at it, a frown forming. Walking towards it, he sat on the seat. Beside him was the advertisement poster display cupboard. It was a narrow, glass fronted, locked cupboard that contained posters advertising everything from Defence Bonds to Pears Soap. Now shards of broken glass stuck out at odd angles from the shattered frame.

He thought of George, a young man who through inclusion in the Auxiliary Unit had found a way to prove his bravery. Changing the poster every week had been part of George's duties as postman. The lad collected Clement's report from the vicarage while delivering the post, then visited the bus shelter to change the poster. While doing this, he wedged the report between the timber frame of the advertising cupboard and the wall of the shelter for an unknown person to retrieve.

Clement stood and checked behind the broken frame but the missing report wasn't there. He lowered his head. George's murder saddened and bewildered him, but the missing report was, in its way, more worrying. Sitting on the seat again, he stared out across the village green. Directly in front of him was *The Crown*. He looked at the old Elizabethan building. Upstairs he could see the tiny windows of the guest bedrooms under the overhanging thatch. His eye fell on one in particular. Number six.

21

It was late and Clement was tired, but he had to see them. A few minutes before eight o'clock he knocked on the door of Peter's house.

'The men are here,' Peter said.

Clement heard the sorrow in his friend's voice, but Peter's tone and expression held more than sadness. There was an element of resignation. The acceptance of death during war was inevitable, but George had not died on the battlefield. He had been murdered and until it was proved otherwise, his murderer was English.

Three faces looked up at Clement as he entered the sitting room. In that instant he saw, and felt, the dis-unity; Reg stood to one side, his right arm resting on the mantelpiece. Clive and Ned were seated but there was no ease between them. The camaraderie Clement had felt at Coleshill had vanished. He hoped it was only temporary. They all stared at him as he sat in one of the chairs.

'I suppose you've heard about George?' he asked.

Heads nodded.

'What's going on, Clement?' Reg asked. 'Was George's death connected to our activities?'

'I don't know. I hope not. However, that's not why I asked you here tonight. I wanted to bring you up-to-date about the invasion.' Clement told them about Gubbins's theories concerning the Germans waiting until they held air supremacy before invasion.

'Well, I wish they would just hurry up and get on with it, if they are going to,' Reg said.

The room was silent. No one really believed Reg wanted an invasion, yet they all understood.

'And George?' Clive asked, voicing what Clement knew was on everyone's mind.

'Unless Stanley is hiding in the forests, it can't be him this time,' Ned Cooper said.

'You're right, Ned. If Stanley and the girl are still together, Fearnley Maughton and its environs would be the last place he would be.'

'Unless that is his thinking,' Ned added.

'Stanley doesn't have the brains for that kind of deception,' Reg said.

Clement flicked a glance at Reg. Even though harsh, he knew Reg's assessment was correct.

'Unless it was about the girl. George was keen on her too,' Clive added.

'Stanley and George have known each other for too long for that. I am concerned about the girl,' Clement added. In his mind he could see Elsie sitting on the bar, her shoe dangling from her toes. 'I don't mean to sound unkind but why would a girl like Elsie be smitten with a lad like Stanley? What could she possibly hope to gain from the liaison? What's more, we don't really know if the girl and Stanley are still together.'

'Well, if not Stanley then who? Does this Chief Inspector Morris have any ideas?' Reg asked.

'He is a thorough man. And an intelligent one. I'm sure he will find the killer soon.'

'Do you think David Russell and George were killed by the same person?' Clive asked.

'Where's the connection, Clive? There isn't one, so that can't be right,' Reg said.

'And what about Constable Newson?' Ned asked.

'Wrong place, wrong time,' Reg added.

Clement glanced around the faces present. He could feel and see the tension. He hoped Coleshill would sort it out. 'I don't know. It is possible someone stumbled on the Operational Base and killed George thinking him an enemy spy. But if the killer of both men was the one person, Reg is correct; what is the link between George and David Russell, and Constable Newson who, it seems, just got in the way?'

'So what happens now, Clement? Are we to be disbanded?' Reg asked.

He looked at Reg. He could see the scepticism - or was it disappointment? - on the man's face. Was Reg too eager to prove his loyalty? Clement chastised himself; with all that had happened, he was beginning to question everything and everyone. Reg was one of the best marksmen Clement had ever seen. The man could score a direct hit from fifty yards without a telescopic sight. He thought of Reg's solo patrol. The man had to be managed. Clement visualised the hole in George's head and Constable Newson's blank visage. He thought of the skirting board in Russell's office. But no matter how accurate Reg's shooting, Clement did not really believe Reg Naylor to be a cold-blooded murderer.

'No. In fact, Gubbins wants you all to go to Coleshill for a few days to hone your skills. If the Germans are waiting to gain air supremacy before invading, the invasion could be on hold for a while. It gives us some much-needed breathing space. Given this and where George's body was found, it is best we stay away from the Operational Base for now. It could all be coincidental, I just don't know. Go to Coleshill, but remain vigilant. And watch each other's backs.'

'You not joining us?' Reg asked.

Clement shook his head, feeling increasingly like an outsider. 'There is something important I must do and about which I can tell you nothing,' he said, hoping it sounded convincing.

The room fell silent again.

'I thought we were a team, Clement?' Peter said.

'Doesn't seem like one to me,' Reg remarked.

'I'm sorry but it has to do with Stanley,' Clement said. 'He must be found. And the girl. And Johnny can get Scotland Yard involved.'

'Stanley's dead, isn't he?' Reg said, staring at Clement. 'If not already, then he will be. He knows too much. You doing it, Clement?'

Clive and Ned were staring at him. Clement could see their incredulity. He believed he mirrored their reaction. 'I don't know where Stanley is and that is God's honest truth.'

But Reg's face was resolute. 'Right! Well, if that's it?'

Reg's reaction annoyed Clement but there was little else he could say. 'Be at Lewes Station at six o'clock tomorrow morning with full packs. That's all for now.'

Reg walked towards the front door and they heard it slam shut.

Clive Wade stood, Ned beside him. 'What Reg said, is it true, Clement?' Clive asked.

'Absolutely not!' Clement said, aghast. 'I do not kill innocent men!' But he could feel the stares.

'That's good enough for me. Sorry, but I had to ask,' Ned said.

'I understand. And thank you, Ned.'

'Do you think Stanley is still alive?' Clive asked.

'I don't know. I hope so. But he must be found. Soon.'

Peter showed Clive and Ned to the door.

The room was empty now except for Boadicea who hadn't moved from her mat in front of the fireplace. It alarmed Clement that Reg thought him capable of tracking and killing Stanley. Especially as he was endeavouring to find some proof that would exonerate the man. Clement had, at times, removed his cleric's collar since the national *Cromwell* alert, but he hadn't abandoned his Christian faith.

Peter returned, and they exchanged glances but neither of them spoke for several minutes. Clement stared at the flames licking the logs in the fireplace. A pine cone cracked in the heat, the popping sound and sudden burst of released embers briefly illuminating the grate.

'At least the Germans haven't yet landed,' Clement said.

'Don't worry, Clement. We'll do what we must. You just find Stanley and who killed George.'

'Thank you, Peter. I appreciate your support.' Clement stood and they walked towards the front door. 'Keep an eye on Reg, will you Peter? I'm concerned his negativity will influence the others.'

The front door closed behind him. Pulling his coat around him to ward off the cold, he pedalled into the night. As he rode he looked upwards. He hadn't heard the low drone of bombers tonight. Above him was a clear night sky studded with stars and the omnipresent moon. As beautiful as it was, the memory of Reg standing beside Peter's mantelpiece and what the man had believed him capable of doing, appalled Clement. Yet that would have been David Russell's fate and it was what they had been trained to do. To Kill. Silently. 'Get used to it,' he muttered. 'It's what you signed up for!' he reminded himself.

He cycled back into the village, the moonlight casting long shadows across his way. No one was about. Late-night travel was discouraged, considered too dangerous and, for those who had vehicles, a waste of valuable petrol.

As he cycled past the common he could smell the burning log fire in *The Crown*. He stared at the building thinking of Elsie Wainwright. The girl was an enigma. Arthur Morris was staying at *The Crown*, and Clement wanted to ask him if they could leave a little earlier. He wanted to see the injured in Lewes hospital before going to London.

Clement opened the public house door. There was the usual group huddled around the bar and seated by the fire place. He scanned the faces present before opening the door to the dining room.

Arthur sat alone in the deserted room, a newspaper spread on the table in front of him, the evening meal long since tidied away.

'It's late to be out, Clement. Everything alright?' Arthur asked.

'Yes. Tomorrow, Arthur, I was wondering if we could leave the village a little earlier than arranged. I should visit those who are still in hospital in Lewes. I feel guilty I haven't seen them before now.'

'Of course. I can spend some time in my office in Lewes and meet you on the platform. There is always plenty of paperwork for a policeman to do.' Morris paused. Lifting the newspaper he slid out a piece of paper with a rough sketch of the village drawn on it. 'Would you mind if I asked you again about the day you found Inspector Russell?'

'Anything to help,' Clement said looking at the sketch. Lines and arrows had been drawn all over the page.

'The vicarage is quite close to the police station,' Morris said.

Clement studied the diagram. He could see that Arthur had pencilled in his home, the police station and other buildings around the village.

'From your perspective, Clement, what was going on in the village last Sunday and Monday?'

Clement thought for a moment. 'That was the fifteenth. They are saying it was the worst day of bombing. We saw bombers and fighters all day and well into the night. Our planes and the Germans. Sortie after sortie. I don't know how our brave boys could tell who was friend and who was foe. Do you know the glow of London could be seen ten miles away? I heard that on the wireless. Hard to believe how London has survived. The sight and noise of those planes overhead placed a pall over the village. By Monday morning everyone was worried. But it is amazing how people react. Some went about their business, while others remained indoors listening to the wireless reports. The tension was undeniable. Invasion and defeat were in everyone's mind. But I am glad to say not on their lips. The village was eerily normal.'

'What did you do that day?'

'Church, of course, in the morning,' he leaned back in the chair remembering. 'In the afternoon, I went for a walk on the Downs. I saw our bank manager, John Knowles. Not a happy situation. The child had been born that day. There was much gossip about the child's paternity in the bar. I went home after that.' He paused. He could not tell Morris about his main concern that day, the retrieval of the list from Russell's safe.

Morris nodded. 'And Monday? Where were you, exactly?'

He couldn't look at Morris. That was the morning he received the telegram with the one word, *Cromwell*, the codeword for all Auxiliary Units to assemble, when life as he knew it changed forever. 'At the vicarage,' he said. 'Then I went to Peter Kempton's office, then to look for Stanley.'

Morris paused. 'Why did you go to see Inspector Russell?'

'I couldn't find Stanley and I thought David might have known where he was.'

Morris picked up his pencil and drew a dotted line from the vicarage to Peter's office building, out to Stanley's cottage then back to the police station.

'Was Constable Matthews there?'

'Yes. No.'

Morris raised his eyebrows.

'I mean, he was on duty, just not behind the desk when I arrived. I didn't have to wait long though.'

'Did Constable Matthews say where he had been?'

'He was in the station. I saw him, through the glass partition, walking back down the corridor. I remember now, he was carrying a dustpan and broom. Of course, the smashed bottle on the doorstep. He must have just cleared it up.'

Morris paused.

'The day of the raid, the seventeenth, you went to check on Stanley. Do you remember anything you thought was out of the ordinary?'

'Other than a German fighter dropping bombs and strafing a quiet English rural village, you mean?'

Morris pulled his lower lip inwards. 'The plane was quite low, I understand?'

'Yes. I did think that was odd. The pilot dropped the two bombs and strafed the village a couple of times then left. Most people were just trying to get out of its way.'

'Did it follow the same path on the second and third runs?'

'Yes, I think so.'

'And most of the damage was around the village green?'

'Yes. One bomb dropped on Peter Kempton's office. It must have been a bigger bomb.'

'Why do you say that?'

'It caused much more damage than the one on Doctor Haswell's garden. Although there was a large hole in the rear wall of Phillip's house, I remember thinking that there wasn't much damage in the street.'

'Did you see anyone near to or enter the police station?

'There was so much confusion. I saw almost all the villagers at one time or another. I did see John Knowles outside *The Crown*. His wife was one of the victims killed in the strafing. I asked him to help me carry the dead on stretchers to the church. We passed the police station several times. Too many times. But I do not remember seeing anyone enter or leave the police station.'

'When did you last see Elsie Wainwright?'

Clement didn't have to think. 'On the Sunday afternoon, in *The Crown*.'

Morris smiled. 'Thank you, Clement.'

'I'm not sure if I have been of any help, Arthur.'

'Timing, Clement. That is how our murderer, or should I say murderers, have done it.'

'You think there is more than one?'

'Without question.'

22

Saturday 21st September

C lement was getting used to Lewes station. Even the stationmaster smiled at him as he sat in the waiting room. Mary had packed two sandwiches and some Italian sardines that her sister Gwen had saved and which he would savour on the journey. He saw the Chief Inspector walk onto the platform.

Morris sat beside him and they exchanged pleasantries. 'You seem quiet this morning, Clement?'

'I have just come from the hospital. The sight of burnt flesh is very sobering, Arthur.'

'Indeed. How is the Doctor coping?'

'The man works long hours. In fact, he was at the hospital even earlier than me this morning.'

'I am yet to meet Doctor Haswell. He is out every time I call to see him,' Morris said.

'Really? I would have liked to have spoken with Phillip myself. I am worried about Mrs Faulkner. She is elderly and has dreadful burns. The Sister says she may be in hospital for months.'

'You didn't see Doctor Haswell?' Morris asked.

'No. But I know he was there. His car was in the parking area at the front when I arrived. I don't suppose you have heard anything about Stanley and Elsie?'

'Nothing as yet,' Morris paused. 'This afternoon, Clement, after we have met with your people, I might go to Scotland Yard. If you need to get away early, I can make my own way back.'

'Of course.'

Morris opened his newspaper. Clement noted it was the previous evening's edition of *The Evening Argus*.

'I have today's paper if you would prefer it, Arthur?'

'Thank you but I'm actually looking at the classified section.'

'You're looking for other work?'

Morris smiled. 'No. I can't imagine what I would do if I was not a policeman. I am however, looking at the Hospital and Medical Appointments.'

'May I ask why?'

'I am wondering why a village Doctor in Sussex advertises in *The Times*. With all the signage removed, I would have thought a Nurse with local knowledge of the area would have been preferable. But, who knows? Perhaps Doctor Haswell advertised in the local paper as well.'

Johnny met them at Victoria Station and they sped off towards Whitehall and the ubiquitous beige and grey stone.

Clement smiled at Miss Bradwynn seated behind her desk in Gubbins's outer office.

'Won't you sit down, gentlemen? The Colonel won't keep you long,' she said. The typewriter clacked away, the bell sounding as the carriage was pushed back with every new line. A buzzer on her desk sounded. 'You can go in now.'

Colonel Gubbins was seated behind a pile of papers on the desk. Clement thought he looked older. Now he was about to add to the man's troubles. Clement introduced Arthur Morris and they sat down.

'We couldn't tell you over the telephone, Clement. But we have decided to stand your cell down. It's just temporary,' Gubbins told him.

Clement felt his face fall. Gubbins must have seen his reaction. 'Your sector will be handled by people who are worth a lot more to the Germans than your team,' Gubbins told him.

Clement swallowed hard. 'And my men, Colonel?'

'Given that two of them are no longer with you, your remaining team will be much safer at Coleshill for the next few days, Clement.'

Clement felt the weight lift from his shoulders.

'Before you begin to tell us what's happening in East Sussex, Clement,' Johnny cut in, 'I must inform you, Chief Inspector that everything you may hear in this office is top secret. While you don't need to know everything about Clement's activities in and around Fearnley Maughton, you should know that there is a secret underground installation frequented by Clement's team in Maughton Forest.'

Morris's head tilted in acknowledgement. 'Thank you for your candour, Commander,' Morris added.

Clement explained the events of the past few days. Morris hadn't interrupted but Clement saw the smallest of reactions on Morris' face when he informed Johnny and Gubbins about the proximity of George's body to the Operational Base. As tragic as George's murder was, it was the disappearance of the report that furrowed the brows.

Gubbins remained silent for several minutes. 'Chief Inspector, it is vital you find Stanley Russell and Elsie Wainwright. Kent and Sussex are our top-priority sectors. If these two people remain at large, they could jeopardise every cell in the country and we simply don't have the personnel to replace them all. Especially now.'

'Have you any leads, Chief Inspector?' Johnny asked.

'The pieces are coming together. I would like Scotland Yard to run a few checks on the bullets we've recovered from the various crime sites.'

'As long as there is no mention of us here or the Auxiliary Units,' Gubbins said.

There wasn't much more to say. Being stood down should have made Clement happy. And as far as it involved his men, it did. But he didn't feel joyful. In fact, failure is what he felt.

He and Arthur Morris left the office. There had been no mention of lunches this time; what's more, Clement was left in little doubt that Gubbins and Johnny were regretting his involvement. No other group, Clement felt sure, had caused so many problems. At least his men were safe and that alone was cause for celebration. He pushed Johnny and Gubbins from his mind. 'There is a place under St Martin-in-the-Fields where we can get some lunch. It will probably be bread and soup but it's not too bad.'

'Thank you, but no. I want to run some checks on those bullets. Even with top priority, it will probably take all day, so I'll make my own way back to Lewes.' Morris paused. 'And rest assured, Clement, I won't mention anything of your clandestine activities.'

Clement smiled, feeling suddenly hungry. He watched Arthur Morris walk away then checked his watch. It was nearly one o'clock. He walked towards Trafalgar Square, heading towards St Martin-in-the-Fields.

Crossing The Strand, he heard the siren start. Slow to begin with, then heart-racing in its urgency. The noise bounced off the stone buildings and reverberated around him. A wave of pigeons lifted from the pavements, their wings loud with panic. People began to run. For a second he didn't know what was happening.

He wheeled around. Above him he heard the repetitive low booming sound, like hundreds of cars spluttering and back-firing. A second later, the ground began to shake.

'Get in the shelter!' someone bellowed.

Clement turned again. A warden was yelling at him. He looked around, in the direction of the angry man's pointed finger.

'I'll show you,' a woman's voice said.

He felt the tug on his arm. A young woman was pulling him along.

'Down here,' she said.

They hurried, with scores of others; like a human ribbon they streamed down the steps into the underground. Below it was dark and smelt of sweat and urine.

'Quickly now,' the girl was saying. 'If we hurry we can find a place to lie down.'

'Lie down?' he mumbled.

'They're early today. I was hoping to have time to wash my hair before reporting back,' the girl said.

'How long does it last?' Clement asked.

'You're not from around here, are you?'

'No. I'm just in London for the day.'

The girl laughed. 'Well, if it is like yesterday, we could be here all night.'

The girl ran forward and pounced on the wooden-planked station seat. 'Come on!' she called. 'We can share the seat. The other night I had to lie on the steps. Bloody Jerries!'

Clement removed his coat and sat beside her.

'Oh! Sorry, Vicar. I didn't know.'

'No harm done,' he said. 'I'm indebted to you for ushering me down here. I wouldn't have known where to go.'

'Anne Chambers,' she said, her hand thrust towards him.

'Reverend Wisdom,' he said smiling, shaking the girl's hand.

The rumble of bombs rattled above them. He glanced around. No one seemed to be paying much attention. Someone had turned on some lights. But the underground was grimy and dingy. He remembered the crypt at Christ Church, Mayfair. Somehow at Christ Church, sitting among the sarcophagi had seemed more normal than sitting and waiting for the forces of good and evil to transform the world above them as they knew it.

He stared at the people. Some sat or lay along the platform. Everyone waited. It was a well-rehearsed routine, but to an onlooker it was the most extraordinary sight. People, probably total strangers, sat side by side along the platform like Gwen's Italian sardines. Women were making tea on small paraffin cookers near a brick column upon which were advertising posters. He stared at one. It showed Weston-Super-Mare, couples sitting idly in deck chairs staring at a golden setting sun and enjoying life. Fate had a cruel sense of humour.

He gazed around the space. Other women were knitting, the needles clicking hard, the repetitive sound bouncing off the hard surfaces then stopping each time the earth shook. He thought of Mary and prayed there were no stray aeroplanes over Fearnley Maughton today. A man stoked his pipe and sat down on a chair as though he was in his own home. What Clement saw was visible resilience, but what he smelled was suppressed fear.

'Tell me about yourself, Vicar?' Anne said, settling on the bench. 'Are you married?'

He smiled at Anne. If the woman was afraid she didn't show it. But then he knew from Coleshill, and his time in the trenches, that some people talk a lot when nervous. Clement nodded. 'Over twenty years. My wife used to work in London, at The Admiralty.' He paused, thinking of Miss Bradwynn. 'What about you?'

The girl stood and removed her coat and threw it over the seat. 'London born and bred, me.'

It wasn't until she sat down that he realised she was wearing a nurse's uniform.

'Do you work hereabouts?' he asked.

She nodded. 'Charing Cross.'

The memory flashed in Clement's mind. Elsie. Elsie said she had worked at Charing Cross. He turned to face Anne.

'I trained at Guys,' Anne went on, 'but I've been delivering babies at Charing Cross ever since. I like London, Vicar. Couldn't live anywhere else. Although there is a rumour at the hospital that if the bombing keeps up they are going to relocate us to Hertfordshire. Wherever that is.'

'I don't suppose you ever worked with an Elizabeth Wainwright?'

'Yes, I knew Elsie.'

The girl's response was so unexpected Clement felt his jaw drop. 'She worked in my village, in East Sussex.'

'Elsie? In the country? Can't be the same Elsie, Vicar. She hated the country. Particularly East Sussex. Too close to her parents. They didn't get on.'

A child was crying, but Clement almost didn't hear the wailing infant. 'She grew up in Eastbourne. Her father was a doctor there,' Clement said trying to confirm the few details he knew about the girl.

'That's right. Both her parents died some time ago.' Anne pulled a biscuit from her pocket and broke it in half. She held it out to him.

He shook his head.

'I put them there during the shift. I don't steal; but if the patients don't eat them, why waste them? Besides, you never know when you might not eat for a while. She nibbled on the biscuit then said, 'She went back there a couple of years ago to see their graves… Elsie, I mean. She met someone. A man. But it didn't work out, so she returned to London. She said she wouldn't leave London ever again. Only get your heart broken, she said.'

'Do you know where she is now?'

Anne stared at him, the large green eyes wide. 'But I thought you knew, Vicar? Elsie's dead.'

23

Clement felt the ground shudder, the sounds amplified and distorted in the railway tunnels. 'What did you say?' he asked aghast.

The rumbling continued. A sudden gust of wind came through the railway tunnel each time the earth shook.

'She jumped off Westminster Bridge. Well, that's what the police said.'

Clement stared at Anne Chambers. 'When?'

'It's got to be three years now. Not long after she came back to London.'

'Can you describe her?'

'What is it, Vicar? You look like you've seen a ghost?'

'Please, Anne, indulge me. Can you describe her?'

'About five feet four inches, twenty-three,' Anne paused, 'Elsie would be twenty-six now, blonde with blue eyes. Pretty. The prettiest girl I ever saw. She wasn't too pretty when they pulled her out of the Thames.'

'Did she have any distinguishing marks?' Clement asked, thinking Anne's brief illustration of Elsie could describe many thousands of pretty girls.

'Elsie? She was about as perfect as God can make a woman, Vicar.'

'Indeed,' he said. But he was thinking of the Elsie Wainwright he knew. 'Was there anything about Elsie that only someone who knew her well would know?'

The girl looked at him, her expression changing. 'Other than being pregnant, you mean?'

'What?'

'What is all this about?' Anne asked.

Clement sat forward on the seat. 'I don't mean to alarm you or reignite unhappy memories, but I have met a young woman who is calling herself Elsie Wainwright. She's wanted by the police.'

'Then whoever she is, she couldn't be the Elsie Wainwright I knew. I lived with her. Shared a room in the Nurses' home with her. There wasn't anything we didn't share about each other. And it was me who identified her. And I know that body was Elsie Wainwright.' Anne paused. 'They said that is why she jumped off Westminster Bridge, because she was pregnant.' Anne shook her head. 'I shouldn't be telling you this, Vicar, but nurses, well, we work with babies. And some women lose babies, poor sods. Naturally, I mean. But there are always a few from the wealthy classes who don't, if you know what I mean.'

What Clement was hearing astounded him. 'It wasn't quite what I meant,' he muttered, his voice subdued. His head spun; not because what Anne had told him very clearly confronted his religious beliefs, nor so much for the evident illegality of it, but because Anne Chambers had confided so much vital information he was having trouble taking it all in.

'You meant was there anything physically different about her?' Anne said, staring at him. 'It was how I knew it was Elsie.' The girl paused. 'She had a mole on the fourth toe of her left foot.' Anne let out a short laugh and shrugged her shoulders. 'She used to wear a sticking plaster around it rather than look at it. It was just a tiny mole, but Elsie hated it.'

'What did the police say had happened to her?'

'Death by suicide. But I don't think so. She had gone to meet him. She told me. She was so excited. She thought he was going to pop the question. But she never came back. The police said she killed herself because of the baby. Not Elsie. She was popular – men fell at her feet. With or without the baby, she'd have found another. Besides, like I said, she didn't have to have it.'

'Did you ever know the man's name?' he asked.

Anne shook her head. 'She wouldn't say. But I know he was in the Navy, based somewhere along the south coast. Classified!' Anne shrugged her shoulders. 'They all say things like that.'

Clement stood. He needed to find Arthur Morris before he left London. And he needed to tell Johnny and Miss Bradwynn what he'd learned.

'Need the lav, Vicar? I'm afraid it's a bucket down here.'

'No. I need to leave.'

Anne Chambers laughed. 'The Warden won't let you leave here until the all-clear sounds.'

Clement sat back down on the hard bench and ran his tongue over his lips to moisten his dry mouth. He still couldn't believe it. But illegal abortions and unwed young women aside, what he had learned about Elsie sent his head spinning. Why had the Elsie he knew attached herself to Stanley? Clement's heart was sinking, and for the first time he began to suspect that the trusting lad had suffered the same fate as his father.

Clement visualised Reg Naylor leaning on Peter Kempton's mantelpiece asking if Stanley was already dead. Was Nurse Anne Chambers correct about Elizabeth Wainwright? Or had Elsie Wainwright wanted to disappear and staged her own death? He thought of the mole. Could that be faked? Could Anne have lied to aid Elsie's disappearance? Clement didn't believe so. Anne had volunteered the information and believed Elsie Wainwright was dead. In his mind he saw the girl sitting on the counter in *The Crown*. His heart was pounding. Had the real Elsie Wainwright been murdered because she resembled the Elsie he knew? If she was not Elsie, then who was she? And why had she come to Fearnley Maughton?

Clement pulled his coat around his body. Thoughts rushed through his mind so quickly he couldn't process them fast enough.

'You alright, Vicar?' Anne asked.

'Yes. Thank you. It doesn't matter. It must be another Elizabeth Wainwright.'

Anne pulled a book from her cape pocket and started to read. He wondered what else Anne Chambers carried in the capacious folds of her nurse's cape. But right now his mind was on Elizabeth Wainwright.

Leaning his head back on the wall, Clement closed his eyes. Elsie Wainwright had come to Fearnley Maughton after answering an advertisement in *The Times*. Why would a girl who did not like the country seek a position in a rural village in East Sussex? The girl Clement knew as Elsie didn't know the real Elsie's dislike for the country, especially East Sussex. That tiny fact alone could be her undoing. He thought of Arthur Morris and the man's patient, diligent investigation. Morris had checked *The Evening Argus* classified section for Hospital and Medical Appointments. "The pieces are coming together," Clement muttered remembering what Morris had said in Gubbins's office. Clement smiled. Chief Inspector Morris was also suspicious of Elsie Wainwright. Clement needed to speak with Morris, but until he could, he forced himself to focus on Elsie and on all the occasions he had met the girl since her arrival in the village. He had noted at the bus stop in Lewes that the girl had very little luggage. She would, if she did not intend to stay long.

Mary had suspected something about the girl. The next time Clement saw Elsie was in the street. But he had not spoken more than a few words to the girl on that occasion. After that he had seen her on the Sunday in church, surrounded by men, then later that same day at *The Crown*. He pictured her in his mind, sitting on the bar-room counter surrounded by men who were eager for the gossip she was happily supplying.

Clement thought back to the day he and Constable Matthews had found Stanley in his cottage holding the knife. Stanley believed the girl had left to pack her possessions then return to his cottage. She did go to *The Crown*, Clement knew that. But where had she gone afterwards? And how had she left the village without being seen? Had it all been staged? Had Elsie killed David Russell and fled? Timing. Morris had talked about timing.

Morris had also talked about there being more than one murderer.

At the time David Russell lay dead, Elsie would have been at *The Crown* packing. Or was she? Had she packed previously? Sometime around when Stanley was heard arguing with his father and before the time of death at around half-past ten, Elsie had disappeared. Clement thought back. What else had happened at that time? Then he remembered the broken bottle. Why had someone smashed a bottle on the police station doorstep? Constable Matthews was a little deaf, yet it was loud enough for him to hear it and investigate.

Clement opened his eyes. The safe keys. Whoever had killed David Russell had already done it. Morris believed, as Clement did, that the murderer had entered by the window and been expected. That had been confirmed in his mind when he stood by the window in the police station attempting to attract the attention of Phillip Haswell. David Russell had been expecting Elsie. The window was open and Russell would have seen the girl arrive.

But once inside, and with Russell unconscious, the open window permitted another to enter. Clement thought of the blow to Russell's head. A woman could have done that. Especially a woman who already knew of David Russell's weakness for a pretty face and who had prearranged the meeting. Russell would not be expecting trouble. In fact, the contrary. It fitted with what Clement had witnessed in *The Crown*. Elsie could have left the police station by the same window and run around the building, smashing the bottle on the steps to bring Constable Matthews to the door. This would give whoever was in David Russell's office time to fetch the keys.

Clement stared at the blackish, soot-stained wall of the underground opposite. Did that mean that whoever had killed David Russell knew where to find the keys? That would implicate a local, especially Stanley. Yet, if Elsie had agreed to elope with Stanley, he would certainly have told her about his inheritance and where it was kept.

Constable Matthews had said that Inspector Russell always kept his office door ajar, but when the constable was standing in the corridor outside the inspector's office, someone had closed the door. Clement knew now that the murderer had closed it. But how were the safe keys replaced? The keys were there when Clement went into the police station. Or had they been? Constable Matthews would surely have noticed their absence. They must have been there. Clement shut his eyes. If Elsie was watching the building, she would have seen himself and Phillip Haswell along with Constable Matthews carry the body of Inspector Russell out of the police station and around the building to Doctor Haswell's car. The police station would have been unattended for a few minutes.

Clement recalled when he had seen her cycle through the village. She came and went, and almost no one took any notice of the district nurse on a bicycle. He remembered Arthur's comment about there always being a witness. The killer could have given the keys to Elsie through the window that faced the High Street. Elsie could then have dropped them into her nurse's cape before entering the station and replacing them on the hook and all before he and Constable Matthews returned to the station to telephone Lewes Police.

It fitted. But how had she acquired the gun? She must have duped Stanley into showing her his pack. Clement remembered seeing it in Stanley's bedroom. Stanley had made no attempt to conceal the pack. She had taken the gun and the knife, but she had only time to place the knife in the scullery drawer before Stanley joined her. The gun she had already taken and hidden somewhere.

Clement blinked several times. He needed to find Morris.

'Had a nap, Vicar? That's the way. Forget about it. It's better that way,' Anne was saying. 'Do you want some tea? The ladies over there are making,' she said. 'It's really brown-coloured water. Best not to ask what. But you can tell yourself its tea. Mind my seat and I'll get us some.'

He smiled. Anne Chambers was a well-meaning girl. A real nurse: helpful and caring.

He watched Anne walk away. There was something different about her. It was in the walk, the way her feet hit the floor; slap slap. She had the slouch of the weary. It told the onlooker that here was a person used to hard physical labour and who spent most of every day on her feet. Elsie had never displayed such a gait. Whilst Clement knew the girl to be an impostor, he did believe she had medical training of some kind. She had delivered the Knowles' baby. But if Anne was the epitome of the over-worked London nurse, then Clement did not believe Elsie had come from London at all. Clement now believed the girl was implicated in the murder of David Russell. Elsie Wainwright became more enigmatic with every passing minute.

224

Did it follow, though, that she was also involved in George's death? If the answer to that was yes, then it had to mean that whoever this girl was, she was still near Fearnley Maughton. Or still in it!

Anne returned and Clement sipped the tea. The liquid looked unappealing but at least it was hot. He remembered the vagrant. Was the vagrant her accomplice? Had he been the man the real Elsie Wainwright had gone to meet on Westminster Bridge? And if Elsie, with or without the vagrant, had the list, what were they planning next? Had Gubbins suspected it and that was why he sent the men to Coleshill?

The All-Clear siren sounded, intruding on his thoughts.

'Well there's a relief, Vicar. We won't be down here all night after all.'

'Do you live far from here, Anne?'

'I live in the Nurses Home, attached to the hospital. I was on a split shift and hoped to have time to wash my hair and get some much-needed air. Some air! The smells of the London underground! Never mind. I wouldn't have met you, Vicar had I not come out. Well, good luck to you.'

Clement lifted his hat. 'Thank you, Anne. You have been such a help. Would you mind if I was to contact you again? About Elsie?'

Anne turned to face him. 'If you can make any sense of it, Vicar, it would put my mind to rest.' Anne lowered her voice, 'because I think she was murdered.'

Clement came up into the light. Trafalgar Square looked much the same. He thanked the Lord for his safe delivery and for Nurse Anne Chambers. Meeting Anne had been a true turning point. Some would say it was luck or coincidence. He felt a smile creep across his lips. Clement called it divine intervention. But now he needed to find Arthur. He wasn't really sure where Scotland Yard was, but he quickened his pace as he walked in the direction he had seen the Chief Inspector take. Asking directions, he found the layered white and red brick building and entered the main door. Fifteen minutes later he was sitting in an office with Arthur Morris.

Clement related what he had learned from Anne Chambers. 'Can you find out what happened to the real Elsie Wainwright?'

'Yes, that is possible. The archived files are downstairs. The raid has delayed the forensic report on the bullets, so we can do it now.'

Clement followed Morris through a labyrinth of stairs and corridors until they stood at a counter in the basement where Morris requested the file on the deceased Elizabeth Wainwright.

'I never thought I would say this, Arthur, but I have to thank the Germans for their early bombing raid today. I would never have questioned the identity of Elsie Wainwright.'

'It has certainly advanced the investigation. And we may just catch them, Clement.'

He wasn't really sure what Arthur had meant by the remark. He would have asked had the woman not returned to the counter with a file in her hands. They sat at a wooden desk, one of many in the archive room.

'Does it say anything about distinguishing marks?' Clement whispered.

Morris' eye scanned the document. He saw Morris raise his eyebrows and knew what that meant, but Elsie

226

Wainwright's pregnancy had no relevance to their current enquiries.

'There are no birthmarks listed,' Morris said.

'Not a birthmark as such,' Clement said and he told Morris about the mole on the fourth toe.

Morris turned the pages to the list of the deceased's possessions. Listed with the clothing and personal effects was a hand-written comment that upon removal of the water-sodden shoes and stockings, a plaster covering had been found on the fourth toe of the left foot but it had revealed a mole, not a wound.

Clement learned back in the chair. 'Was Elsie Wainwright murdered?'

'Can't answer that, Clement.'

'But you will investigate?'

'Perhaps. My current priority is to find the girl purporting to be Elsie Wainwright, and Stanley Russell. It must be considered that Stanley might be another victim. Shall we call the imposter *Jane,* for now?'

Clement was thinking more Jezebel. 'Why Jane?'

'Plain Jane,' Morris answered. 'A simple name for a most complex woman.'

Clement smiled and began to share his thoughts on how *Jane* had entered the police station, and his theory about the smashed bottle.

'Did you think to ask Anne Chambers where we can find her in future?' Morris asked.

'She lives in the Nurses Home at Charing Cross Hospital.'

'Good.'

'You seem convinced that Elsie, sorry *Jane*, is not acting alone,' Clement said, but his statement had more to do with confirming the suspicion rather than challenging it.

'I am pleased you have come to the same conclusion, Clement.'

They left the archives office and returned upstairs to the visiting police officer's room. On the desk was a beige envelope marked for the attention of Chief Inspector Morris. He tore open the envelope, his alert eyes flowing over the document. Morris lifted his head, the report in his hand. 'Nine millimetre. All three from the same weapon.'

'A Sten?' Clement asked.

Morris shook his head. The intense brown eyes settled on Clement. 'Luger.'

24

Morris opened the train door and they stepped onto the platform of Lewes Station. Clement glanced at the station clock. It was just before seven.

'Are you returning to Fearnley Maughton tonight, Arthur?'

'Yes. Can I offer you a lift?'

'Thank you. That would be most kind.'

'Could you give me half an hour or so while I attend to some paperwork?'

'Of course. In fact, I'll use the time to visit some more of the injured at the hospital.'

'I'll collect you from there then. Around half past seven.' Arthur said.

They walked away from the station and separated, Morris going on into the town. Clement turned left, up the steep hill towards the hospital. The girl - *Jane* as they were now calling her - occupied his thoughts. Had it not been for the air raid in London and the chance meeting with Nurse Anne Chambers, Clement would never have questioned the girl's identity.

Clement stared down at his feet as he walked, his mind sifting the facts as told to him by Anne Chambers. Anne had said that Elsie's death was three years ago. He slowed, his gaze still on his boots. Surely, if there was a connection between the real Elsie and *Jane*, it could only be coincidental. If not, and *Jane* was a German collaborator, then arranging for the death of her look-a-like implied a complex and sinister plan that had been implemented years previously.

Clement began to wonder what could be so important to commit murder, install an impostor and wait three years? Three years ago the war hadn't even begun. He thought of the man with the classified job in Elsie Wainwright's life and the Naval installation Clement now knew about at Cuckmere Haven. Had it been there three years ago? If so it would be important enough for the Germans to want to know about it. Had *Jane* taken the money from the safe, Clement may have thought her just a thief. Now he wasn't so sure. Looking up, he realised he was standing in front of the old stone gates of the hospital. He walked towards the front entrance.

Reaching forward to grasp the handle of the door, Clement stopped and turned. Off to his right he saw the Doctor's car parked in the front. Clement shook his head. He hadn't seen much of Phillip, but, Clement surmised that since the attack on the village, the man had been kept busy. He checked his watch. Arthur had told him to be at the hospital's front door at half-past seven. It didn't give him much time, but he wanted to see Mrs Faulkner again. He opened the heavy, glass-fronted hospital door. The smell of ether and floor wax filled his nostrils as he walked down the corridor, his gaze on the shiny blue and white striated linoleum.

He stayed with the old lady just five minutes. She had expressed her gratitude that he had visited her twice in one day. But something the old lady had said worried him. Clement made his excuses and left the bedside. Quickening his step, he hurried towards the Matron's office. 'Can you tell me where Doctor Haswell is, Matron?'

'I haven't seen him all day, Reverend Wisdom.'

'I saw his car parked out the front this morning, and it is there now. He must be here. Could you find out if he is in the hospital?'

'Is something wrong, Reverend?'

'I just need to speak to him,' Clement replied but he could hear the panic in his voice. He cleared his throat trying to suppress his rising fears for the man's safety. His mind flashed to the day the fighter strafed the village. Phillip had been a tower of strength. By the grace of God, he had been in his garden when the second bomb landed on the Anderson Shelter. The Matron picked up the telephone and Clement waited while the woman rang every ward.

No one had seen him.

Clement left the Matron's office and hurried down the corridor towards the front door. He could hear the woman running behind him.

He walked towards the car. He wasn't sure what he expected to see. He peered in the driver's side window, but Haswell wasn't there. Then he placed his hand on the engine. It felt cold. 'We must telephone Chief Inspector Morris.'

'Do you think something has happened to Doctor Haswell?'

'Matron, could you find out if anyone saw the doctor arrive? And don't touch the car!'

Clement ran back into the hospital and headed straight for the switchboard operator. He felt his heart pounding in his ears. As he waited for Arthur Morris to answer the telephone, his mind raced. Something insidious was happening around him, its tentacles enveloping him and those he knew and cared for. George's dead body flashed into his mind. Everything was connected, Clement just didn't know how. Arthur's steady logical mind would bring reason. He ended the call and went back outside.

Within minutes Morris and a constable stepped from the police car.

'What is it, Clement?' Arthur asked.

He nodded in the direction of Phillip's car. 'Doctor Haswell's car. It was parked here this morning, I saw it. And it is still there. The engine is cold. And no one in the hospital has seen him today.'

The hospital door opened and the Matron joined them. 'I asked the Evening Supervisor to check with all the Ward Sisters, Chief Inspector. They all say that Doctor Haswell has not been in the hospital since lunchtime yesterday.'

Morris turned and walked towards the car. 'Did you touch the car, Clement?'

'I looked in, then touched the bonnet but when I saw nothing, I telephoned you.'

'Matron, could you ask your staff if anyone saw the doctor leave the hospital on Friday?' Morris asked.

The Matron nodded and left.

Morris opened the driver's door and looked in.

'Anything?' Clement asked as Morris checked the car's interior.

Morris closed the door. 'Nothing unusual.' Walking around the car, Morris reached for the latch to open the car's boot.

The lid lifted.

Morris reeled back.

Clement stepped forward and stared in. A dark haired man in a navy overcoat with epaulettes lay coiled in the boot, his hands bound behind his back, a bullet hole between his eyes.

Neither Clement nor Morris spoke. Clement couldn't take his eyes from the man's face: the grey-white pallor of death, the out-of-place, repellent purple hole between the eyes, the dishevelled hair. He screwed his eyes shut. In his mind's eye he could see George lying on the forest floor staring heavenward in death, the exact same gunshot wound; life terminated in an instant. *In the midst of life we are in death*, so the Order for the Burial of the Dead said. Clement had never before realised just how profound those words were. He blinked and forced himself to look again at the man in the boot of Phillip Haswell's car.

Clement stared at the coat, the rankless epaulettes: the vagrant. The deceased was not old. Neither was he a boy. This man was of enlisting age. Clement ran his eye along the contours of the body. From what he could see, the man appeared to be in good physical condition with little evidence of malnourishment. Nor did he appear unkempt. Only the navy coat with epaulettes alluded to this man being the vagrant seen by his men in Maughton Forest. His eye looked along the trousers to the shoes. The soles showed no sign of excess wear and despite the beginnings of a beard about the man's face, Clement was not convinced the deceased was a vagrant at all. If the man had deserted, it was recent.

Leaning forward Clement looked at the man's hands. Bruising around the wrists indicated that he had been bound before death. The nails were short and from what he could see, clean. Clement looked again at the face. Did the beard suggest the man had fled into the forest? And if so, why?

Morris closed the boot. 'Clement, when the Matron returns, would you ask her to contact the Coroner? And Constable, please arrange for the car to be moved into the police yard.'

The constable nodded and left.

Clement could see Arthur Morris was deep in thought and didn't interrupt the man's steady concentration. The Matron appeared on the steps and Clement went to speak with her.

He rejoined Morris by the car and waited for the Chief Inspector to look at him.

'Apparently no one saw Doctor Haswell leave the hospital.'

'Do you know the deceased man, Clement?'

'Not one of mine. He could be the vagrant my men saw, although other than the beard, this man doesn't look like a vagrant to me. The sighting of a homeless man wearing a navy coat with epaulettes was in our report to Gubbins.' Clement stopped speaking. 'Of course, that report didn't reach him.' He paused. 'Two deaths because of a report?'

Morris pursed his lips. 'It would appear so. And both killed at the same location. And possibly the same time.'

'How do you know that?' Clement asked.

Morris sprung the latch on the boot again and reaching in, placed his hand on the dead man's coat. Lifting the fabric, Morris pointed to several leaves in varying stages of decomposition stuck to the man's coat and socks.

'The second bullet!'

Morris nodded. 'I think it likely.'

'Why didn't the murderer remove the bullets this time?'

'Good question, Clement. And as I said at the time, I believe our murderer wants us to know something. It is almost as if he's leaving clues for us. He is undoubtedly aware of your subterranean base.' Morris squinted his eyes. 'But does he want to be identified?'

'He wants to be caught?'

'Not quite what I said.' Morris replaced the man's coat and closed the boot again. 'I do not believe there will be any more murders. Whatever the murderer or murderers came for, they now have.'

'How do you know that?'

'Because *Jane* has disappeared. I believe she was brought into the village for a reason, and whatever the reason was, it has either already transpired or it is no longer relevant. But first we must identify this man. Then we can work on the motive.'

Clement swallowed hard. 'And Phillip Haswell?'

'I don't know, yet.'

Clement watched Morris scrutinise the vehicle, the stern gaze tracing every contour. Did Morris suspect Phillip Haswell? How was Phillip implicated and why had he advertised for a nurse in *The Times*? Surely Morris was right in thinking that a local girl would have been more appropriate. Phillip would, equally surely, have known that.

'Do you have any ideas where *Jane* has gone?' Clement asked.

'None, yet.'

Clement said good night to Arthur and walked up Church Lane. He felt bone weary. One death was shocking. But four was too many for a murderer to remain at large. If Arthur was right, the murderer wanted to be identified, although not caught. But how could the murderer remain uncaptured once identified? Only leaving England would safeguard such a man.

And, what of Phillip? Clement could not bring himself to think of a fifth death. Or was it six? His thoughts turned to Stanley. Like George, a good and decent young man who had not deserved such a fate. George's cold body flashed before Clement's eyes again. The stare. The finality of murder. He felt overwhelmed by what was happening around him. He would never forget it. Cold-blooded murder had nothing to do with defence.

And now Phillip was missing.

Clement let himself into his home. The hallway was dark. For a horrible moment his heart jumped. 'Mary?' he shouted. He made his way to the kitchen and switched on the light. A note sat propped against the mustard pot on the kitchen table - Mary had gone to Windsor during the day and was not returning till Sunday by the late train. The hours spent underground with Anne Chambers and the ghastly discovery in Phillip's car had combined to delay him. He folded the note and let it fall onto the tablecloth, feeling wretched.

He made his supper and carried it to his study. Sipping the warm drink, he remembered the hot brown drink in London's underground. Leaning his head against the antimacassar, he closed his eyes. *Jane* and another had killed David Russell. And Constable Newson. And by assisting Stanley to escape, had ensured that he had, in absentia, taken the blame for the murder of his father and the constable from Lewes.

Clement took another sip. If *Jane* and her accomplice had implicated Stanley for the murders, why would they want Stanley with them? Was he a hostage? As far as Clement knew, when people were taken as hostages, a demand of some kind followed. And, again as far as he knew, no such demand had been received. Besides, with Stanley's father dead who would pay the ransom?

Clement stared into the cold fire place. Had the gullible lad gone willingly? Clement knew Stanley loved the girl. He reflected on the day he had spoken with Stanley in the cell at the police station. Stanley had been prepared to hang for the girl. Would he commit murder? Did that also include George's murder?

Clement refused to believe it. Stanley had been used as surely as the real Elsie Wainwright. But where was Stanley? Clement placed the cup onto the tray and closed his eyes, melancholia settling into his heart. He now accepted the heavy realization that Stanley was probably dead and may never be found. He could hear the clock in the hall, ticking by the seconds. Death had no use for time. He opened his eyes. 'May never be found,' he said aloud. The realization hit him. Clive's words that night at the Operational Base reverberated in his mind. What had Clive said? "If it had happened during the raid, no one would be any the wiser". Clive had been referring to the murder of David Russell, but had it also been the fate of the son?

25

Sunday 22nd September

The telephone was ringing. Clement threw back the bed covers and pushed his feet into his slippers. Reaching for his dressing gown, he pulled the garment on as he descended the stairs. The house was still in darkness and he had no idea of the hour.

'Hello?'

'Clement. I'm sorry to disturb you so early. Can you be dressed and outside in fifteen minutes?'

'Arthur?' Clement mumbled.

'I would like your assistance with something,' Morris told him.

'Actually, Arthur I wanted to see you today. I've been thinking about Stanley. I am concerned that he might have met the same fate as the others.'

'I'll be around in fifteen minutes.'

Morris rang off and Clement replaced the receiver. He wandered into the kitchen to check the time. The overpowering weight of anxiety about Stanley and now Phillip made Clement feel old. Almost by instinct, he filled the kettle and placed it on the stove then lit the gas. Walking to the sink, he splashed his face with icy water, the freezing liquid penetrating his flesh. With his realization about Stanley, he prayed that Arthur had not found Phillip dead in some squalid place, for whatever Arthur had to say to him at four o'clock in the morning could not be good.

Twelve minutes later Clement was outside. A light breeze brushed his unshaven face and he shivered. It was still dark, but he could hear the familiar sound of the swaying trees that surrounded *All Saints*. He pulled his coat around him. Winter approached. Bad times were always endured better in the summer months. He heard the light footsteps and turning saw the familiar silhouette of Arthur Morris walking up Church Lane towards him.

'What's happened?' Clement asked in a low voice.

'I received a telephone call late last night from your Commander Winthorpe, Clement. *Jane* has been sighted.'

'Stanley?' Clement asked, hoping to hear his suspicions were wrong.

Morris shook his head.

'Where is she?' he asked. But he was wondering why Johnny had telephoned Morris with the news.

'She was spotted on a train and is being followed. But that is only partly why I called you. I need your assistance, Clement. Rather, I need you as a witness.'

He stared at Morris uncertain what was coming next. 'How can I help, Arthur?'

'I want to break into someone's house.'

'Pardon me?'

240

'I realise it is unusual, but I don't want prying eyes and I don't have time for official documentation.'

'Whose house?'

'Phillip Haswell's.'

It was the name Clement dreaded hearing. 'You think he's dead too?'

Morris looked away, down Church Lane. 'You mentioned that there was something you wanted to ask me about, concerning Stanley Russell?'

'It was something one of my men said,' and he told Morris about Clive's remark.

Morris stood staring into the night sky. 'You could well be right.'

'What do you expect to find in Phillip's house, Arthur?' he whispered, closing the gate to the vicarage.

'I would just like to see inside the house. And as I said, there is no time for official documentation to be sought.'

Clement felt the hollow anxiety of dread. 'You think his body is there?'

Arthur didn't reply.

They walked down Church Lane. It was only a short distance. No one was yet in the street and the blackout curtains in the neighbouring houses were still drawn. Clement looked down the High Street to the village green. Even though the moon was waning, there was sufficient light by which to see. Behind him he heard a door open. He spun around and saw the large, young constable from Lewes standing in the police station doorway.

Morris motioned to the constable, who without waiting for further instructions, walked towards the front door of Phillip's house. The large man slammed his shoulder several times into the surgery door. A minute later the old, panelled door gave way under the constable's considerable force, the timber door-jams splintering around the lock.

The constable then straightened his jacket and returned to the police station, closing the door. Clement followed Morris into the house.

The corridor was dark and cold. A strong draught flowed through the house, the open door to the street turning the hallway into a wind tunnel. Clement shivered. A window somewhere was rattling. He remembered the damaged rear wall. Morris flicked on a torch and Clement followed the Chief Inspector into the surgery at the front of the house.

The room looked as though it had been cleaned since Clement had seen it last. A makeshift kitchen had been set up in the corner. Arthur's torch scanned the floor. But Phillip Haswell was not in his surgery. They turned to leave the room.

'A moment, Arthur. Shine your torch there,' Clement said pointing behind the doctor's desk. Phillip's medical bag sat on a shelf. Its presence reinforced Clement's worst fears.

Morris left the room and Clement could hear the measured tread in the hallway. He joined the Chief Inspector in the room opposite. It had once been a sitting room, but it was now used as the waiting room. Chairs lined the walls. Near the fireplace was a desk. A chair was placed under the desk as would be done when the occupant had gone for the day. He saw Morris staring at him, the familiar enquiring tilt to the head.

'Nothing looks any different to how is always does,' Clement whispered.

Morris opened the next door; a store room with patient records. Again, nothing appeared disturbed or unusual and there was no sign of any dust or debris from the damaged rear wall. Opposite the storeroom was the staircase. Sweeping the torch from side to side they went upstairs. Off the landing were four bedrooms.

Clement had never been upstairs but he could see there were two rooms at the front on either side of the landing and another two smaller rooms at the side and rear of the building. All the doors were open. Morris stood in the doorway to the bedroom that overlooked the front of the house. Clement joined him. Arthur directed the torch beam onto the bed.

Clement stared at the empty bed as Morris walked across the room and opened the wardrobe. Phillip's clothes hung on hangers. Clement felt his anxiety rising. He knew Phillip was unlikely to travel without his Doctor's bag, but no one would travel, even for a short time, without clothing. Clement glanced at Morris then strode towards a chest of drawers and opened each. In every drawer were underclothes and vests and other assorted gentleman's intimate dressing requirements. He turned and saw the shoes lined up under a washstand.

A pain was developing in Clement's chest. He forced himself to breathe. Leaving Morris in Phillip's bedroom, he went into the room on the opposite side that also overlooked the front. Like Peter Kempton's house, it was filled with old patient records. Clement stepped back into the hallway and went to the smaller bedroom adjacent to the stairwell. He stared at the bed there, the walls, the cupboards and drawers. He opened the wardrobe. Nothing hung there. He went to the room at the rear. It contained a couch, a few old wooden chairs and

243

a radiator. He could smell the brick dust. Returning to the small bedroom, he stared inside. No one, it seemed, routinely occupied this room, but there was something about it that appeared familiar. Clement walked back to Phillip's bedroom and stood in the doorway.

Morris joined him. 'What is it, Clement?'

'The bed in the next room. Something about it. I just wanted to compare it to Phillip's.'

Morris flicked the torch onto Phillip's bed again. Two pillows with white and pink ribboned covers sat side by side on the double bed. For one moment Clement felt ashamed for trespassing on Phillip's tangible memories of his departed wife. What would he say to justify such an intrusion if Phillip returned at that very moment? But the bed, although made, was not well made. And Clement knew from Mary, that if one went away even for a short period of time, beds had to be stripped, blankets and quilts folded and mattresses rolled. Phillip's bed looked exactly as though he expected to return. The blanket was roughly tucked in on all sides and a pink quilt lay folded over the end.

'What is concerning you, Clement?'

'Come and have a look at this.'

They went back to the small bedroom. Against one wall was a single bed. It was an iron framed hospital bed, utilitarian and austere.

'Look at the corners,' he pointed. The bed in room number six at *The Crown* flashing into his mind. 'Neat, without a wrinkle anywhere there shouldn't be one.'

Morris turned to face him. 'Hospital corners. Well spotted, Clement. I will make a detective out of you yet.'

'Is that your intention, Arthur?'

Morris' head tilted. 'Nothing in this wardrobe, I suppose.'

'No. I checked,' Clement said. He looked at Morris's face and knew what the Chief Inspector was thinking. 'But why would she be here?'

'Do you know if Doctor Haswell had anyone to do for him?'

Leaving the room, they stood in the upper hall. 'I don't know,' Clement muttered. It was possible, but Phillip had never told Clement of any domestic help. In fact, he recalled that Phillip often complained about housework. That always amused Mary.

Walking back along the hallway to the rear bedroom, he stared at the blanket that had been nailed up covering the damaged rear wall that was awaiting repair. It still had the dust of damaged brickwork on the window sills and furniture. Only the rooms with public access and the two bedrooms upstairs had been cleaned. 'Why didn't Phillip know?'

'Clement?'

'The day the fighter strafed the village, Phillip told me he didn't know Elsie, that is *Jane,* had left the village. Why wouldn't she be at work on a Tuesday?'

'Another good question.'

They went downstairs and walked through the old kitchen. Clement's apprehension was rapidly changing to doubt. Also suspicion. Even betrayal. Of friendship certainly. The cold of the morning seeped into his bones.

The rear wall of the kitchen and scullery had been boarded up, but again no repairs had been carried out. Why, when the rest of the village was almost fully repaired, had no work been done here? Was it because

Phillip Haswell knew he wasn't going to be in Fearnley Maughton for much longer? Clement felt ill.

'Clement, the day of the strafing raid, you said you came to find Doctor Haswell. Where exactly did you find him?' Arthur asked.

'In the garden. His front door was open as usual.' Clement paused, reliving the day he had ran into the doctor's house. He stared at Morris. 'Why was the destruction here so much less than the bomb that demolished Peter's office?'

'More good questions,' Morris said, and stepped outside.

The first tinges of dawn were lighting the heavens. Morris flicked off the torch and they stood gazing down into the crater that had been Phillip Haswell's Anderson Shelter.

Clement drew his collar up around his neck to ward off the cold air.

'Did you hear this bomb hit, Clement?'

'Yes, it was a moment after the other one.'

Both men stood staring at the hole in the ground as the daylight increased around them.

'Would you, with your knowledge of explosives, say that it was possible for a fighter to drop two bombs of different tonnage in rapid succession?'

'I am not an aeronautical expert, Arthur, but I do know that a fighter plane can carry bombs. Not really heavy ones and not many. But I do know that light aeroplanes, like fighters, need to be balanced to take off. If it was carrying two bombs, I suppose they would be the same weight.'

'I have visited the site of Mr Kempton's office. It was a two-storey building, I understand?'

Clement nodded.

'Have you been there since the bomb landed?' Arthur asked.

'Yes. I offered to help Peter carry anything that survived the blast, but there was nothing left. The whole building vanished, and everything in it.'

'How deep was the crater?'

'Deep. About twice as deep as this. The hole is wide. And of course, filled with rubble.'

Clement and Morris stared at the crater that had once been the Anderson shelter. The hole contained the metal sheeting, and a quantity of earth and grass, which had once formed the bomb shelter's roof, and now covered the crater's floor. Clement turned around and saw the fragmented brick and timber walls of the garden shed lying on the ground where they had fallen.

'It is fortunate that Phillip was not in the shelter at the time,' he said. 'Nor still in the shed.'

'Where was he exactly?' Morris asked.

Clement's gaze went to where he had found Phillip standing in the garden. In the muted morning light, Clement saw the beans. *Beans and carrots...* Phillip had told Clement that he had been pulling up carrots when the bomb hit. Clement told Morris.

Leaving Morris staring at the crater, Clement wandered along the path and walked the rows of beans and potatoes. He stood in the middle of the patch and stared around at all the vegetables growing in the garden, the first streaks of sunlight hitting the tree tops.

'Have you found something?' Morris called.

'It's what I haven't found, Arthur,' Clement called. 'There are no carrots.'

26

D awn was breaking and the rising sun had turned black night to pale day. Clement closed his eyes and leaned back in his chair. Even the familiar click of his door could not deliver its usual soothing response.

It had been just after first light when Arthur jumped into the crater that had once been the Anderson Shelter in Phillip Haswell's garden. Clement still could not believe it. He visualised the twisted, burnt wires and valves of what had once been a transmitter radio buried deep in the soil and rubble of the Anderson Shelter.

Clement wrapped his hands around the warm tea cup. He felt numb. He felt betrayed and foolish. He remembered a verse from Ecclesiastes about anger being in the lap of fools. But Phillip was not an angry man. Neither was he foolish. At least the Phillip Haswell Clement had known wasn't. Perhaps, as the Good Book taught, it was only the foolish who expressed anger. The truly wicked never displayed rage. Theirs was the smiling faced, festering hatred of the psychopathic mind that contrived and manipulated while maintaining a detached, even charming, cool head. How could he have so misjudged the man?

Elsie Wainwright. The real one had met a man in Eastbourne and had conceived his child. Had that man been Phillip? Had he lured the real Elsie to Westminster Bridge then pushed the girl to her death? Clement thought of the pink and white pillow cases. The depth of the man's deception astounded.

Clement now knew how Elsie had left Fearnley Maughton without being seen. If Phillip's car held the body of a man, it would hold a woman. A woman who had returned to London to hide. But where was she now? Morris had said she had been spotted on a train, but he had not said in which direction that train had been travelling. *Jane*, was being followed. And if *Jane* was to rendezvous with Phillip, they would be caught.

Morris had said that finding the nurse was the turning point. Clement believed *Jane* had taken the opportunity to flee the village during the strafing raid, having made arrangements for Phillip to follow at a time and opportunity that would not raise suspicion. Clement took in a deep breath. What they had done between them was staggering in its heartlessness and complexity.

Together, they had ordered the raid to disguise the detonation of the shelter which destroyed the wireless. And Peter's building, because of its distinctive colour and architecture, had identified the village for the pilot and acted as a diversion. *Jane,* having killed Constable Newson, then freed Stanley and took him to Peter's office via the rear lane, knowing a bomb would fall on the house where Stanley and anyone else in the building - including Clement's friend, Peter - would be killed, their remains beyond recognition. And the bombing of Peter's office building would be the signal to blow up the Anderson Shelter.

Such cruelty and wickedness confounded reason.

The doorbell sounded.

Clement opened his eyes, feeling utterly drained. The clock in the hallway chimed nine. Standing, he went to open his front door. 'Arthur?'

'Could I have a word?'

'Of course, come in.' Clement closed the door.

'Given what we have learned about Doctor Haswell, I wondered if you have also realised that the raid might not have been accidental?'

Clement nodded.

'It is possible Mr Kempton's office building could have been used for more than identifying Fearnley Maughton to the pilot.'

'I thought the same thing, Arthur.'

'I have arranged a team of men to do some digging on the site of Mr Kempton's former office. Do you know when Mr Kempton is due back?'

'Not specifically. But it won't be before Monday afternoon at the earliest,' Clement said. With all that had happened he had not thought about his men. They were safe, and for now that was enough.

'Would you know if Mr Kempton was in his office on the morning of the raid, before the bomb actually landed?'

Clement thought back. 'Thankfully no. He was with the team at the base.'

Morris nodded. 'Do you think he would have any concerns about us digging on the site?'

Clement shook his head. 'If Stanley was killed there, Peter would be the first person to assist with the digging.'

'It's Sunday. Will you be taking the church service today?'

'No. Reverend Battersby will be here soon. He is taking matins for me.'

'There is no need for you to come to the site. However, if I find anything of an unfortunate nature, I will come and find you.'

Through his open study window, Clement heard the footsteps before the doorbell rang. He rose from his desk and went to the door. Arthur Morris stood on the doorstep. The man's face was downcast and Clement feared the worst.

'Come in, Arthur.'

Morris stepped inside and Clement closed the door.

'It would appear that only Mr Kempton's secretary was in the office the day of the raid. However, Miss Forster has told me that now she has had time to reflect on that day's events, she remembers hearing noises upstairs. Before she could investigate the source, she heard the aeroplane and left the building to run to the assembly point at *The Crown*. Clement, fragments of bone have been unearthed,' Morris paused. 'And a blood-stained shoe.'

'I'll get my hat and coat.'

Following Morris into the village, Clement stood on the edge of the crater. A crowd had formed around the site. Lumps of stone and splintered timber lay in crude stacks along the ground. In several boxes beside the crater were hundreds of torn leather strips of book bindings, while twisted pieces of office equipment lay stacked nearby. Arthur went to one side of the vast hole and lifted an object from one of the boxes. It was a blood-stained shoe without laces. Clement recognised it immediately; Stanley had such large feet.

Clement felt the lump in his throat. When so many young men were dying in the skies above them, defending the nation, Stanley's death was so needless. And so wicked. A trusting lad had fallen in love with a girl; the most natural thing in the world. Clement glanced at Arthur and nodded.

'What was upstairs in Mr Kempton's office?' Morris asked.

'Storage rooms filled with old files. They would once have been bedrooms long ago. Peter has been the solicitor in Fearnley Maughton for at least twenty years. I think he purchased the building at the same time as he purchased the practice and it has operated out of the same location for generations. There must have been thousands of files up there. No wonder there was so much destruction. It was a fire waiting to happen.'

'But enough room for someone to hide?'

'Peter doesn't live on the site, so yes, there would have been enough room. And, of course, there was an external staircase to the upper floor. It had once been the servant's entrance. No doubt Phillip and the girl wanted Peter dead too. Like George and Stanley and the rest of my men. I cannot tell you how grateful I am that Peter wasn't here at the time. We have lost too many from the village. Is that what it is all about, Arthur? Eliminating the men of my team? I didn't realise the Germans saw us as such a threat. I am so pleased my men are safely away from here at present. How did *Jane* get out of the building, do you think?'

'She would most likely have known when the strafing raid was to happen and would have made some excuse to leave Stanley here alone.'

Clement felt such revulsion toward the girl. He abhorred *Jane* more than Phillip who, it now appeared had orchestrated the whole thing, for *Jane* had crushed Stanley's heart, not just his body.

'When did she leave the village?' Clement asked.

'I don't know, but possibly the next day when Haswell left Fearnley Maughton on one of his routine trips to Lewes to see the strafing victims. Given the bed in the second bedroom, it would appear that *Jane* hid at Doctor Haswell's until she could leave the village in the Doctor's car.' Morris paused. 'There is something else, Clement. But perhaps we should return to the vicarage.'

Clement picked his way over the rubble and they walked away from the destruction, back to his home. As he closed the door to his study he heard the click. Its pacifying effect was returning. He gestured towards the armchair in his study and Morris sat down.

Clement saw Morris's procrastination; the lips being sucked in, first the top then the other. The room was quiet and cold.

'Where is Mary?' Morris asked.

A cold dread coursed through Clement's body from scalp to toes. He heard himself answer. 'In Windsor, with her sister, Gwen.' But his heart was thumping. And panic was rising. His head spun. 'Why do you ask?'

'I thought in view of the current situation, you may appreciate your wife being with you. I telephoned the police in Windsor this morning and asked them to send a police vehicle around to her sister's place and drive your wife home.' Morris paused, his face contorted with painful duty. 'She's not there, Clement.' Morris paused. 'The neighbours confirm she hasn't been there for some time.'

27

'Drink the brandy, Clement.'

Clement stared at the glass in Morris's hand. His mouth was dry and he felt as if he'd been flattened in the rubble of Peter's house.

'I think it is time we spoke again to Commander Winthorpe,' Morris said. 'I'll call from here, if that is alright with you?'

'Johnny? Why would you call Johnny?'

'Rest here, Clement. I am sorry to have shocked you but there was no other way.' Morris paused. 'Try not to get ahead of yourself. It could all be completely innocent. I'm sure she will be found safe and sound.'

Clement looked up at Morris, his mind reeling. What did the Chief Inspector suspect? Mary had gone to Windsor, to Gwen's. Leaning forward, he grasped the armrests of the chair, his hands shaking, then stood. He wanted to telephone Gwen. There had to be some mistake. He knew he had phoned Gwen's number previously. Then, the lines had been crossed, that was all. Besides, Mary had answered the second time. How was that possible if she had not been at Gwen's house? The neighbours were mistaken. He stared at Morris's concerned face. 'Dear God! You think they have kidnapped Mary?'

'It should not be ruled out.'

Hurrying into the hall, he dialled Gwen's number. 'Hello Gwen. It's Clement. Is Mary with you?' he asked, trying to sound calm.

'No. I haven't seen her in weeks, Clement. Is everything alright?'

'Yes, Gwen. She went up to London shopping and said that if she had time she would call in on you. Nothing to worry about.' He knew the excuse was ridiculous, but it was all he could think of on the spur of the moment. His head was spinning. It did not make any sense. Why would she lie? 'I don't know what to think, Arthur.'

'I think, Clement, that there is more to what has been happening than we have been told. We should speak again with Commander Winthorpe. Perhaps he can shed some light on it all.'

'If you think so, Arthur.' But Clement's pulse was still racing and his head ached. He took a long deep breath, and walking back to his study, sat down. Why would Mary have lied to him? It made no sense. He took another sip of brandy. They had been married over twenty years. They shared everything. He knew her. He looked around the familiar room feeling the realization of a deception revealed.

Arthur Morris sat in the chair beside him. 'I have to ask myself a question, Clement. Well, two questions, really. Why did Commander Winthorpe telephone me to say that he was having *Jane* followed and not you? And how did he know it was *Jane*?'

Clement placed the glass on the table beside him and pondered what Arthur had just said. He thought back to when Johnny had come to Fearnley Maughton. That was before he and Mary had met the girl they had known as Elsie Wainwright at the bus shelter in Lewes. Clement sat upright, frowning. Johnny had never met *Jane*. 'Only someone from the village could recognise *Jane* as Elsie. Unless,' Clement paused. 'He knew her beforehand.'

Morris's head was nodding. 'My thoughts also, Clement.'

Clement slumped back in the chair, overwhelmed. He felt bone weary. Surely it wasn't possible that Johnny had betrayed him? Had Johnny killed the very people he had helped to unite? And where was Mary? Clement's limbs felt heavy and he could feel the blood draining from his face. He stared through the drawn curtains to the day beyond. Everything around him was like walking into a spider's web - felt but unseen. Whichever way he looked, he couldn't see the way clear.

'First things first, Clement. We telephone Commander Winthorpe and go from there,' Morris was saying.

Clement stood and walked into the hallway but his footsteps felt as if he was walking on quicksand. He reached for the telephone and dialled the number. 'Commander Winthorpe, please.'

The telephone line clicked and crackled. He spoke to three male voices before he heard Johnny's voice on the line.

He placed his hand over the mouthpiece and nodded to Arthur as Johnny said hello.

'Something else happened, Clement?' Johnny asked.

'Tell me something, Johnny. Who is following *Jane*?'

There was a short pause.

'We have several people on it. They change every hour or so,' Johnny said.

'Are you going to tell me who?' he asked, his voice becoming insistent.

'Not over the phone.'

Clement could hear other voices on the line. They seemed to be in the background and he fancied that Johnny was at some meeting and had taken the call in a public place. At least, Clement hoped that was the case. 'Chief Inspector Morris thinks we don't have much time. The main suspect has not been seen since lunchtime yesterday.'

There was a pause.

'Where are you, Clement?' Johnny asked.

'At home. Chief Inspector Morris is with me.'

'Can you and the Chief Inspector be at Lewes Police Station within the hour?' Johnny asked.

'Yes,' he said.

Clement heard the line go dead. He turned to Morris. 'I think Commander Winthorpe is not in London. In fact, he could be quite close by.'

Morris nodded.

'This is more than murder, isn't it, Arthur. We are talking espionage, aren't we?'

'Quite possibly.'

Clement went to the kitchen and made a pot of tea, but everything in the kitchen reminded him of Mary. 'Combe Martin!' he said, holding the tea pot in mid-air.

Morris looked up. 'The West Country?'

'Of course. That is where she is, Arthur,' he said stirring the pot. 'I asked her to go there a week or so ago, when I thought the invasion was at hand. There is no telephone there, but I can get a message to her through the postmistress.' His mind flashed to Ilene Greenwood. 'In fact, the postmistress will probably know where she is. They all seem to know everything.'

Morris smiled. 'May I use the telephone first, Clement? I would like to call the Chief Superintendents in all the coastal towns and ask them to keep a look out for two people answering the descriptions of *Jane* and Doctor Haswell.'

Thirty minutes later they drove out of Fearnley Maughton. Clement had never felt so despondent or so exhausted in his whole life. Even the trenches of France had not had the same effect upon him. His call to Combe Martin had only resulted in the postmistress confirming that she hadn't seen Mary. Was Morris correct? Was it espionage? He felt completely bewildered by the turn of events. His thoughts went to Mary. He loved her, and he believed she loved him. What had caused her to lie to him? Yet, if he was fair, he had withheld his involvement in the Auxiliary Units from her. They had been married twenty years. They finished each other's sentences, such was their affinity. That Mary should have a double life was unfathomable. He felt alone and betrayed.

Morris pulled the car into the police parking area at the rear of the Lewes Police Station, and pulling on the handbrake, turned off the engine. From his seat in the car, Clement could see both Inspector Russell's car and Doctor Haswell's parked in the police compound. He got out of the car and stared at the vehicles. For the first time he realised how similar they were. Walking towards them he stared at the tyres on both.

'I told you I would make a detective out of you, Clement,' Morris said.

'Are they identical?'

'No. Doctor Haswell's car is a Humber Super Snipe, to be precise, and Inspector Russell's is an Austin Twelve. But they both have long wheel bases and four doors and six side windows. They have similar front wheel arches and both have a rounded shape over the boot. And, perhaps more importantly, they are both black. Only the grilles are different. With both cars parked front to curb, as they were in the rear lane behind the police station in Fearnley Maughton, the grilles are not visible. And with the wartime modifications that are required of all vehicles, the cars do look remarkably similar.'

'So it was Inspector Russell's car that drove into Maughton Forest?'

Morris shook his head. 'No, I don't believe so. While the body was found in Doctor Haswell's car, I do not believe it was either the Doctor's car or Inspector Russell's that was in the forest.'

Clement stared at Morris. 'If not either of these cars, then whose?'

'Another good question, Clement.'

'What is going on, Arthur?'

'Do you know something interesting?'

'What is that?'

'When we brought Inspector Russell's car to Lewes we had to jump-start it. The car keys are missing. They were not on Inspector Russell, neither were they in or on his desk. Nor were they in the safe. Nor at Inspector Russell's home. Constable Matthews says that the Inspector kept the keys to his car on his person. However,

I am also informed that Inspector Russell's car keys have a distinctive key ring with a Celtic cross medallion.'

'You think the car was used?' Clement asked.

'I do. Find the car keys and we find the murderer.'

'But if the murderer returned the safe keys, why wouldn't he replace the car keys?'

'Because the car was used after Inspector Russell's body was removed from the police station.'

'How?'

'I'm not sure yet,' Morris replied. They heard the sound of an approaching vehicle. 'But I think we are about to find out.' Morris tilted his head in the direction of a black car that was pulling into the police yard. 'That must be the fastest trip from London on record, if that is where Commander Winthorpe came from.'

Johnny got out of the vehicle wearing his Royal Navy uniform and greeted Clement. Together, they walked into the police station and followed Morris to an office at the end of a long corridor.

'You came from London, Commander?' Morris asked, removing his overcoat and hanging his hat on the stand in his office.

Johnny shook his head. 'Not even I can drive that fast, Chief Inspector. In fact, I have been at a meeting at Petworth on an unrelated matter. I couldn't say over the phone, Clement, but *Jane* is heading south east. Possibly Eastbourne. But it could be somewhere further east. Tell me what's been happening.'

Clement told Johnny what he and Morris had found in the Anderson Shelter. 'All the murder victims are from the village except one, the man my men believed to be a vagrant. A description of him was in our report that was stolen, and for which at least two people have died.'

'Is the body of the vagrant still in the mortuary?' Johnny asked.

'I have arranged for you to be taken to Lewes Hospital's mortuary to see the body of the seaman, as we are calling him, on your arrival,' Arthur told Johnny. 'Perhaps we should do this first. Once you confirm the identity of your man, if it is your man, perhaps you would like to inform us what is really behind the murders in Fearnley Maughton?'

Clement saw Johnny lean back in the chair. He was staring at Morris, a slow smile spreading over his lips.

Forty minutes later they were back in Morris's office.

'How were you so sure he was my man, Chief Inspector?' Johnny asked.

Morris held Johnny's gaze. 'If he had been a deserter, I would have been given a name and a description. And I would have had a visit from the Military Police. Likewise, if he had been a German spy I would have been deluged with telephone calls from London and Special Branch. That no one was asking about this man led me to only one conclusion.'

Johnny smiled. 'Quite so. And a lesson for us all, Chief Inspector. The seaman, or the man you believed to be a vagrant, Clement, was Naval Lieutenant Roger Ellis. Ellis is, or rather was, one of my men. Sorry, Clement, but church duties for me have really taken a back seat. And the Archdeacon thing is only for the duration of the war. It allows me to travel around Britain in clerical garb when a degree of secrecy is called for, and I always have a place to stay away from hotels and other more public places. Ellis was stationed at a top secret location in Cuckmere Haven, known as *His Majesty's Ship Forward*. It is there that all Royal Navy battle plans are formalised. So you see just how vital it is that the facility at *Forward* remains secret. However, it had become apparent from intercepted German chatter that the enemy had become aware of some activity at Cuckmere Haven. That being the case, we saw little point in trying to conceal it from them. In fact, rather than attempting to hide it and thereby making the Germans even more curious, we saw it as a golden opportunity. It has taken over a year for Ellis to establish his cover and, more importantly, for his information to be believed. His death is a major blow.'

'He was feeding misinformation?' Clement asked.

Johnny nodded. 'Yes. We know he had a contact in Fearnley Maughton, although we never knew who. The contact went by the code name *Phoebe*. Ellis would deliver the information to *Phoebe* in Maughton Forest. That contact would then send the information onto the Abwehr by radio. Ellis had become suspicious about *Phoebe* and reported it to me. The interesting thing about our work is not only listening to what is said but also what isn't. *Phoebe* had changed and even failed to make the rendezvous on several occasions. Never a good sign. Changes in habit have to be investigated. Perhaps Ellis asked too many questions and *Phoebe* became suspicious. Unfortunately, we will never know the answer to that. And, Ellis, of course, was the only person who could identify *Phoebe*.

'Doctor Haswell,' Clement said thinking of the times he had seen Phillip Haswell drive away from Fearnley

Maughton. He had always believed the Doctor was visiting the sick in Lewes or doing rounds, not keeping appointments with Naval Lieutenants.

'He must have seen the Royal Engineers on one of his rendezvous in the forest, and found the Operational Base,' Clement said thinking of George.

'Yes. But knowing *Phoebe's* real name now is of little use. We suspect the bird has flown, although we do not know where, precisely. We hope he will rendezvous with Jane, which is why we haven't apprehended her as yet. Don't want her disappearing before she makes contact with Doctor Haswell, if he really is *Phoebe*.'

'Is there any doubt?' Morris asked.

'Until the individual is caught, there is always the possibility of error.' Johnny added.

'Who recognised *Jane*?' he asked.

'Just one of my people.'

'I understand you grew up on the coast, Clement?' Johnny said. 'Considering *Jane* is heading east, it could be useful if you were to come along.'

'Of course.' Clement couldn't stop thinking about Phillip Haswell. 'He lived among us in Fearnley Maughton for three years. Why now? What changed?'

'It could have been the establishment of the Auxiliary Units,' Johnny said. 'But I don't think so. Especially as Doctor Haswell could not have known about the team's existence. Or perhaps someone was just getting too close.'

'Or he had what he came for?' Morris added.

Johnny raised his eyebrows. 'Perhaps. But I think he would have remained in situ for the duration of the war. It is my opinion that he would only break cover if he had a vital piece of information that could not be sent by wireless, or if he was in danger of discovery. I feel certain that the strafing run was arranged for no other reason than to blow up the radio transmitter.'

'And the murders of George and Stanley, David Russell and Constable Newson?' Clement asked.

'It would seem that *Jane* was called in to assist Haswell's escape and to aid in any other sabotage. Perhaps the murders of members of your team, Clement, were for no other reason than that Stanley Russell had told her about the group and shown the girl the weapons. While the Auxiliary Unit could well have been the catalyst for Haswell's flight, the information from Cuckmere Haven would appear to be the real reason for Doctor Haswell to break cover.' He paused. 'But I don't think so. I think that is what we are meant to think. While *Phoebe* was receiving what he believed to be accurate information, why would he leave? But, if *Phoebe* learned of the existence of Coleshill and its location, that would be a real coup for the Abwehr and an excellent reason for breaking cover. Every cell in the country would be wiped out and the training camp targeted. The elimination of Coleshill and every Auxiliary Unit cell would render us vulnerable to invasion. If they can win the war in the air before we can properly regroup and rearm after Dunkirk, there would not be much stopping them on the ground. It would be a complete walkover. And even if we did somehow stop the Germans from landing, the elimination of Coleshill and its work would set our war effort back at least twelve months. This knowledge is a major coup for the Germans. Certainly worth breaking cover for. They will probably award him the Iron Cross.

'Stanley must have told *Jane*,' said Morris. 'She certainly knew about his pack. And finding the list in Inspector Russell's safe gave her the names of the other members of the team. It is the only answer.'

'But Stanley didn't know about the existence of the list,' Clement told them. 'Moreover, the list contained nothing else but names. No mission, no regimental identification...' Clement stopped speaking.

'Clement?' Johnny asked.

'It was in an official envelope. Ministry of Home Security. That would have been enough for them to open the letter.'

'How did they know it was there?' Johnny asked.

The room was silent.

'Inspector Russell must have told someone. He was the only other person who knew it existed. Other than me and Johnny and Gubbins.'

'Perhaps they opened the safe as a matter of course,' Morris said.

'Well, no point speculating on it now,' Johnny said. 'We have a Nurse and a Doctor to find as a matter of priority.'

The large constable appeared in the doorway. 'Sorry to interrupt, Sir, but there is an urgent telephone call for Commander Winthorpe.'

'May I?' Johnny asked gesturing towards Morris' telephone on the desk.

Morris nodded.

Three minutes later Johnny replaced the receiver. 'Do you have enough petrol for a trip to the coast right now, Chief Inspector?'

'I can get it. Where to, exactly?' Morris asked.

'That was Gubbins on the phone,' Johnny said. 'He has just heard from Y-section. Y-section listens in on our enemy's conversations. They have correlated some chatter they heard a day or so ago with a deciphered Jerry message to a U-Boat in the North Sea. There is to be a pick up. Scheduled for the high tide at zero four hundred hours tomorrow morning.'

'Where?' Morris asked.

'Winchelsea Beach.'

'Are you with us, Clement?' Morris asked.

Clement nodded. He felt exhausted. They had been awake since four o'clock in the morning, but he was not going to miss confronting Phillip Haswell. Clement pictured all the dead and injured from the strafing raid. George Evans's pale face was locked forever in his memory. Lieutenant Ellis, Constable Newson. Even David Russell. But the one he particularly wanted to avenge was Stanley. Gullible Stanley, whose only crime was to fall in love.

'And,' Johnny added. 'Elsie - or *Jane* as you are calling her - is on a train for Rye.'

267

28

Leaving Lewes Police Station, they walked towards the waiting police car. Clement checked his watch. Four o'clock. In another twelve hours he would be on Winchelsea Beach. His mind drifted back to his childhood and the hours he had spent with his mother wandering along the shore collecting whatever the tide brought in. He remembered them with such affection. Halcyon days, he thought, but no longer. His memories now of Winchelsea Beach would forever be tainted with betrayal.

Whenever Clement thought about Phillip Haswell, he felt nauseous. How could he not have known Phillip's true leanings? It reinforced his belief that no one really knows the people with whom one spends one's life. His mind turned to Mary. He wanted to speak to her; to learn why she had lied. He had tried calling the vicarage but the telephone in the front hall had rung and rung without answer. And now they could wait no longer.

He looked across to Arthur Morris sitting with him in the back seat of the car. Johnny had taken the front seat beside the police driver. Morris had his eyes closed but Clement was sure he was not asleep. 'How was Inspector Russell's car used?'

Morris opened his eyes. 'Not one hundred percent sure, but I think it was where Lieutenant Ellis was stored overnight, before being transferred into the Doctor's car. Remember I told you; there is nearly always a witness. But unless it is blatant, that witness may not even be aware of what they are seeing. And as the police station is at one end of the village, a car could come and go in that back lane without raising suspicion. In fact, as long as the cars are similar and are parked in the same place, it usually assumed by any casual observer that it is the car belonging to either Doctor Haswell or Inspector Russell. But what if the cars were switched in their parking places or even substituted for a few hours...would anyone take any notice?'

Clement stared through the window at nothing much reflecting on what Morris had just said. 'I saw Phillip drive away on Friday. It was when Peter and I were in your office at the police station. The day we found George. I even waved to him. Though I couldn't say if it was his car or not. But it was his car in Lewes Hospital. And the body of Lieutenant Ellis must have already been in the boot of his car when Phillip left Fearnley Maughton.'

'Not necessarily. And it is possible that Doctor Haswell might not have known the body was there.'

'You think Haswell is innocent?' Clement asked.

'I don't know yet.'

'Either way, Lieutenant Ellis was put into Doctor Haswell's car on the previous night,' Clement added.

'That would be a safe assumption.' Morris closed his eyes.

'Brought out of the forest in David Russell's car then transferred to Doctor Haswell's car during the night,' Clement said, almost to himself.

Morris opened his eyes a second time. 'Again, not necessarily. As I said earlier, Clement, I do not believe it was Inspector Russell's car that went into the forest. There was no sign of leaf matter in the tyre treads of either car. Of course, the tyres might have been washed but someone would have witnessed that. However, I do believe that Inspector Russell's car was used for storage and retrieval.'

Clement remembered he had seen Phillip driving into the rear lane one evening. Was he really sure it had been Phillip's car? It may even not have been the Doctor driving. Morris had said it was all about timing. Clement leaned his head back, reflecting on that night. He had seen the headlights and made the assumption it was Phillip Haswell. When was that? Clement thought. It had been the night he had cycled out to Peter's to enquire about the report. George was already dead, lying in the leaves of Maughton Forest. And what of Lieutenant Ellis? Was he already in the boot of Haswell's car?

The police car drove into Rye just on dusk. Stepping from the car outside Rye Police Station, Clement breathed in the salty air. He knew every corner, every twisting byway in the town. His eyes darted to his left. Against the skyline he could see the spire of St Mary's, his father's old church, in the dwindling light. He had no wish to go there; the place held too many memories. Closing the car door, he walked with Morris and Johnny towards the front of Rye Police Station.

'Since you telephoned earlier, Sir,' the police Sergeant said, 'we've had the railway station under constant surveillance.'

'Thank you, Sergeant,' Morris said.

'Now, how can we be of assistance?' the Sergeant asked.

'We will need a room to formulate our plans and any maps of the town and area you have. Ordnance Survey maps would be especially helpful.'

'I'll see what I can do, Sir. In the meantime, I'll arrange some tea and something for you all to eat.'

'Thank you, Sergeant,' Morris replied.

'Is there a telephone I can use,' Johnny asked.

'Yes. In the Inspector's office,' the Sergeant said, pointing to the door further down the corridor.

'Has *Jane* been sighted?' Clement asked.

'Yes, but not intercepted.'

'Where?'

'Not far as it happens. *The Standard Inn* in The Mint.'

'I know it,' Clement said. 'She will probably take the Needles Passage to Wish Street then across the Strand Quay for Winchelsea. It is only about three miles.'

'You have someone watching her, Sergeant?' Morris asked.

'One of my people, actually, Chief Inspector,' Johnny said re-entering the room. 'They followed *Jane* to the inn and took rooms. When *Jane* makes her move, they'll telephone us here.'

'What about Phillip Haswell?' Clement asked.

'Hasn't been sighted yet,' the Sergeant answered. 'We have checked all the inns. But, of course, he could be using an alias. The description of the suspect could fit any number of men in the town.'

'Only Reverend Wisdom would recognise Doctor Haswell in the dark,' Morris said.

Clement frowned remembering what Arthur had told him about Phillip always being unavailable. He tried to remember the sequence of events, but they had been so rapid, his memory had become confused.

Morris had always said it was about timing. Clement thought back. The Chief Inspector had arrived in the village the afternoon of David Russell's death and Phillip Haswell had not left the village until the following Friday. Four days. Yet in those few, event-filled days, Phillip Haswell had evaded Morris. Despite Clement's earlier doubts about Haswell's betrayal, the evidence was undeniable.

'At least we know where *Jane* is,' Johnny said. 'If Haswell and the girl are to rendezvous, it will either be here or on Winchelsea Beach. But they will not make their move for a few hours yet. It's a waiting game for now. One thing is certain, they will be on the beach at zero four hundred hours tomorrow morning because that submarine will not wait any longer than its prescribed time.' Johnny helped himself to some tea.

It would be a long night.

'Could I also use the telephone, Sergeant?' Clement asked. The Sergeant led him to a vacant room further along the corridor. Clement closed the door. The room held only a desk, a chair and a telephone. He dialled his home number and waited but no one answered.

Clement said a quiet prayer for Mary and for his men at Coleshill. And he prayed for himself, Morris and Johnny for whatever happened this night, it would end badly for someone. He glanced up at the half frosted window in the room. From the diminishing light outside he could tell it was now nearly dark.

He rejoined the group as the Sergeant unrolled a map of Rye and spread it out over the table. They gathered around. A pencil mark had already been drawn on one street, indicating *The Standard Inn* on The Mint.

'How many people do you have available, Commander?' Morris asked Johnny.

'Just the two. But both are seasoned operatives. *Jane* will not detect them. Sergeant, do you have a police motorcycle?'

'Yes, but no petrol, Commander.'

'Have your constable drain some from our car. It would be best to have it available, as a diversion, if required.'

'Would you prefer, Commander Winthorpe that this was handled as a security matter or a police matter?' Morris asked.

Clement glanced at Johnny.

'Police matter is best, I think,' Johnny answered.

Clement saw Morris tilt his head. The gesture was familiar to Clement now and one Morris used to indicate his scepticism.

'If we are to have any hope of apprehending the suspects, some of us must be in place on the beach well before four o'clock,' Johnny said.

'You are proposing we divide, Commander?' Morris asked.

'I am suggesting that I leave Rye earlier taking the motorcycle and conceal myself at the northern end of Winchelsea Beach. That way I am in place should any

273

unforeseen problems occur. Once Clement has identified Haswell and the rendezvous taken place, you both then make your dash for the beach.'

'Could we not apprehend them before they arrive at the beach? Say, here at the bridge?' Morris asked, his finger on the map.

'I agree that would be easier all around. But we would need to be sure that *Jane* and Haswell have already joined up. What if they go separately to the beach? If the rendezvous is in any way compromised, Haswell or the girl could abort and we would lose them both. Clement, is there more than one way to Winchelsea Beach?'

'Yes. The road, of course, and there is an inland walking track that crosses the dunes.'

'Whilst I think it more likely they would use the road at such an hour, we cannot be sure,' Johnny said.

'The beach it is, then,' Morris added. 'Once your people confirm that *Jane* has left the inn, and Clement has identified Haswell, he and I will go to Winchelsea Beach. We can conceal ourselves somewhere along The Ridge.' Morris's finger pointed to the strip of roadway on the map that hugged the beach front. 'It is a bit exposed, but that should not be too great a problem at night. We will also see the landing craft sent to collect them. Clement, the beach at Winchelsea is it sand or shingle?'

'Shingle.'

'Pity.'

'What about ordnance?' Clement asked, looking at the Sergeant.

The Sergeant spread another map on the table. Small green circles dotted the beach. 'The larger circles are anti-tank mines,' the Sergeant told them.

'And the smaller ones with spikes?' Clement asked.

'Anti-personnel.'

Clement studied the clusters of green circles spaced along the beach. Each mine had been placed at approximately twenty-foot intervals along the land-side edge of the beach about ten feet in from the roadway. He could feel his eyes widening. Whilst the anti-tank mines presented no problem for a man on foot, it was a different story for the anti-personnel explosives and ordnance survey maps were notoriously inaccurate.

'How far apart are the anti-tank mines from the anti-personnel mines?' Morris asked.

'About a yard either side,' the Sergeant replied.

Clement flicked a glance at Morris and Johnny. Fleeting though it was, their eyes held the same reaction. If he had not believed the mission to be suicidal before, he did now.

Johnny was the first to speak. 'As soon as the targets are on the beach, we move in around them. Once I see them pass me, I will start the motorcycle. When you hear the motor, you can run onto the beach. What is the wind forecast for tonight, Sergeant?'

'Around two knots, Commander, south south-west. So quite calm.'

There was silence for some minutes. Clement glanced at the faces of the men alongside whom he was soon likely to die. He thought their expressions mirrored his own. He had seen it before, in the trenches, moments before the whistle sounded. The interesting thing about impossible missions, he believed, was the silent acceptance of them. Fear disappears when death is inevitable. At least, that had been his experience of the men with whom he had served. There was a job to be done. That was all they needed to know.

'When they hear the motorcycle they will start to run, surely,' Clement added.

'It doesn't give us much time,' Johnny agreed. 'But by then everyone is exposed. It should be expected that they will be armed. And the boatman may well have a machine gun mounted in the craft.'

Clement remembered the two-week life expectancy. Now it was a matter of hours. He wriggled his ankle. But a knife, even a commando knife, was a risky venture on the beach with a younger man who was also the enemy. And not worth a farthing against a mounted machine gun. A Sten was what he needed. 'Sergeant, do you have any binoculars?'

'I can arrange that, Sir.'

'A Sten gun would have been useful,' Clement added, thinking of his pack in the filing cabinet in the church office.

'Already thought of, Clement,' Johnny said. 'And both my operatives have pistols, as do I.'

'Right. So, Clement and I will position ourselves midway along the roadway, adjacent to the beach and opposite the most northern groyne. The topographical map shows a ditch on the opposite side of the road, from which there should be a clear view of the beach and both sides of the groyne. According to the ordnance survey map there is a gap between the buried mines directly opposite the line of sight from the ditch to the groyne pylons. Commander Winthorpe, as you will be at the beach before us, can you cut the wire there in advance? That way you will know exactly where Clement and I will station ourselves. Once we see *Jane* and Haswell, we can

276

cross the road and run onto the beach in a straight line to the pylons. We should have a reasonable chance of cutting them off.'

'Sir, all the horizontal boards on the groynes have been removed. Only the uprights remain,' the Sergeant put in.

'How tall are these pylons?' Morris asked.

'Well over a man's height, Sir, and spaced about ten feet apart.'

'But enough to offer some protection?' Clement asked.

'Limited,' the Sergeant added.

'Morris is right,' Johnny said. 'The landing craft may not beach. It could stand offshore but the pylons offer the only protection while the targets swim out and board the dinghy.'

'Would the Germans know the locations of the mines?' Clement asked.

'It is wise to assume they do,' Johnny said.

Johnny must have seen Clement's sceptical expression.

'Intelligence of that sort is much prized and highly paid for, Clement. We cannot assume that everyone is a patriot.' Johnny paused. 'Paid for,' he muttered.

Clement looked up. 'Using five pound notes, perhaps?'

'It is possible, Clement,' Johnny responded, 'those notes would be very useful for any other future German spies arriving in England.'

Clement wondered about the notes. Not that he believed the whole business had ever been about money. But if five pound notes lined the pockets of *Jane* and

Phillip, the money would provide a tangible link to the murder of David Russell.

The room was quiet. Clement knew they were all wondering what lay ahead on Winchelsea Beach. He did not believe Phillip and *Jane* would ever allow themselves to be caught. Much less stand trial for either espionage or murder. The best Clement could hope for was to kill them before they, or the machine gun in the dinghy, killed him. His thoughts disturbed him. Several times since Clement had become involved in the Auxiliary Units he had said that he felt less and less like a vicar. Once, he could never have imagined even thinking such thoughts. He remembered Gubbins's words about killing. But this had become personal; Phillip Haswell was a man he knew, or at least thought he knew. He pushed his feelings aside and tried to remain detached, hoping his motives were not revenge but duty. He understood now why Johnny had referred to them as "targets". It depersonalised what they were about to do, for regardless of what Clement thought, both targets were the enemy, and the location of Coleshill had to remain a secret. That was what he had signed on to do; to defend and, if necessary, to die to protect his country from Nazi aggression.

'Sergeant, would you inform the local Home Guard of our activities tonight? It is better that they know and stay away,' Morris said.

The Sergeant made an entry in his note book.

'Where do you think Haswell is hiding?' Clement asked.

'You are our Rye expert, Clement. Where would you go?' Morris asked.

Clement stared at the map of the streets he knew so well. 'I do not believe he would be close to *The Standard* in case *Jane* was picked up. But I do believe he could be somewhere where he could see her departure. Will they walk to Winchelsea Beach?'

'I think it likely,' Morris said. 'If not, they would have to steal a car or motorcycle which would be too noisy and too great a risk of there being no petrol in it.'

'And they can't afford to miss the rendezvous,' Clement added, almost to himself. 'It's my opinion that they will leave Rye separately and join up once away from the town.' He stared at the map. In his mind, he walked the streets, the waterfront and the Winchelsea Road. He studied the perimeter of the town, especially on the seaward side.

The view from Ypres Tower spanned more than two hundred and seventy degrees across the surrounding environs and more than one hundred and eighty degrees across the harbour, but at night the shifting sands were too dangerous for anyone not familiar with them. Besides, the local Home Guard had a post in Ypres Tower and at the foot of Watchbell Steps on the eastern end of the Strand Quay.

Watchbell Steps. 'Of course,' Clement muttered. They led from Watchbell Street down the steep escarpment to the waterfront. He also knew of the tunnels that connected the houses of Watchbell Street with the infamous smugglers haunt, *The Mermaid Inn,* in Mermaid Street at the end of which was the lane known as The Mint.

'There,' Clement said, pointing to the steps. With his left index finger on the steps at the end of Watchbell

Street, his right finger traced the route of *Jane*'s anticipated departure. '*Jane* leaves *The Standard* and walks from the inn towards the Needles Passage then into Wish Street and across the Tillingham River to Winchelsea Road. Phillip is watching from the steps in Watchbell Street. Even in the darkness, with a pair of binoculars and with the moonlight reflecting off the water, there is sufficient light to see her cross the bridge. Especially since *Jane's* departure will most likely be at a specific time. But Haswell will not take the steps to the waterfront because of the Home Guard sentry. Once Haswell sees her, he returns to the house at the end of Watchbell Street and takes the underground tunnels to *The Mermaid*. Then he leaves the inn and walks down to the Strand Quay to cross the Tillingham, the Home Guard sentry now behind him and obscured from sight.'

'You're sure about the tunnels?'

Clement nodded, but he was thinking of his mother and all the stories she told him about Rye's smuggling past.

'Sergeant, telephone the Captain of the Home Guard and tell him to remove the sentry on duty tonight at the foot of the Watchbell Steps between the hours of midnight and four o'clock tomorrow morning. I do not want another unnecessary death,' Morris said.

'Where exactly does this tunnel surface, Clement?' Johnny asked.

'Behind a bookcase in one of the bedrooms at *The Mermaid*. I have seen it. Phillip takes the tunnels from Watchbell Street to *The Mermaid,* then runs the short distance towards the bridge over the Tillingham. Once across, he joins *Jane* on the Winchelsea Road.'

'How do you want to play this, Chief Inspector?' Johnny asked.

Morris stared at the map. 'It would be wise to check the steps near Watchbell Street.'

'The local boys should do it,' Clement said, interrupting Morris. 'If Phillip sees any of us, especially me, he could vanish. The local police should station themselves in a house in Watchbell Street with a view of the steps. Once they see Haswell, or any man watching the seafront return to the house with the tunnel, they could telephone you here at the police station. However, the Sergeant and I should position ourselves in another house opposite *The Mermaid* as soon as we know *Jane* has left *The Standard*. We will need as much time as possible to get into position. Sergeant, can you arrange it with a patriotic resident?'

'Leave that to us,' the Sergeant said.

Clement continued. 'Phillip's departure from Watchbell Street will be but minutes after sighting *Jane* crossing the bridge. I estimate that the Sergeant and I have about three to five minutes before Phillip emerges in Mermaid Street. Once I identify Phillip and see him leave *The Mermaid*, the Sergeant and I will return to the police station and you and I, Arthur, will run overland for Winchelsea Beach. Johnny, you should go at midnight. That will give you more than enough time to locate the best and safest course across the beach and cut a section of barbed wire for us. When Arthur and I arrive at the beach, we will locate the ditch adjacent to the cut wire opposite our surveillance post. Then we wait for *Jane* and Phillip to arrive.'

They stared at the map of the ancient town.

Phillip Haswell flashed into Clement's mind again. Was the location of Coleshill really what it had all been about? Phillip Haswell had not recently been won over to Nazism by the prospect of a negotiated peace to mitigate grievous times. Phillip and *Jane* had killed the real Elsie Wainwright in order to contrive and maintain a history for him; a legend, Clement believed was the word they used for such deceptions.

Haswell had been sent in by the Germans years earlier to watch and wait and provide information that was so valuable that the Nazis would wait a long time to acquire it. Even if the location was known, the secret of what really went on at HMS Forward, was still intact thanks to Lieutenant Ellis's misinformation. But the existence of Coleshill and what happened there, especially now with the invasion imminent, was what it really had been about. That was why Phoebe had broken cover.

29

Monday 23rd September

I'll go now,' Johnny said, reaching for his coat. 'It's just turned midnight. Once I see the targets, I'll start the motorcycle. If there is anything unexpected, I'll flick on the head light.'

Clement shook hands with Johnny.

'See you on the beach, Clement, Chief Inspector. Oh! And Clement, sometimes things don't go as expected. Just be prepared. Always best.'

Clement smiled. He understood such missions almost never went according to plan. But he took Johnny's remarks in the manner in which he believed they had been intended - as reassurance. Johnny left the room, his footsteps diminishing along the corridor. Clement flicked a glance at Arthur Morris who was checking his police-issue service revolver. Morris placed extra ammunition in his pocket. Clement knew the weapon would be next to useless, but he couldn't say as much.

He closed his eyes, his mind was on Mary; on happier days when he knew where his wife was and what she was doing. He also thought of his men. At least he knew where they were. Having Reg and his ability with the rifle with them would have been useful. Clement leaned back in the chair and silently repeated his favourite line from *Henry V*.

The resourceful Sergeant had found two Home Guard uniforms for him and Morris. While the cloth was rough, it was incredibly warm and Clement thought it fitted better than his own. By the time he and Morris returned to the interview room wearing the uniforms, the Sergeant had replaced the pot of tea.

Clement sipped the warm drink. What he really needed was sleep. He couldn't. Not yet. When it was over he would sleep like a baby. He wondered whether it would be in this life or the next.

He turned his mind to the weapons Johnny had brought. Clement stood and pulled them out of the pack, lining them up along the table. The Sten was closest to his hand. He felt the familiar coolness of the barrel, then attached the magazine of ammunition. His preparation was routine. He didn't expect trouble. Not this time. The initial sortie was for reconnaissance only. Despite this, he would not go unprepared. He heard Major Bannon's voice telling him that preparation and adaptability are the keys to a successful mission. Keys. His mind drifted to Inspector Russell's car keys and what Morris has said about them. Finding the five pound notes on *Jane* or Phillip implicated them, but the car keys with the Celtic cross would see them hang, if they were not already dead by morning.

Clement wriggled his foot, the feel of the Fairbairn Sykes knife strapped to his inner left leg digging into his calf. He ran his gaze over the remaining weapons. He intended to take three grenades and four more magazines of ammunition when they went to Winchelsea Beach. His eye rested on the trip wires, and explosives. But there was no time for laying explosives, besides there were enough already on the beach. He glanced at the knuckle duster, stiletto and garrotte. The knuckle duster could be useful but the others he decided to leave behind. Stealth might have been possible if the beach was sand, but it was impossible to disguise running footsteps on shingle. The small, rounded stones had a way of subsiding and slipping beneath one's feet. As a child he had loved both the feel and the sound of the crunching, sliding stones. But now their sound meant death. Frontal attack was the only way, and that required as much bravado as it did bullets.

He checked his watch. Thirty minutes had passed since Johnny had left the police station. Clement guessed it would be another hour and a half before they received word that *Jane* had left *The Standard*.

As the temperature dropped, Morris went to lie down in one of the cells. The wait was tedious. It made one sleepy yet heightened the nerves. Despite Clement's body yearning for the panacea of sleep, adrenaline kept him awake. He hoped it would last for a few hours yet. Swinging his feet onto a chair, he leaned back and pulling his uniform jacket about him, closed his eyes.

The telephone rang.

From further along the corridor, Clement could hear the Sergeant's even, determined footsteps.

'*Jane* has left *The Standard*,' the Sergeant said, entering the office.

Morris joined him. Clement glanced at the clock on the wall. Two o'clock. Reaching for the Sten gun, he checked it one more time then fitted the silencer.

Clement smiled at Morris; a man he had come to respect and admire. 'Be ready to leave the moment we return, Arthur.'

Morris nodded. 'I'll be ready. And Clement, good luck.'

Clement and the Sergeant ran along the corridor, opened the door and stepped into the street. Cinque Port Street was deserted. A cool wind slapped their faces as they ran into Market Road. Crossing High Street, they ran up West Street, their distorted shadows leaping over the cobblestones in the moonlight like the departed spirits of the smugglers' gangs. Clement knew their footsteps were echoing off the buildings, but there was little he could do about it.

As they approached Mermaid Street, Clement began to tip-toe along the cobbles. Slowing at the corner, he ran his fingers along the Sten and slipped the catch. Peering around the edge of the corner building, he saw that Mermaid Street was deserted. Rounding the corner, he leaned against the walls and stared down the descending, narrow street, his eye scanning and checking every window and doorway in the darkness. He edged forward and glanced upwards. The roof line of the houses was visible against the moonlit sky. But the light did not penetrate into the narrow streets. In the darkness, human forms blended into night air. His ears strained for any sounds of movement.

Beckoning behind him to the Sergeant, Clement hunched low and they ran along the cobbles to the door step of a house diagonally opposite *The Mermaid Inn.*

Clement kept his Sten gun close to his chest, his finger poised on the trigger. Glancing around, the Sergeant tapped on the door. A man of advanced years opened it and Clement and the Sergeant slipped inside. It had taken them three minutes to reach the house.

'Thank you for helping us tonight,' Clement said. He didn't know the couple's names, but he could see their wide-eyed enthusiasm. The old man pointed to the stairs and they ran up to the bedroom at the front of the house that overlooked the street. A minute later the telephone rang and he heard the old man answer. Clement squatted by the window and waited.

'The man has left Watchbell Steps,' the resident said, entering the room.

Clement nodded.

The man left. Staying by the window seat, Clement opened the window and leaned his head out, his gaze on the front door of *The Mermaid*. The street was deserted and still. He checked his watch. In the dim light, the street below exuded its sinister past. Silent - macabre even - in the black-blue light. He gripped his Sten, recalling the terrifying tales his mother had told him when just a boy of the infamous Hawkhurst gang who tortured and murdered anyone who dared oppose their smuggling activities. *The Mermaid*, even then, had been the chosen haunt of criminals. He saw the inn's door open.

Two figures stepped out into the street, their boots tapping on the cobblestones, a wisp of condensed air escaping from their warm mouths.

Clement stared at the dark shapes.

'Is that him?' the Sergeant whispered.

Clement leaned further forward, his torso out the window. Staring at the backs of the two men wrapped in coats with hats pulled down over their heads, he fixed his gaze on their silhouettes. He had not expected two men. He squinted, his eyes straining for any sign of recognition. Were they innocent people walking the streets? But who walked streets during wartime at two o'clock in the morning? Clement stared again at the darkened shapes as they walked away from the inn and down the street towards the waterfront, their shadows elongating as they went, the moonlight picking up their presence.

Clement continued to stare. Time was passing. He needed to make his decision. He squinted at the forms, his concentration absolute. The figures were almost at the junction of Mermaid Street and The Mint. He visualised the day of the strafing run, when he had watched Phillip Haswell run towards the village green. Were these the same narrow shoulders? Clement shifted his stare to the other man. This man had a slight but noticeable limp and although he wore a heavy coat, Clement knew, by the man's large frame, he was not Phillip Haswell. But there was something else. Something odd about the way the men walked. Clement frowned. Were they too close? He couldn't see the thinner man's arms. He rubbed at the crease in his forehead. 'That's him!' he said but he felt something was not right. He stood and without waiting for the Sergeant, ran from the room and descended the stairs. Opening the front door of the obliging resident, Clement stood in the doorway and checked the street. The two men had disappeared from Mermaid Street and were now somewhere close to the waterfront and out of his sight. Turning right, he ran to the top of the street and sprinted towards Cinque Ports Street.

Three minutes later he ran into the police station. Morris looked up as he entered the room.

'There are two men!' Clement said.

'Two?!'

He nodded. 'Are you ready?' he asked Morris while grabbing the weapons lined up along the table.

'Yes.'

Almost without thinking, Clement slipped the knuckle duster, three grenades and four magazines of ammunition into the webbing around his waist, and strapped a pouch containing the binoculars to his right thigh. Glancing at Morris, Clement held the Sten in front of him, and they hurried from the police station into the night.

They ran as far as Wish Street, pausing just before the last building. Leaning against the cold wall, Clement peered around the corner. He scanned the open space between the last building in Wish Street and the Tillingham Bridge, then he concentrated on the opposite side of the river. If he had been Phillip Haswell, he would wait in some obscure hiding place on the other side just to make sure no one was following, before running along the Winchelsea Road. He scrutinised the low bushes on the other shore for movement.

'What's happening?' Morris whispered.

Clement reached for the binoculars and scanned the opposite shoreline. He saw the huddled forms. Three shapes coalesced into one dark mass, then parted again into three. Standing, the three separated and began to run. *Jane* was on the far left, the slight shape immediately recognisable. From the running gait of the centre figure Clement recognised Haswell. The other man was hunched and the limp seemed to be more pronounced.

He was carrying something. As Clement stared, the moonlight caught the object. A glint of light, just a second in duration but it was enough. The large man held a machine gun. Within seconds the group had disappeared from sight.

Clement signalled Morris. They ran across the bridge. Running through low scrub land, they headed south-east for Winchelsea Beach. Clement's eyes darted between his feet and the night air in front of him. He could hear Morris's breathing as they ran. Flaring his nostrils, Clement breathed in the salty air. He had not run along this stretch of land since boyhood, but nothing was different. The short-cuts and tracks to the beach had not changed in forty years.

From the top of the beach head, he and Morris lay belly down in the grass. He fancied he could hear the gulls, but he knew it was his imagination. Reaching for the binoculars again he scanned the barbed wire, looking for the break Johnny had cut through it two hours previously.

'We need to get closer.'

Clement replaced the binoculars in their pouch and stood. He could see the old, wooden pylons about fifty yards along the beach, black like tall burned tree trunks against the shingles. Hunching, they ran through the long grass towards the ridge opposite the line of pylons. Clement stopped and scanned the beach before he and Morris descended from the scrub land, across the track and onto the ridge overlooking the beach.

Opposite the now deconstructed groyne was a narrow ditch. It had once been used as a drain in the event of an unusually high tide. He and Morris lay there, their bodies spread on the sloped wall. Clement flattened himself into the ground and, lying on his belly, raised the binoculars to check the length of the barbed wire barricade. He smiled when he saw the break in its defence. Johnny had cut a gap for them, and had even placed some driftwood over the fallen, razor-sharp wire.

Morris dropped beside him, pressing his back into the ditch. 'Anything?'

Clement handed the binoculars to him and pointed to where Johnny had cut the wire. 'Any sign of the submarine?' Morris asked.

Clement shook his head. He hadn't expected there to be anything yet, he just wanted to be familiar with the beach and the structures on it. He scanned its deserted length. In the half-light he could see the low waves crashing onto the shingles and creeping up the beach with the tide. Halfway along the beach were the remains of a fishing shed and another series of pylons. He focused the binoculars again on the ones opposite their position. There were the remnants of twelve pylons. He knew, from his boyhood, that each pylon was taller than a man but the horizontal planks that formed the groyne had been removed, just as the Sergeant had said. Five of the pylons stood on the beach out of the water, seven extending into the waves. A boat could tie up to the outer one but there would be little in the way of protection from onshore attack. An individual, however, would be afforded some protection. Clement looked out to sea. The night sky and the sea had merged into one dark mass. Had it not been for the moon's half-light, he believed they would see nothing. Silver flecks of light played over the water.

Clement checked the time. Two forty-five.

The wind blew in Clement's face. He should have been feeling nervous, but he was surprised by his sense of calm. He felt alert and alive, almost like a young man again. But above all, he felt in control. Was it just that he was on familiar ground? Perhaps he felt the familiarity of past actions? He had lain in trenches before, his eyes scanning horizons for German raiding parties. Now in the dead of night he searched for German submarine periscopes. Somewhere out there, just beneath the surface was a German U-boat waiting for the allotted time.

Holding the Sten in his right hand, he again checked the time. Zero, two, fifty-eight hours. 'Have you done this sort of thing before, Arthur?'

'I was once involved in an altercation involving guns. But not one with a German submarine.'

'Are you an accurate shot?'

'Yes. Although I am not sure how I will fare against automatic weapons.'

The ensuing silence told Clement they both knew how it could go. He gazed upwards and silently recited the *Lord's Prayer*. It is amazing how many stars are visible when there is no ambient light. He wondered why he had spent so little time doing things like star-gazing. The view at night would be spectacular from the Downs. He closed his eyes. He would never see it now.

'What do you think of our chances, Clement?'

'Not good.'

Time passed, the only sound was the lapping water; the rhythm of the endless waves on the shingle shoreline. Clement closed his eyes and rolled over and listened to the hypnotic sound. Soothing, gentle. He burrowed his shoulders into the shallow depression seeking any

292

measure of comfort the cold earth afforded. The temperature dropped. So did the conversation; there was nothing to say. Besides, voices at night carry for miles, especially with the light wind. Clement pushed his hand under his coat and flicked on the torch to check his watch. Zero, three, forty-five hours. Soon. Fifteen minutes to zero hour. He rolled onto his belly and holding the binoculars once more scanned the foreshore. Morris lay on the grass beside him, his hat over this face, his police service revolver in his grip. He nudged Morris who rolled over, his eyes staring out to sea.

'Do you see anything?' Morris whispered.

'Not yet. But it won't be long.' Clement shivered. It seemed colder to him but perhaps it was just that he knew the time was approaching. He'd read somewhere that night is coldest at four o'clock. He trained the binoculars on the shoreline, scanning right to left, then out to sea, scanning and sweeping over the waves. Moonlight, silver and bright, cut into the scene, like a dagger plunging from the horizon and pointing straight at them. The light played and sparkled over the ever-moving surface.

It appeared; the thin, black periscope slicing through the water. Then the dark hull began to rise from the depths. Even though Clement was expecting the submarine, actually seeing it sent shudders through his body. He lowered the binoculars and stared into the night.

'What is it?' Arthur whispered.

'They have arrived.' He passed the binoculars to Morris. 'The submarine, not the targets,' he said, reminding himself that Phillip Haswell was his enemy.

Clement checked his watch again. Zero, three, fifty-eight. The trio would be on the beach within seconds.

He held the binoculars again to his face and relocated the periscope. What he saw made his heart skip a beat. In the moonlight the dark form took on a shape and a presence of satanic evil. He had never felt or witnessed anything like it. The black mass, sinister and silent rose before him. It had appeared without any sound and was lying in wait for its prize. Clement's open mouth was dry and he knew his eyes were wide. He could feel his eyelids had opened so wide it was almost uncomfortable. But the sight was mesmerising.

'How far off the shoreline is it?' Arthur asked.

'About half a mile.'

Clement watched as the conning tower hatch opened. A minute later he saw a silhouette climb out and descend onto the submarine's deck. A small dinghy was lowered and the man climbed over the side of the submarine and into it. Clement watched the conning tower. No one else left the deadly hulk.

A crunching sound cut into the cold air. In an instant the mesmeric hold of the submarine on his concentration vanished. Several sets of feet were running over the shingle. He held the binoculars steady and focused on the sound of running feet.

'Now!' he said, grabbing his Sten. He and Morris stood, and ran forward. As they crossed the road they cleared the ridge top and descended on to the beach. The motorcycle engine roared somewhere off to his left. A shaft of light from the motorcycle's headlights coursed over the beach. Clement stopped and he saw the beam of light cut into the night. In its glare he saw legs, torsos, then arms, running, two men, one woman. Within seconds, gunfire exploded in rapid staccato cracks. He saw one of the men turn and drop to the beach, the flash from the muzzle of the gun strobing yellow in the blackness as the bullets sprayed the beach. Clement heard the motorcycle engine still going but the machine was stuck in the shingle, lying stationery in the loose surface. Bullets shattered the sides, and the headlight was extinguished. Within a second the fuel tank exploded, the noise and searing light piercing the night around them. For one second Clement could see three figures on the shingle at the water's edge. Another round of bullets sprayed the burning motorcycle. Clement wondered about Johnny. In the confusion, he and Morris ran for the break in the barbed wire, his feet falling on anything, his eyes searching for the driftwood plank over the barbed wire. Rushing forward, Clement crossed the break, the shingle sliding and slipping beneath his feet. 'Arthur, stay behind me and off to my right,' he shouted, turning his head back to see the Chief Inspector only a few paces behind him. The machinegun fire stopped.

In the silence, Clement fell to the beach, the Sten in his grasp. He heard Morris fall onto the shingle behind him. He couldn't see the group now. In the confusion he and Morris had advanced across the beach about fifty yards. Lying on the shingle, listening to his own breathing, Clement was convinced that his enemy did not know of his or Morris's presence.

Everything was silent. He waited. He could hear, in the light wind, the sound of oars in the water followed by a bump. Repeated. The light wind was bringing the sounds to them. He knew it was the dinghy. The small craft was hitting the last pylon, the waves buffeting the boat against the wooden pole.

Then he heard running feet.

As the feet ran across the shore the rapid firing started again, the yellow strobing flashing, coursing across the shoreline. Clement thought the firing was random, and he guessed his position was still unknown to the gunman. He could hear the bullets hissing and pinging off the shingle. He lay on the beach, his head down and waited for the barrage to stop. Turning his head to one side, he saw the gunman strafe the beach again. The yellow flicker of the bullets leaving the muzzle exploded in the night and he caught a glimpse of the man, backlit from the firing weapon. An outline of the face only, but it was enough.

'Stop firing!' a panic-stricken voice screamed into the night air.

Clement recognised Phillip's voice in the hysterical shriek. It shocked him for one moment. Standing and holding the Sten to his shoulder, Clement fired at the face he had known for three years. Two sharp cracks sounded in the night. He saw Phillip fall. Clement dropped and rolled several times to his left over the round, hard stones. But the hail of bullets was not directed at him. He rolled once more. The firing started again. A further round of shots strafed across the beach, followed by the sound of running feet. But the pattern was different. Someone was injured. The running was laboured. Clement looked up from his position lying on the shingle wondering if the man with the limp had been shot. The yellow flashes were coming from behind one of the pylons. The pattern continued. Running. Firing. With each round a spray of short, staccato shots flew across the stretch of beach, but the gunman was moving to the next pylon with each burst. Clement could tell that the firing was wild and not aimed with any accuracy. He watched the glow from the muzzle move further towards the sea. He could hear Morris behind him, then another set of feet. He hoped Johnny's. Standing, Clement ran forward, dropped to the ground again and lined the Sten up with the pylon at the end of the old groyne.

The low sound of an engine filled the night. Clement thought it was a diesel motor; the slow chugging sound of a small launch. From where he lay on the shingle, he looked up. Out of the blackness a search light lit up the shoreline. He lowered his head, his Sten on his chest, and rolled sideways away from the shaft of light, their position no longer unknown. Lowering his head, he waited for the rapid fire. Bullets skited across the shingle, pinging off the stones. The light was on the pylons now. Each one was illuminated in turn until he saw them, bright, in the intense beam break cover and run into the low waves.

Clement could not tell if the launch was friend of foe, but it no longer mattered. He would use it. He stood again and ran forward. The old rotting pylons of the groyne stood out, brighter than day in the blinding light. He heard splashing. Then he saw two people, a woman and a man holding hands as they ran into the water. He saw the man toss the weapon into the sea and swim towards the dinghy. They had separated, the woman still behind the last pylon. Machine-gun fire coursed from the motor launch. Clement could hear the bullets splashing and skipping across the water; the high-pitched spitting continued, several rounds hitting the water-sodden timbers of the pylons.

Clement stayed low. He rolled sideways, then two seconds later he rolled away once more as the bullets fired again. Although he could not be sure, the bullets from the launch did not appear to be directed at the beach. Keeping his head down, he looked back. The light strobed across the beach again, then swept over the water. In an instant he had seen Morris and Johnny lying flat on the beach behind him, lit up in the glare. Clement stood, and running forward, fired the Sten, sending a sweeping spray of bullets into the sea.

The light swung off the beach and onto the water. Morris had been off to Clement's right, lying flat on the shingle and about twenty feet behind him. To his left Johnny was closer, a Sten in his hand. Clement did not know if either or both were hit. He stared into the night. The launch worried him. The light went away from the shore again and onto the water surface. He looked up. In the distance he could see the outline of the submarine; its sinister dark presence impassive to the mayhem around it. The man in the dinghy was standing now, his blonde hair caught in the fierce glare of the launch's light. The man was firing in a wide arc, defiantly spraying bullets across the water towards the motor launch. Clement rolled again, over and over, away from where he had lain on the stony beach. Lying his head along the barrel of the Sten, he closed one eye and stared down the sight at the dinghy. Pulling the trigger, he heard the bullets skimming the water. He rolled again, left then right. The man in the dinghy once again directed his fire onto the beach, the bullets striking where Morris and Johnny had been pinned down. The strafing continued, the yellow light from the machine gun indicating the arc of the gunman's aim. Spitting bullets were still hitting the water.

Clement guessed the man who had swum towards the dinghy was now either dead or in the craft, but the girl, if not already dead, was still behind the pylon. He wondered why the men would sacrifice themselves waiting for her. He stood and ran forward, firing at the last pylon, running across the shingle towards the water's edge. The bullet hit hard. Clement's upper arm was stinging as though he had been bitten by a large dog. It felt warm. He dropped again. He couldn't see the girl behind the pylon. Holding the Sten to his right shoulder, he laid his head along the barrel, his eye on the sight. His arm felt heavy and painful, but he fired again into the night in the direction of the dinghy and unleashed the remaining contents of the magazine.

The search light flashed again. Clement saw to his left, the man in the dinghy was down. With the boatman down, the two escapees would have to swim to the boat, board it and row away themselves. But for some reason the limping man, if he was alive and in the dingy, was waiting for the girl. In that instant Clement knew he had them. He looked again at the dead boatman, whose body was half in and half out of the water. Another flash of the spotlight revealed the limping man hunched over in the dinghy, his body still as the boat floundered in the waves.

Clement fitted a new magazine and fired the Sten. He saw the hunched body move only slightly with the impact of the bullets. The girl, *Jane*, was in the water, an arm raised in the waves.

It was over.

The motor launch's engine roared and although Clement could no longer see the craft, he heard it disappear into the night. Lying on the beach, he grabbed his binoculars and scanned the sea, about a half mile offshore. The black conning tower was sliding down into the waves. He watched it, spell bound, until it disappeared.

'Everyone alright?'

It was Johnny's voice.

'Yes,' Morris responded.

'Fine,' Clement heard himself reply but he wanted *Jane*. And he wanted the dead traitor, the unknown third person. Standing, Clement reached for another magazine in his belt and reloaded the Sten as he ran forward crossing the shingle. He heard his boots splash into the water and felt the rush of cold water around his ankles. He held the Sten chest-high and let off another round of bullets into the air. 'They are all dead and you have nowhere to go! Swim to the beach and come out of the water with your hands over your head!' he shouted. He kept the barrel of the gun on the girl as she swam towards the shoreline.

Johnny stood and, running forward towards the girl, dragged her to her feet.

Clement tossed the Sten back towards the beach and plunged into the sea. He ignored the pain in his upper arm and swam out through the waves towards the dinghy, grabbed the rope on the bow of the small craft and pulled it towards the shore.

A line of people now stood on the beach. From their naval uniforms Clement guessed they were Johnny's people. He glanced at Arthur Morris. Chief Inspector Morris had been allowed to do his bit, but it had been Johnny's call all along. Strangely, Clement found it insulting. More for Morris than himself. The unknown silent men moved forward into the water and dragged the dinghy high up the beach. Two men now had *Jane* at gunpoint. Clement glanced at the girl, but he needed to know. Standing, he clutched his bleeding arm and walked towards the craft. Morris was beside him. The Chief Inspector reached forward, and grasping the coat of the dead man, rolled the body over and switched on a torch.

30

Clement felt himself starting to shake. He lurched backwards, his lungs sucking in the cold air, his mind reeling. Before him, in the dinghy, lay Peter Kempton, his fixed unseeing gaze staring into the night sky, his body ripped apart by bullets. The pain in Clement's arm was intense now and he wasn't sure if he was falling. He could hear the waves. He could hear the sound of feet on the shingle. The waves; always the waves: incessantly caressing the shore and the ears. But he could no longer see; everything was dark now. Yet he could hear voices. He had no concept of the physical world around him. Time had stopped. The gentle hush of the waves penetrated his consciousness. He seemed to be falling. He heard the soft thud. He was floating, downwards, and it was hot: his skin prickled with the heat. Something hard was under his head and he could hear raised voices above him. He closed his eyes.

'Clement?'

It was a voice Clement knew.

'Can you hear me, Clement? Everything is alright. You are safe now,' Mary said.

He tried to speak but a stab of intense pain coursed through him. Despite this, he smiled. Mary. For a few seconds he allowed the sound of her voice to linger. But in his mind he saw the running legs. Crunching. Running feet over shingles. Strobing yellow flashes. Machine-gun fire. Rapid. Fall! Roll left. Roll right. Shafts of piercing light. The yellow light flashed in his memory. They were exposed, the blinding light lit them up like actors on a stage. Shoot at the beam. 'Get it out or we'll all be dead!' he screamed. The blonde man in the dinghy was firing. Now the man lay slumped over the gunwale. U-boats. Phillip. Was he dead? The searing light from Johnny's exploding motorcycle. Johnny. Roll right! Roll left! Fire! *Jane*. He had to get *Jane*. Pain, hot and stabbing. 'Stop!' he shouted. He felt a restraining hand on his chest. Someone was beside him. He felt the needle enter his arm. The pain was subsiding. He slept.

For some minutes he watched her knitting, the needles clicking, the thread unravelling.

'Mary?' he said.

The needles stopped and she leaned forward and kissed his forehead.

'What time is it?' he asked.

'About eleven o'clock,' Mary said.

'What day is it?'

'Tuesday.'

'Where were you?' he asked, reaching for her hand.

'In London, Clement. I still do some work for The Admiralty. Johnny Winthorpe recruited me last year along with many other former secretaries. I'm sorry,

Clement but I was not permitted to tell you. And Gwen knows nothing about it. I haven't had to do anything until recently. And certainly nothing as exciting as you. I follow people and courier things. It was I who spotted *Jane*. I saw her at Victoria Station as I was returning home, that unmistakable travel bag was in her hand. So I followed her onto the train. But not before I got a message to Johnny via the station master.'

Clement understood all her absences now. 'I suppose it was you who put my name forward to Gubbins?'

She smiled.

He struggled to sit up. 'Where are we?'

'Rye Hospital. You were shot, Clement. We will be home tomorrow if the Doctor says you are well enough to be moved.'

Doctor. Phillip Haswell. 'Is Phillip dead?'

'Yes,' she said. He could hear the sad note in her voice. He wondered why. He looked around the hospital room. They were alone. 'Am I the only sick man in Rye?'

'Johnny arranged the private room.'

The door opened and Arthur Morris entered. 'How are you, Clement?'

'I'll live, Arthur. What's happening?'

'Commander Winthorpe is still in Rye. He and I have been interrogating the girl. Her real name is Katarina Klausmann and she has confessed to luring Stanley Russell to his death. Bundles of five-pound notes were in her pockets. Stanley died at Mr Kempton's office in the raid as we thought. But it appears that there is another sad note to all this.'

'Which is?'

'It appears that Phillip Haswell was innocent.'

Clement stared at Morris. 'What?'

Morris nodded. 'I'm afraid so. When we picked up his body on the beach, we found that his hands were bound. And just like Stanley was framed for the death of his father, so Phillip was made to appear like the German infiltrator. It may be, Clement, that it was not you who killed Phillip. There are several bullets wounds in Doctor Haswell's body, some at point-blank range. It is possible that they shot him but wanted you to think you were responsible. The Coroner's report will confirm which shot killed Doctor Haswell.'

Clement fell back on the pillow. Could betrayal get any worse? The depth of it was confounding. It was as though someone had taken a cricket bat to his head. The door swung open and Johnny entered the room

'Arthur has told me about Phillip Haswell,' Clement said. 'Is it possible...' Clement paused. He couldn't speak the name. '*He*...was another victim?'

Johnny shook his head, but it was Arthur who spoke. 'We found the keys to Inspector Russell's car in Peter Kempton's pocket. There's no doubt, I'm afraid.'

Clement heard the words but he could no longer comprehend. Whether or not he had fired the fatal shot that had killed Phillip Haswell didn't change what Clement had done. He had intended to kill the man he believed was a murderer and a traitor. Now he would have to live with that. But he had been betrayed by another. He felt the pain in his chest. 'It tells me who, Arthur. But it doesn't tell me why. Neither does it tell me why Peter kept Phillip with them. They disposed of Stanley without conscience, why not Phillip?'

Morris shrugged. 'It may have been purely for insurance, in case Katarina was caught, Phillip could be traded. Or it could have been for his medical skills. Mr

Kempton had a long gash to his leg. It would have been painful, and we suspect it was caused by a sharp edge or even the side of a boot being slammed into Mr Kempton's leg, perhaps inflicted by Doctor Haswell himself, trying to escape. We shall never know the answer to that.'

'So it was Peter's car that went into the forest?'

'Yes. My Sergeant found the car in a side street near the hospital. The tyres had leaf matter stuck in the tyre treads.'

'But his wife was Jewish?'

'A lie, Clement,' Johnny said. 'Katarina is quite a handful but she eventually told us what we wanted to know. I suppose she is hopeful of a mitigated sentence. Unlikely. It appears that Peter Kempton's wife Muriel is alive and well and working for the Abwehr. Of course, his name isn't Kempton. It is Klausmann, Pieter Klausmann. The girl we were calling *Jane*, is his daughter by his first wife.'

'That is why he waited,' Clement muttered remembering the dinghy. 'But Peter is English? Everything about him is English. Even his dog.'

Johnny shook his head. 'Peter is German. He didn't come to England until after he married Muriel. His daughter, Katarina, remained with her mother, Peter's first wife, in Germany but Peter did stay in contact with his daughter. Katarina Klausmann came to England on holidays before the war, but Peter was careful never to bring his daughter to Fearnley Maughton. The Germans then sent Katarina to England the year before war broke out.'

'The year Muriel was supposed to have died in Switzerland,' Clement said. 'What about Elsie Wainwright and the man from Eastbourne?'

Morris continued. 'After you informed us that the real Elsie Wainwright was dead, we located her grave. She was buried alongside her parents in Eastbourne Cemetery. We exhumed her remains yesterday. The real Elizabeth Wainwright is dead, just as Anne Chambers said. All the Klausmanns had to do was locate a single, dead girl of the same age as Katarina. They would have researched her background, perhaps they found a photograph of the late Doctor and Mrs Wainwright and their daughter in local newspaper records. The fact that the girl was a nurse was a bonus with Katarina having trained in Germany. As long as she stayed away from Eastbourne and of course anyone who actually knew the Wainwrights, no one would ever be the wiser.'

'Your chance meeting with Nurse Chambers in the underground shortened our search for the girl considerably,' Johnny added. 'Miss Bradwynn and her team would, I have no doubt, have arrived at the correct conclusion eventually, but by then it would have been too late and Katarina and her father would have been safely back in Germany.'

'And the man in Elsie's life wasn't Phillip Haswell?' Clement asked.

Morris shook his head. 'It appears not. The murders of Inspector David Russell, George Evans, Stanley Russell, Constable Newson and Lieutenant Ellis and the kidnapping and possible murder of Phillip Haswell, were all by the hand of Pieter Klausmann.'

Clement stared at the foot of the bed, his mind reeling. It was as though they were talking about a stranger;

a dead but unknown enemy agent. Not a man who had been his friend for twenty years. Clement couldn't comprehend it now, but he knew he wouldn't stop thinking about it. He would trawl in his memory twenty years of chats, of times spent walking the Downs, of philosophical debates, life ambitions, politics, the war, anything and everything that would help him to understand. But right now, today, all Clement felt was utter betrayal. Tomorrow it would be anger. Next week, he hoped it would not be hatred.

'Ecclesiastes,' he muttered. He shook his head and looked up at Morris. 'How did,' Clement paused, '*he* find out about the list? I told no one.'

'It was a routine visit to Brighton Police Station to see a client arrested for theft,' Morris answered. 'According to Katarina, her father saw, while having tea with the Chief Superintendent in Brighton Police Station, an envelope on the man's desk with the Ministry of Home Security crest in the top left corner. When the Chief Superintendent left the room for a few minutes, Mr Kempton opened the letter and saw it contained a list of names. On return to Fearnley Maughton, he decided to check David Russell's office to see if a similar list existed. When Mr Kempton saw the names, he knew what the lists were about and in view of the list in Brighton Police Station, it was a fairly safe assumption that there would be similar lists with other senior police officers around the country. He also realised that he would need an accomplice, so he arranged for his daughter to get a job in the village by talking Haswell into believing he needed a nurse and that he should advertise in The Times. Kempton then arranged for Katarina to visit David Russell in his office which she did, entering through the window. After Katarina rendered Inspector Russell unconscious, Mr Kempton entered the police station, also through the window, opened the safe and removed the list.

'The odd thing is,' Johnny interrupted, 'that in every sector other than yours and Brighton, the local police chief personally vetted the selected men. The patrol leader in Brighton had reservations about their police chief, just as you did, Clement. This is why Gubbins so readily agreed to the sealed list idea. Of course, Peter had also attended the course at Coleshill and not only knew what was taught there, but also - and more importantly - the location. Perhaps he never intended to kill David Russell, just render the man unconscious, but whatever happened, Klausmann killed Russell, then had to devise a plan to implicate someone else and extricate himself from the scene. You might recall, Clement,' Johnny added, 'it was Peter you asked to assist the Royal Engineers to choose a suitable place for the Operational Base. Peter had been meeting with Lieutenant Ellis for some time in Maughton Forest, so he did not want the Auxiliary Unit group stumbling on his rendezvous with the naval lieutenant. So Peter made the Operational Base location convenient for his purposes. However, when George stumbled on Peter receiving information from Lieutenant Ellis, both George and Lieutenant Ellis were doomed.'

Clement looked at Johnny. 'But Peter was in the Operational Base the day David Russell was killed, on patrol with other members of the team.' He paused. 'No, he wasn't. Reg did the solo patrol to Cuckmere Haven; I remember now. Reg said they had become separated. Peter must have doubled back into the village. He would have had plenty of time. Peter was good at camouflage. He also compiled the watches and who patrolled with whom. I even left him in charge on more than one occasion.' Clement stared at the window in the white painted room. 'But why now?'

Johnny sat on the edge of the bed. 'In a word, Clement, *Scallywags*. Peter believed the invasion was happening. We had sent out the official code word, *Cromwell* for all units to assemble. Peter knew what the Nazi's would encounter on arrival and wanted to warn them. He also knew he could not risk his radio message being intercepted, so he decided it was time to leave. It would have been a major coup for the Jerries if he had succeeded. And a disaster if they had ever discovered the real purpose of *HMS Forward*. We will miss the opportunity to mislead. Never mind. There will be others. And perhaps Peter Kempton thought you would find out about him if he stayed much longer.

Once Kempton made the decision to leave, he radioed for the fighter to destroy his own office, and the gullible Stanley Russell, then he hid the radio in Doctor Haswell's Anderson shelter. The fighter did the rest. And when you and Chief Inspector Morris discovered the wires in the rubble, of course you suspected Haswell. It is possible that Klausmann was hiding in the garden when the fighter strafed the village, and saw Phillip holding the carrots. Perhaps it had been Klausmann's intention to kill Haswell, but when he found the Doctor in the garden during the raid, he decided to make full use of the unsuspecting man. Kempton would also have overheard your conversation. Once you and Haswell left the garden to attend to the strafing victims, Klausmann was free to remove all the carrots from the plot, which, if Haswell was questioned, would implicate the man further. Peter then returned to the Operational Base. Placing the dead Ellis into Doctor Haswell's car was all the evidence needed to implicate Haswell as the enemy agent.'

Clement's heart was heavy. He wasn't sure whose bullet had actually killed Peter Kempton, or whatever name the man chose to use, but Clement believed he had killed Phillip Haswell. In a way, Kempton had killed him too. He looked up at Johnny and Arthur Morris. 'I knew Peter Kempton for many years. Played chess with the man every week. How is it possible I did not know about his Nazi leanings or that he was not an Englishman?'

'Don't beat yourself up too much over it, Clement. Klausmann fooled more than just you,' Johnny said. 'As a result of his fooling the psychological assessments at Coleshill, we are re-evaluating our procedures there.'

'Everything about him was English,' he said. 'How could I have missed it?'

'While Klausmann was born in Germany, he preferred living in England. But when the war came, Muriel who, of course, spoke English, offered her services to the Abwehr and a credible story was devised to explain her absence. Peter evidently decided that his Nazi fervour could best be demonstrated by remaining in England. He visited Germany on the anniversary of Muriel's supposed death, to see his wife and his daughter and to update his handlers. Klausmann was about as convincing an enemy agent as could be devised. His death will, no doubt, be a major loss to the Reich. We hope not to have too many more like him.'

'And the team?' Clement said, looking at Johnny.

'The invasion has not happened as yet so there is plenty of time to make decisions about the fate of the remaining members of your group. Just get well and we can talk again as soon as you are stronger.'

Clement shook hands with Johnny. He watched the brisk gait of his old friend from seminary school leave the hospital room. Clement considered that for Johnny and men like him, the war had become their *raison d'être*. Clement glanced at Arthur Morris.

The Chief Inspector held out his hand in farewell. 'Thank you for all your assistance, Clement. I could not have done it without you.'

Clement smiled. 'I'm not sure that is correct, Arthur. But perhaps, if you have some spare time, we could play some chess?'

Morris reached for his hat and smiled. Nodding to Mary, he left.

Clement lay in the bed in the old Rye Hospice, staring at the river and several small fishing boats lined up on the expansive sands. He could hear the gulls now, but their distinctive and formerly comforting cry did not help. He turned his head and smiled at Mary. He watched her deft fingers slide and twist the wool over the knitting needles, the familiar shape of a sock now evident. She and thousands of women like her was what it was all about. Home. And security. A land free from fear and treachery. He closed his eyes. Yet all he could see in his mind's eye was the dark form of the menacing U-boat. The effect of the craft was like something he had never previously experienced. Its presence was more than foreboding. He believed it was actually satanic. And it wasn't just a memory for him. He could feel the cold dread of its presence even now, days after the sinister craft had sunk back into the water; its invisible malevolence lingered. It represented the antitheses of everything decent men valued and cherished. What kind of world lay ahead if the Nazis won the war? And what sort of people devised such a pernicious regime that contrived to have men deceive and entrap. It was an alien and sinister force which had to be stopped.

He gazed up at the ceiling, the soft pillows under his head. How long could Britain hold out against such wickedness? Days? He hoped years. He hoped forever. But one thing was certain; life as he knew it would never be the same. The war that had seemed so remote for him had been brought to his doorstep. No longer was it the enemy in the sky or a faceless man who dropped bombs on the innocent. Peter Kempton had seen to that. The impersonal had become profoundly personal.

Clement looked out over the water as the evening light fell. But the war was not yet over. In fact, for many it had only just begun. He now believed it would not be over for many months, if not years to come. It was time for him to open his eyes. He loved Fearnley Maughton, and its people, but now he knew where his future lay. And it was not in the church pulpit.

Acknowledgements

My sincere thanks go to Peter for his unfailing support, to Sarah and Elizabeth for their enthusiasm and encouragement and to Daniel for his advice on all things military. My thanks also go to Barbara Dein and the Venerable Terry Dein and also the Reverend Robert Jones for their theological guidance.

I would also like to thank my wonderful editor and friend Janet Laurence, Ian Hooper of Leschenault Press and to Stewart Angell for sharing with me his knowledge of the Auxiliary Units and to the many people I interviewed about life in wartime Britain.

Author's Note

The Auxiliary Units were created in 1940 in response to the impending threat of a German invasion of Great Britain. They were not disbanded until 1944. With hindsight, we know that these units never had to face the enemy on home soil but this in no way diminishes the courage and bravery that these men demonstrated. They were prepared to die for their country and kept their involvement in these units secret.

While much of what I have written about the Auxiliary Units in *In Spite of All Terror* is factual, other parts are entirely fictitious. Likewise, some is open to speculation. The notion of killing the local senior policeman came from an online search and while the article is keen to dispel this as myth, any hint of murder is a flame to the crime writer moth.